Badlanders

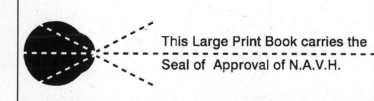

This Large Print Book carries the
Seal of Approval of N.A.V.H.

BADLANDERS

DAVID ROBBINS

THORNDIKE PRESS
A part of Gale, Cengage Learning

GALE
CENGAGE Learning·

Farmington Hills, Mich • San Francisco • New York • Waterville, Maine
Meriden, Conn • Mason, Ohio • Chicago

GALE
CENGAGE Learning®

LIBRARY OF CONGRESS CATALOGING-IN-PUBLICATION DATA

Robbins, David, 1950–
    Badlanders / by David Robbins. — Large print edition.
      pages ; cm. — (Thorndike Press large print western)
    ISBN 978-1-4104-7687-6 (hardcover) — ISBN 1-4104-7687-1 (hardcover)
    1. Large type books. I. Title.
PS3568.O22288B33 2015
813'.54—dc23   2014043861

Published in 2015 by arrangement with NAL Signet, a member of Penguin Group (USA) LLC, a Penguin Random House Company

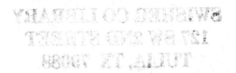

Printed in Mexico
1 2 3 4 5 6 7 19 18 17 16 15

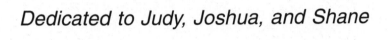

Dedicated to Judy, Joshua, and Shane

1

A pale moon had just risen into the darkening sky when the three men rode into Whiskey Flats.

The single dusty street was flanked by a couple of log cabins, several shacks, and the only building that showed any light. A crudely painted sign announced it was the Three Aces. Under it was the claim that DRINKS ARE CHEAP and under that the news that the saloon boasted THE ONLY DOXIE BETWEEN HERE AND UTAH. Several horses were tied at the hitch rail, and a cat was licking itself under the overhang.

The three riders drew rein and looked at the sign.

"Gentlemen, I believe we've found civilization at last," declared the shortest, grinning. He had a florid face and wide whiskers, and wore a bowler, a suit, and Hessian boots. "Which one of you wants to go first with the doxie?"

The other two were as different from the short man as the pale moon was from the sun. Both were big and broad-shouldered. Both had the weathered aspect of men who spent a lot of time outdoors. And both wore six-shooters, while the man in the bowler did not. There their similarities ended.

"I reckon I'll pass," said the one with curly sandy hair. He had brown eyes and a jaw like an anvil. A Stetson that had seen a lot of use crowned his head. His clothes were those of a typical cowhand and had seen as much use as his hat. His revolver was an over-the-counter Colt, as plain as the man himself.

A savvy onlooker wouldn't peg the last rider as a cowboy, although he did work cattle. His hair was long and straight and black as pitch. His eyes were a startling blue. His hat was black, his shirt the same, his pants gray. A savvy onlooker would also notice that there was nothing plain about his six-gun. A nickel-plated Colt with pearl grips, it nestled high and slightly forward on his right hip. His right hand was never far from his holster.

The man in the bowler chuckled. "How can you let an opportunity like this go by?" he teased the sandy-haired man. "A doxie, by heaven."

"You're plumb amusin', Mr. Wells," the sandy-haired cowboy said in a tone that suggested Wells wasn't.

"And you, Mr. Bonner, are much too serious," Wells said. "You need to learn to see the humor in things."

"Do I, now?"

"Indeed." Wells motioned expansively at the saloon and the cabins and shacks and the benighted wilds beyond. "Think of where we are. In the middle of the Badlands. Hundreds of miles from anywhere, and we find an outpost of humanity advertising the wares of a wanton woman as if she were the Holy Grail of life."

"How you talk, Mr. Wells."

Wells laughed. "I'm a cynic, I'm afraid. Which is why the incongruities of life delight me so."

"The what?"

"Never mind, Neal." Wells dismounted with the awkward form of someone not accustomed to going about on horseback. Looping the reins, he smacked at his clothes, raising puffs of dust.

Neal Bonner alighted with the fluid ease of a true horseman. Glancing at their black-haired companion with the pearl-handled Colt, he said, "Are you fixin' to stay out here and admire the stars or would you care to join us?"

The black-haired man's thin lips quirked, and he swung down. His movements had a pantherish quality, with no wasted movement. He was down, his reins tied off, and his thumbs hooked in his gun belt, all seemingly in the same motion.

Wells had finished smacking and turned. "Let me do the talking. That's why they sent me, after all. But interject where you feel necessary." He glanced at the black-haired man. "As for you. Mr. Jericho, you hardly ever speak anyway, so that won't be an issue with you."

"No mister," Jericho said.

About to go in, Wells paused. "Sorry?"

"It's just 'Jericho.' I told you before."

"And you think I'm peculiar?" Wells said to Neal. Chuckling, he strode to the batwings.

Neal grinned at Jericho. "Easterners."

"For a rooster, he's tolerable," Jericho said.

Inside the saloon, everyone had stopped what they were doing to stare at Wells. At the bar were two older men in grimy clothes with the blurry eyes of heavy drinkers. They smiled in a friendly manner.

There was nothing friendly about the four poker players at a corner table. They bore the stamp of hard cases, their flinty eyes regarding the newcomer with predatory interest.

Wells stepped to where a balding bartender was stacking shot glasses into a pyramid. "How do you do, sir? My name is Franklyn Wells. It's a pleasure to make your acquaintance."

The bartender was carefully aligning a glass and didn't look up. "Can't you see I'm busy? I'll fetch you a drink in a minute."

"It's not liquor I'm interested in so much as information," Wells said. "You see, I represent the Portland Whaling Consortium, and I'm —"

Raising his head above the glasses, the bartender arched an eyebrow. "Whalin', did I hear you say?"

"Yes, you did," Wells confirmed. "And I —"

"You mean those big fish that those fellers on ships harpoon for their oil and whatnot?"

"Well, actually, they're mammals," Franklyn Wells said. "But yes, and you see —"

The barman raised his voice so the men at the table and the bar would be sure to hear. "If it's whales you're after, we have plenty over at Bear Creek. Just the other day I saw one swimmin' in the shallows."

The two old men cackled and several of

the hard cases playing poker smirked.

The one who didn't pushed back his chair and approached. As thin as a broomstick, he had a hooked nose and wore a Remington rigged for a cross draw. His store-bought clothes hadn't been washed since he bought them and his teeth were as yellow as sunflowers. "What do we have here?"

"Didn't you hear him, Dyson?" the barman said. "He's one of them whalers."

"No, actually, I'm not," Wells said. "I represent the Portland Whaling Consortium. "They are whalers. Or, rather, they were. The whaling trade has about died off, as I'm sure you're aware, thanks to kerosene. However, some of the former captains of some of those whaling vessels are looking to invest their considerable capital. The consortium is in the process of establishing the Badlands Land and Cattle Company to take advantage of the coming boom."

"Will you listen to you?" Dyson said. "You sure love to jabber." His hand darted out, and he snatched the bowler.

"Here, now. What are you doing?"

"I'm about to have me some fun," Dyson said. Tossing the bowler to the floor, he placed his hand on his Remington. "Let's see how many times I can make it skip."

"I'd rather you didn't," Wells said. "It cost

me a pretty penny."

"What's to stop me?" Dyson taunted.

"How about me?" Neal had entered unnoticed and stood just inside the batwings. Ignoring the men at the table and the bar, he strode over, picked up the bowler, and jammed it onto Wells's head. "You lost your hat."

Dyson took a step back and tensed as if he expected Neal to draw. When Neal didn't, he looked Neal up and down and said, "You look like the real article, but you must be another weak sister."

"My folks used to say that I'm as strong as an ox," Neal remarked.

"But not very smart," Dyson said, and snapped his fingers at his friends at the table. They were quick to rise and come over, spreading as they came so they were between Neal and Wells and the batwings.

"We're not huntin' trouble," Neal said.

"No, sir," Franklyn Wells said, bobbing his head. "All we want is some information, if you would be so kind."

Dyson curled his lip in contempt. "You rile me, little man. You and your city clothes, and pretendin' to be so damn polite, even when you've been insulted. It ain't natural."

"Sure ain't," a heavyset man in buckskins said. He had a Sharps in the crook of his arm, and wore a beaver hat.

Neal moved in front of Franklyn Wells. "You can insult us all you want, but we won't be prodded. Answer Mr. Wells or things will get ugly."

"What will you do?" the man in the beaver hat asked. "Slap leather against all four of us?"

"Slappin' is my job," said a new voice.

Jericho stood just inside the batwings, his arms at his sides, as casual as could be. But there was nothing casual about the glint in his blue eyes. He moved his right arm slightly, and the pearl grips on his Colt gleamed bright in the light.

"Who are you and how do you fit in?" Dyson demanded.

"I squish flies," Jericho said.

"I'd like to see you try," the man in the beaver hat declared.

"Careful, now, Stimms," Dyson said. "I don't like the looks of this one."

Stimms turned toward Jericho and placed his thumb on the hammer of his Sharps. "You heard him say he can squish us. Who does he think he is? That fancy Colt don't scare me none."

"It should," Neal said.

Just then someone coughed, as if to get their attention.

Another man had come out of a hall to the back. Uncommonly handsome, he was attired in a frock coat such as gamblers wore, and a white shirt with frills. He wore no gun that anyone could see.

His arm was around the waist of a woman twice his age. Once, she had been beautiful, but the ravages of years on the line hadn't been kind. Her dress, too, was past its prime, and here and there red thread showed where patchwork held it together. "Strangers, by God, Beaumont."

"I can see that, darlin'," Beaumont said. "And someone has started a fracas without my say-so."

"We were only havin' a little fun," Dyson said quickly.

"In my saloon," Beaumont said.

"You were in the back with her," Dyson said. "We know better than to disturb you when she's relaxin' you, as you like to say."

"I have a name," the woman said. "It's Darietta."

"Hush, darlin'," Beaumont said. Letting go, he smoothed his expensive jacket and came over and offered his hand to Franklyn Wells. "I always judge a man by his clothes, and yours, sir, cost more than both of your friends' combined. Beaumont Adams, at your service."

"Some civility, at last," Wells exclaimed happily. "I'm delighted to make your acquaintance. "These other gentlemen seemed intent on — what's the expression? Bucking us out in gore?"

"You don't need to worry there," Neal said. "That's why I brought Jericho along."

"Introduce me to your friends," Beaumont said to Wells.

"Certainly. The man who just addressed you is Mr. Neal Bonner. He was foreman at the Diamond T Ranch in the panhandle country until my employers hired him away to work for them. They say he's forgotten more about cattle raising than most men ever learn."

"Do tell," Beaumont said. He indicated Jericho. "Who is he and what does he do?"

"He squishes things," Neal said.

"How interestin'," Beaumont said. "Did you hear them, Dyson? And you, Stimms? Don't you find it interestin', too?"

Dyson and Stimms looked at each other in confusion.

"How about you finish your card game while I deal with these gents?" Beaumont said.

The pair offered no argument. If anything, they were anxious to please.

"My word," Franklyn Wells said. "Look at

them scurry. You'd think they were scared to death of you."

"You would, wouldn't you?" Beaumont said. Smiling, he clapped Wells on the back. "How about I treat you to drinks?"

"As I was telling the bartender," Wells said, "we're really only in need of information."

"I insist," Beaumont said. "To make up for the shabby treatment you received from those in my employ." His hand still on Wells's back, he ushered him to the bar. The two old men hastily moved aside. "Floyd, a bottle of the best brandy for my new friends."

"The best?" the bartender said.

"Do I have to tell you twice?"

Floyd blanched. "No, sir." He picked a bottle from the back of a shelf thronged with all kinds.

"I took you for a brandy man," Beaumont said to Wells. "But if you'd rather have whiskey or somethin' else, say the word."

"Brandy is fine," Franklyn Wells said.

"What would your friends like?"

"None for me, thanks," Neal said. "I'm workin'."

"How about your blue-eyed partner yonder?" Beaumont said. "Does he drink or does he only squish?"

"He doesn't drink when he's on a job, neither," Neal said. "But yes, he's the best squisher I know."

"Is he someone I'd have heard of?"

"Down to Texas you would have. But not in these parts," Neal said, adding, "Yet."

"Do tell," Beaumont Adams said. "This gets more interestin' by the minute."

2

Lice McCoy was dozing in his chair in front of his fireplace when his dog commenced to bark and growl. It took a bit for the barking and growling to seep through Lice's besotted brain and to bring him out of the chair with an oath. Shaking his head to clear it, he went to the gun rack and took down his shotgun. "Must be that damn bear again," he muttered.

Lice always kept the shotgun loaded. He lived miles from anywhere in the heart of the Badlands and never knew but when hostiles or a wild animal might pay him an unwanted visit. The bear was the latest to give him fits. A big black, and not, thank the Lord, a griz, it had been nosing around his place a couple of times now, even though he'd fired in the air once to scare it off.

"This time I'll shoot it dead," Lice vowed as he moved to the front door to his small cabin.

"Lice" was his nickname. His given name was Isaiah Pickford McCoy. His mother had called all seven of her children after biblical prophets. Lice never liked his much. He liked being called Lice even less. But then, he never liked to take a bath, either, which was why he always crawled with lice and was forever picking them off. So the nickname stuck.

Now, stepping out into the cool of the night, Lice leveled his shotgun and hollered, "Where are you, bear?" He hoped his shout would be enough to drive it off.

His mongrel, tied at a corner of the cabin, was still raising a racket, its hackles raised and teeth bared.

"Where is that critter?" Lice said, sidling to his dog's side. He didn't have a name for the dog. He just called it "Dog" and let it go at that. Thinking up a name was hard work, and work was one thing Lice avoided if he could.

Dog rumbled deep in his chest.

Lice peered in the direction the dog was looking and gave a mild start. It wasn't the black bear, after all. Two riders were approaching. His first thought was that they must be Injuns, but no, he could make out hats and saddles. His second thought was that they must be owl hoots. "Hold it right there."

The pair complied and the smaller of the two called out, "Would you be Mr. McCoy? Mr. Isaiah McCoy?"

"Who the hell are you?" Lice demanded. He didn't like visitors. He didn't like people, period. Which was why he lived so far from everybody. He wanted to be alone and to be left alone. Unfortunately his constant craving for alcohol meant he had to go into town every couple of weeks for a bottle. But that was a small price to pay when the rest of the time he lived in cherished solitude.

"Franklyn Wells, pleased to meet you," the small man said cheerily.

"What do you want?" Lice didn't like having his dozing interrupted. "It's damn late to be traipsin' over the countryside."

"We're here specifically to see you, Mr. McCoy," Wells replied. "I apologize for the lateness of the hour, but we've come a very long way and I wanted to conclude our business as soon as possible."

"What sort of business do you have with me that you show up now? It must be pushin' ten o'clock."

"I'll gladly tell you all about it if you'll lower that cannon," Wells said.

"Not hardly," Lice said. "How do I know

you ain't outlaws?"

The other rider spoke in a deep, low voice. "Would outlaws ride right up like this? Use your head, old-timer."

"I am usin' it," Lice rejoined angrily. "Some outlaws are trickier than others. You might have rode up thinkin' I'd think you must be honest folk, and then you gun me in the back."

"We're not here to harm you in any way," Wells said. "I assure you."

Lice snorted. "You expect me to take the word of a gent I don't know from Adam? You must reckon I'm stupid."

"Please," Wells said. "Lower that shotgun so we can talk."

"You have one minute to tell me what you're doin' on my place and then I let fly with buckshot," Lice said.

The other rider raised his deep voice. "Enough of this. Jericho."

"Jericho?" Lice repeated. "That's a city, not a prophet, you lunkhead. Don't you know your Bible any better than —" He suddenly stopped. A hard object had been pressed to the side of his head, and he heard a gun hammer click.

"I'll say this only once," said someone in a manner that sent a shiver down Lice's spine. "Hand the howitzer to me or I splatter your brains."

Lice believed him. "Sure, mister," he said quickly. "Go easy with that hardware." He held the shotgun to one side, careful to keep the barrels pointed at the ground. A hand reached out and took it, and the object gouging his head went away.

"Come on in, Neal. The old tom cat has been declawed."

Lice looked at the man who had taken his shotgun, and swallowed. He flattered himself that he was good at reading folks, and this one was a curly wolf if ever he saw one. Raising his hands, he said, "Take whatever else you want. Just don't kill me."

The man in the black hat and shirt was holding a pearl-handled Colt in one hand and the shotgun in the other. Unexpectedly, he twirled the Colt forward a few times and then backward and slid it into his holster with a flourish, all as naturally as breathing. "No one's goin' to kill you, you old goat."

Lice was terribly confused. He decided to keep quiet and await developments. The man at his side scared him. He knew a gun hand when he saw one.

The other pair rode up and dismounted.

"Let's try this again," Franklyn Wells said. "You can lower your arms. I was serious when I told you we're here on business."

His confusion climbing, Lice shook. He also shook the hand of the man with the deep voice, a big cowboy with as strong a grip as Lice ever felt. "It sure is strange, you showin' up out of the blue like this."

"How about if we go inside and I explain everything?" Wells proposed.

Lice was relieved when only the little fella and the big cowboy followed him in. The gun shark stayed outside. Lice indicated his table with its two chairs and stepped to his own by the fireplace. Crossing his legs, he folded his hands in his lap and waited.

The scary fella had given the shotgun to the big cowboy and now the cowboy propped it against a wall.

"This is Neal Bonner, by the way," Franklyn Wells introduced him. "He'll be the ramrod, I believe it's called, for the Badlands Land and Cattle Company."

"The what?"

Wells took a seat and set his bowler on the table. "The firm I represent. I'm a lawyer. I'm here on their behalf to make you a generous offer."

"Mister," Lice said, "I hope to hell I'm drunk and dreamin' all this, because it makes no kind of sense."

"Permit me to enlighten you," Wells said. "The BLCC needs land, and lots of it.

Some months ago, Mr. Bonner and I looked over this part of the Badlands, and he's of the opinion that it can be turned into a profitable cattle enterprise. Nearly all of it qualifies under the Homestead Act and can be filed on, with two exceptions. The first is Whiskey Flats. The second is your homestead."

Lice didn't know where this was leading, so he didn't say anything.

"My employers regard the town as an eventual supply hub for their ranch. But your homestead is another matter. Your land is at the very heart of their proposed enterprise."

"I don't mind havin' a rancher for a neighbor," Lice said.

"They'd rather avoid that situation, if they could."

"How's that again?"

"Think of it, Mr. McCoy. The Diamond B will have thousands of head of cattle. Perhaps hundreds of thousands if all goes well. And if your homestead is in the middle of the ranch, they'll be trampling all over your property unless you put up a fence. Not only that, the cattle will have to be driven around you to get from one place to another. Does that sound logical to you?"

"I don't know about logic, but I know I

like it here," Lice said.

"I don't blame you," Wells said. "This site of yours is ideally located." He paused. "You have your own well, we're given to understand."

Lice nodded. "I dug it my own self. Plumb surprised me, how the water came pourin' out of the ground like it did."

"Water is one thing my employers need to ensure that their ranch is a success. Which is another reason why they've authorized me to offer you a substantial amount to buy you out."

"Is that why you came all this way?"

"None other," Wells confirmed.

Lice became angry. He'd meant it when he said he liked living there. The winters were harsh, but he always stocked up on firewood and bottles and got by until spring. "You can turn around and go back again. I'm not sellin' out. Not now. Not ever."

"You haven't heard my offer yet," Wells said.

"I don't want to hear it."

Undeterred, Wells said, "They've left the amount to my discretion. And after meeting you, and this short talk we've had, I feel confident in proposing to purchase your homestead for the princely sum of three thousand dollars."

Lice was dumbfounded. That was more than he'd ever had at one time at any point in his entire life. More than he could ever dream of having. It was far more than his property was worth. Which made him suspicious. "Why so much?"

"I've already told you," Wells said. "It wouldn't do to have your place in the middle of the ranch. Plus, you have water, a valuable commodity. My employers can afford to be generous to expedite things."

"Lordy, the words you use," Lice said.

"Big words or little, they all mean the same. Three thousand dollars. What do you say?"

"I don't know," Lice said. He honestly and truly didn't want to sell. But three thousand! His mind reeled at how many bottles he could buy. To say nothing of a new rifle and some new clothes and a new pipe. His brain flooded with images of his richness.

"I happen to have the money in my saddle-bags," Wells mentioned. "All you will have to do is sign several documents I've brought and the money is yours."

"You have it with you?" Lice said. "You must have been awful confident I'd sell out."

"Not that so much," Wells said, "as I believe in always being prepared. I brought the money in case you agreed. It saves me having to ride all the way back and then pay you a second visit."

"That's smart," Lice had to agree.

"What do you say?"

"I still don't know," Lice said. "How much time do I have to think it over?"

"Take all night if you have to," Wells said. "My friends and I will make camp just a little ways off, and I'll come over in the morning to hear your decision. Does that sound reasonable to you?"

"It does," Lice said. He'd be the first to admit he wasn't much of a thinker. Not a quick one, anyhow. He did his pondering nice and slow and came to his decisions only after a lot of deliberation. "I'm obliged."

"No, Mr. McCoy," Wells said, "we're the ones who are grateful that you'll consider our offer." He stood. "I'll leave you to get to it. It's been a terribly long day and I would like to turn in." Shifting, he said, "Coming, Neal?"

"Hold on," Lice said. "I'd like to talk to the cowpoke alone, if you don't mind."

Franklyn Wells stopped in midstep. "Whatever for?"

"That's between him and me."

Wells looked at Neal Bonner and shrugged. "I don't see why you need to, but

I don't see any reason not to, either. I'll wait with Jericho." He touched the brim of his bowler and went out.

"Is it me or does that gent have the talkin' talent of a patent medicine man?" Lice joked.

"He does at that," Neal said.

"Which is why I want to talk to you," Lice confessed. "You have an honest face. That law wrangler is too oily and that gun gent is spooky. But you're normal, like me."

"You can't know how I am," Neal said. "I haven't hardly said a thing since I got here."

"See? You're even honest about that," Lice said. "So tell me. What do you think of this here offer of theirs?"

"It's generous," Neal said. "The filing fee for your homestead was, what, eighteen dollars? You don't have more than a hundred in improvements, if that. And you haven't done a lick of farmin' or ranchin', as required by the law."

"There's the cabin," Lice said. But the cowboy was right. He'd done the bare minimum.

"Which they'll likely tear down to make room for their own buildings," Neal said.

"But I like livin' here," Lice said yet again.

"I don't blame you. It's quiet and peaceful. If I had a place of my own, I'd likely live off from everybody, too. Only I'd raise cows for a livin'." Neal gazed at the cabin's simple furnishings. "I reckon you aimed to live out your days here. But the thing is, you can do that most anywhere. You can find another spot, build another cabin, and have enough money to last out your born days, besides."

"You're not sayin' that just because you stand to be their foreman?"

"You asked my opinion," Neal said. "And the other thing is, no one else will ever make you an offer like this one. Not unless another conglomerate comes along, and how likely is that? This is one of those once-in-a-lifetime deals. Just like their offer to make me their foreman."

"I told you that you were honest," Lice said, and smiled.

"What will you do, old-timer?" Neal asked.

"What any sensible coon would do."

3

Beaumont Adams had claimed his usual table and was treating himself to a glass of his best stock. Taking a long swallow, he smacked his lips, smiled with contentment, and began whistling the tune to "Home on the Range."

Darietta sat beside him, her elbow on her knee, her chin in her hand. It was obvious she was bored and trying not to show it. His whistling perked her interest. "What's gotten into you, Beau?"

"How do you mean, darlin'?"

"Why are you so happy all of a sudden?"

"Nothin' sudden about it," Beaumont answered. "If you'd been payin' attention when those three gents were in here, you'd know why. But because you're as dumb as a stump, you don't."

"Here, now," Darietta said. "You have no cause to insult me."

"You work for me, darlin'," Beaumont

said. "I'll insult you all I want." He went on whistling but stopped when the batwings parted and in came Dyson and Stimms.

They made straight for his table.

The only other person in the saloon was Floyd, the barkeep.

"It was like you said, boss," Dyson began.

Beaumont held up a hand. "Take off your hats."

"How's that?" Dyson said.

"There's a lady present," Beaumont said. "The proper thing for a gentleman is to take off his hat in her presence."

"It's only Darietta," Stimms said.

"She's just a whore," Dyson said.

Beaumont's smile faded. He placed both arms on the table and there was a *thunk,* as of something hard hitting the wood. "Do I have to tell you twice?"

"No, sir," Dyson said, and slicked his hat off as quick as could be.

Stimms, his face scrunched in bewilderment, removed his beaver hat and looked at it as if he couldn't believe it wasn't on his head. "This beats all."

Beaumont sat back and chuckled. "In light of all the changes I foresee for Whiskey Flats, you need to learn more manners, boys." He gestured. "Enough of that. Tell me what happened. Don't leave anything out."

"There's not a heap to tell," Dyson said. "We followed them, like you wanted. It weren't hard since we knew where they were goin'."

Stimms nodded. "We were careful not to get too close, like you told us."

"They went straightaway to McCoy's," Dyson said. "We saw the old buzzard come out and wave his shotgun at them, but that cowhand with the fancy Colt stuck it to his head and took the shotgun away."

"Did he, now?" Beaumont said, laughing. "And quit callin' him a cowhand. He might work cows, but he's more than that."

"More how?" Dyson asked.

"He's a squisher. Don't you remember? But go on."

Stimms said, "We couldn't hear what they were sayin', but we could see some of it from the light that spilled out the window."

"The other cowboy and the little feller went inside and were in there awhile." Dyson took up the account. "Then the little feller came back out. Him and this squisher made camp and then the cowboy joined them and they turned in."

"We took turns keepin' watch," Stimms said. "Along about daybreak they were up and about, and not long after, Lice came out of his cabin and they jawed a spell and Lice and the little one shook hands and went back inside. Maybe half an hour later the little one came back out. He was foldin' papers and appeared happy as can be."

"Do tell," Beaumont said.

Dyson nodded. "That's about all except for the three of them threw on their saddles and came this way, but they circled Whiskey Flats and kept on goin'."

"Just like you said they would," Stimms said.

"How did you know they wouldn't stop?" Dyson asked.

Beaumont began refilling his glass. "They had no reason to. They'd gotten what they were after. That little feller, as you called him, would want to get the news to his bosses right away."

"What news?" Dyson asked.

About to raise the glass, Beaumont regarded the pair with disappointment. "Pitiful. You don't have a brain between you. I always have to do the thinkin'. A gold mine has been dropped in our laps and you're too dumb to see it."

"Those fellers were cowmen," Dyson said. "How did gold get into this?"

"Have a seat," Beaumont said.

34

"At your very own table?" Dyson said in surprise. "The last peckerwood who did that, you shot."

"He was drunk and wouldn't get up when I told him to," Beaumont said. "Have a seat before you make me mad."

With the air of men roosting on shards of glass, the pair obeyed.

"Now, then," Beaumont said, "I'm goin' to explain things to you two and Darietta here. You're the closest thing I have to lieutenants and you need to know."

"To what?" Stimms interrupted.

Beaumont frowned. "Ever hear of the army?"

"Why, sure. Everybody has," Stimms said. "Are you sayin' we're one? How can that be when there're only three of us?"

"Honest to God, I could shoot you."

"I'm only tryin' to savvy, is all," Stimms said. "To be smarter, like you're always sayin' you want us to be."

"I had that comin'," Beaumont said, and sighed. "All right. You know how the army has generals and colonels and captains and such?" He didn't wait for them to respond. "Think of me as the general and you as my lieutenants."

"Oh!" Stimms exclaimed as if it were the greatest revelation ever. "Now I get it.

35

Lieutenant Stimms. I like the sound of that."

Beaumont drummed his fingers on the table.

"What?" Stimms said.

"Back in your buffalo huntin' days, did you accidentally shoot yourself in the head?"

Stimms's eyebrows tried to climb into his beaver hat. "If I'd done that, I wouldn't be sittin' here. A Sharps doesn't shoot bird-shot. It leaves a hole you could stick your fist through."

"I can see the hole," Beaumont said.

"Where?" Stimms placed a hand to the side of his head.

Beaumont extended his arm across the table and jabbed his finger into the middle of Stimms's forehead. "Right there."

Stimms colored, and Dyson laughed.

"Now, then. Where was I?" Beaumont paused. "If you'll recollect, Mr. Wells informed us that the Badlands Land and Cattle Company plans to start up a ranch. You were right here. You heard him, the same as I did."

"So?" Dyson said.

"So it hasn't occurred to you how that will change things? There will be someone to run it, maybe his family, and that fore-man, and fifty to sixty hands, if not more. Plus those that do work besides tendin' cows. Some of them will have families, too. All of them will need things. Supplies and clothes and tools and the like."

"It's too bad there's not a general store hereabouts," Stimms said. "The owner would make a lot of money."

"Yes, I will," Beaumont said.

"You own the saloon, boss," Stimms said. "Why would you give it up to run a general store? You like whiskey more than you do pickles."

"I really could just shoot you."

"I think I savvy," Dyson said. "Beaumont is plannin' to open his own store plus have the saloon. Am I right?"

"You're now my captain," Beaumont said.

Darietta snorted. "If that's all it takes, you should make me a general. Because if I know you, you won't stop there. You've been sayin' since I met you how you'd like to run your own town someday, or some such nonsense."

Beaumont Adams smiled, then uncoiled like a striking rattler and backhanded Darietta across the face. He hit her so hard both she and her chair flipped backward, with her screaming in stark terror. The chair turned as she fell and came down on top of her. She went to cast it off, but Beaumont sprang and pressed on the chair's legs, forcing the back of the chair against her neck and chest. "Talk to me like that again," he growled. "I dare you."

Chalk white, Darietta stopped struggling and got out, "I didn't mean nothin'. Honest."

"Since when is it nonsense to want to be rich? Since when is it nonsense to want to be king of the mountain?"

"It's not! It's not!" Darietta squealed. "I apologize. Let me up. Please. This chair is hurtin' me."

Beaumont bore down with all his weight. "Good. Maybe the pain will teach you a lesson." Stepping back, he kicked the chair and it slid half a dozen feet. "What do you know, you dumb cow? What do you know about anything? All you've ever done is spread your legs for money, and you barely ever make enough to get by doin' that." He balled his fists as if to hit her. "I have big plans. Grand plans. Runnin' this two-bit saloon isn't enough. I only own it because the man who built it didn't have the sense to give me a half interest and run it for the both of us."

"So you snuffed his wick," Dyson said, and laughed. "I still recollect the look on his face when you shot him between the eyes."

Beaumont stepped back, his fury fading. "I never intended to stay on. Figured I'd save enough to head for greener pastures. But now all that has changed. Now a godsend has been dropped in my lap and I aim to make the most of it."

"The godsend bein' the new ranch," Dyson said.

Beaumont nodded, then bent and offered his hand to Darietta. She shrank back, afraid to take it. "Let me help you, damn you. I shouldn't have knocked you down, but you made me lose my temper and you know what happens when I do."

"Don't ever make the boss mad," Stimms chided her. "He ain't nice when he's mad."

"Out of the mouth of idiots," Beaumont said, and held his hand lower. "Do you really want to make me mad a second time?"

Shaking her head, Darietta let him pull her to her feet. When he swiped at a stray bang, she recoiled.

"Stupid cow." Beaumont reclaimed his sat. "Someone pick up her chair. Floyd, keep the brandy comin'. If I know Lice Mc-Coy, it won't be long before he pays us a visit."

It was the next day, shortly after noon, that the man they were waiting for rode up to the hitch rail, visible out the front window.

Beaumont Adams was at his table with Darietta. "Get in the back," he commanded, and she left without a word.

Beaming happily, Lice alighted, wrapped his reins, grabbed his saddlebags and slung them over a shoulder, and sauntered to the batwings. Pushing through, he called out, "Barkeep! Set me up with a bottle of Monongahela. And not the cheap stuff, neither."

Beaumont Adams raised an arm. "Bring the bottle over here, and a glass, too. It will be on me. That is, if you don't mind, Lice."

"Mind a free drink?" Lice said, and chuckled. "That'll be the day. You don't need to, though. I have the money to pay."

Beaumont patted an empty chair next to him. "I insist. It's the least I can do for the man who has been the cause of my deliverance."

"You're what, now?" Lice asked, coming over. He placed his saddlebags on the table and sank down.

"My deliverer," Beaumont said.

"Like in the Bible, you mean?" Lice said. "Hell, you must have me confused with that travelin' parson who came through here about a year ago."

"Oh, it's you, sure enough." Beaumont filled the glass Floyd brought and slid it to Lice. "Here you go. Drink hearty. And while you're at it, I'm curious. How much did they offer you?"

"Who is this 'they'?" Lice asked.

"Play innocent if you want, but everyone knows," Beaumont said. "Or didn't they tell you they stopped here to ask how to find your place? I treated them to drinks, and the short one let it drop about the ranch and how they were hopin' to buy your land."

"Darned leaky mouth," Lice grumbled.

"I'll ask you again," Beaumont said. "Not that it's any of my business, but I'd very much like to know how high they went. I shouldn't think more than a thousand."

Lice snickered. "Shows how much you know."

"Fifteen hundred, then," Beaumont said. "Any more than that, they'd have to be loco."

"Maybe I'm smarter than you give me credit for," Lice boasted. "Maybe I held out for twice that."

Beaumont shook his head in amazement. "Three thousand dollars? Is that what you're tellin' me? And all of it there in your saddlebags?"

"Three thousand, yes," Lice confirmed,

and caught himself. "Wait. I never said anything about my saddlebags."

"You didn't have to. You've never brought them in with you before. Only one reason you would. You don't want to let the money out of your sight. But you had to have a few drinks to celebrate, so here you are, and my nest egg, besides."

"*Your* nest egg?"

"I need money to improve my saloon and to start up a general store, among other things. Between what I have socked away and your three thousand, I should just about have enough."

"What in hell makes you think I'm goin' to give you my money?" Lice snapped. "I'd have to be addlepated to do a thing like that."

"No," Beaumont Adams said. "You'd just have to be dead." So saying, he gave a sharp flick of his right arm and a derringer appeared in his hand. Lice bleated and started to throw up his hands, and Beaumont shot him in the face.

4

The Badlands.

Thousands of square miles of what some would call the most godforsaken country anywhere. To others they were a magnificent display of the Almighty's handiwork in the natural world.

Rocky buttes and towering mesas brushed the clouds. Winding canyons and deep ravines slashed the earth. Washes were dry most of the year but not all. Ridges criss-crossed every which way. Occasional streams accounted for green valleys nestled amid the brown of rock and earth.

The Badlands Land and Cattle Company had chosen their range wisely. It contained a lot of green. There were more year-round streams than elsewhere, and wells produced plentifully. A lot of work was called for, but the Diamond B promised to become a thriving enterprise if managed wisely.

That was where Alexander Jessup came

in. Jessup had no experience running a ranch — that was why the BLCC hired Neal Bonner — but Jessup did have an impeccable record at managing large businesses. Even better, he'd demonstrated a talent for turning a profit from every business he was involved with.

"Alexander the Great," his peers had dubbed him. It was a measure of the man that he regarded it as a title, not a nickname. "Am I not Alexander the Great?" became one of his pet replies when someone questioned his judgment.

When the consortium approached him about managing their new cattle venture, Alexander was overseeing a chain of dairy farms. He'd organized them so efficiently he dominated the dairy market in New York City and other large Eastern cities.

Alexander lived with his two grown daughters in a mansion on the Hudson River, a mansion he'd named Macedonia, and had a sign put up to that effect.

The consortium sent Franklyn Wells to negotiate, and Alexander told him he could make his case over dinner.

Wells was dazzled by the luxury the Jessups seemed to take for granted. After a sumptuous three-course meal, the men lit cigars, sat back, and got to it. After presenting the particulars of the consortium's offer, Wells ended with "We realize we're asking a lot. Cattle raising in the West is nothing like the dairy empire you've established."

"Nonsense," Jessup replied. "Cows are cows."

"Be that as it may, we've hired Neal Bonner, one of the best ranch foremen west of the Mississippi, to be your second-in-command, as it were. He knows all there is to know about ranching, and then some."

Alexander Jessup harrumphed. "In the first place, I don't have seconds-in-command. I lead, others follow. If you want him to be foreman, fine. But he'll take orders from me like everyone else."

"Of course," Wells said.

"In the second place, what I don't know about ranching I'll soon learn. In case your background on me is incomplete, I'm a very quick study. It's one of the secrets to my success."

"Am I to take it that you agree to our terms, then?"

"Provided your consortium agrees to mine," Alexander replied. "I shall operate at my complete discretion. They may advise me as they see fit, but the final decision in matters relating to the ranch is mine and mine alone." He had held up a hand when Wells went to speak. "A house must be provided. I don't expect another Macedonia, but I won't live in a hovel. The house must be ready in advance of my arrival." Jessup paused. "My daughters go with me. They accompany me everywhere, and are indispensable. Both are outstanding businesswomen in their own right. You might have heard I had them privately tutored by some of the best instructors in the country."

"I have, in fact, heard that," Wells said.

"If I can't take them, I won't go."

"The consortium wouldn't think of refusing your request."

"Then I must ask," Alexander said. "What are the perils involved? Not for me, but for them. Besides the obvious."

"The obvious?" Wells repeated.

"Men."

"Oh." Franklyn Wells coughed. "Well, there will be the climate. It's a lot harsher than what you're accustomed to, with temperature extremes in the summers and winters."

Alexander dismissed that with a wave of his hand. "We won't let a little weather bother us. Go on. What about hostiles?"

"The nearest tribe are the Dakotas, or the Sioux, as they are more commonly known."

"The ones who wiped out Custer?"

"They had a part in it, yes. But General Crook and that other fellow, Miles, have put an end to their depredations. Their raiding days are over."

"Anything else?"

Wells tapped his cigar on his ashtray. "There is one thing I should mention. I've never lived in the West, you understand. But I went to Texas to make our offer to Neal Bonner, and learned a lot about the nature of the men who do. You see, Mr. Bonner had conditions of his own, and one of them was that he bring his pard, as he calls him, along. The gentleman's name is Jericho. He's what they call a shootist."

"I'm unfamiliar with the term."

"Jericho is uncommonly proficient with a firearm."

"I'm not sure I understand," Alexander said. "From what I hear, everyone in the West wears a gun. Every male, that is."

"Many do, as I saw with my own eyes," Wells said. "But few are any shakes at it, as Mr. Bonner would say. Jericho is. They're quite reticent about it, but I was able to learn that Jericho has turned five to ten men toes up, as another of their quaint expressions has it."

"Wait," Alexander said. "You're saying this

Jericho is a killer?"

"At least five times over, probably more."

"And I'm to have him in my employ?"

"No Jericho, no Neal Bonner, and we need Mr. Bonner. And you need Jericho."

"That's ridiculous."

"Hear me out." Wells took a puff and blew a smoke ring. "You asked about the dangers. I'm enlightening you. One of them has to do with the character of the men out there, or the lack thereof. You see, Mr. Jessup, the West is home to many bad men. Gunmen, confidence men, cheats, cardsharps, thieves of every stripe, and, more to the point, rustlers. They're much more common than you can possibly imagine, and they are why you need a man like Jericho on your payroll."

"I'm still not sure I understand," Alexander admitted.

"Think of him as a deterrent. Those who live outside the law will be much less likely to give you trouble when they know that they must ultimately deal with Jericho."

"You're serious?"

"Westerners aren't like us," Wells said. "Their character, their fundamental natures are different. They're highly self-reliant. They respect three traits in a man more than any others. His honesty, his devotion

48

to keeping his word, and how lethal he is."

"By God, you are serious."

"Never more so. Shootists, they call them, are held in great esteem, and widely feared by the criminal element. I'm sure you've heard of Wild Bill Hickok, shot down in Deadwood not that many years ago. With a man like him on your payroll, no bad man would dare come near you or the Diamond B."

"This Jericho is as widely feared as Hickok?"

"Oh, goodness no. But he does have a reputation. And as Mr. Bonner put it to me, once Jericho has bedded down a few coyotes of the human variety, you should have no more trouble with any of their kind."

"You make it sound as if it's a foregone conclusion we will have trouble." Alexander thoughtfully contemplated the glowing tip of his own cigar. "Very well. I'll let this Jericho work for me, but only because you've assured me we need Bonner and Bonner wants him along. But Jericho will pull his weight, like everyone else."

"You need not be concerned in that regard. Jericho will work cattle along with the rest of the punchers."

"Good. Then I look forward to the challenge. How soon before the house is ready?"

"Six months, give or take," Wells said. "Mr. Bonner is at this very moment driving several thousand head of cattle from Texas to the Badlands to serve as the nucleus of the Diamond B's herd."

"It's settled, then." Alexander blew a smoke ring of his own. "Assure your investors that they've chosen wisely. I've yet to fail at anything I've undertaken."

"They have every confidence in you," Franklyn Wells declared.

Now, over five months later, Alexander Jessup still brimmed with confidence. As the stage that was taking him and his daughters to Whiskey Flats clattered and bounced along the rutted and winding excuse for a road, he gazed out over the Badlands and felt an unusual stirring in his breast.

"A penny for your thoughts, Father?" asked one of the two young women who sat across from him.

Born three years apart, they were night and day.

The older, Edana, had hair like spun gold that hung past her shoulders in a lustrous wave. Her eyes were green, like Alexander's. She had an oval face with high cheekbones, thin lips, and not much chin. Her expression was nearly always earnest, and she seldom laughed.

By contrast, her younger sister, Isolda, nearly always wore a smirk, as if the world were a source of constant amusement. She had her mother's looks: curly black hair, brown eyes, a wide forehead, and full lips. Where her sister went in for plain dresses and ordinary shoes, Isolda liked to wear dresses with lace at the cuffs, and shoes with higher heels.

"If a penny isn't enough," Edana said when her father didn't reply, "I can make it a dollar."

"Ninety-nine cents profit," Isolda said. "I'd jump at it were I you, Father."

Alexander smiled with genuine affection. "I was thinking of your mother, girls, and how much she would have loved this scenery."

"It is pretty," Edana said, "in an austere sort of way."

"Don't start with Mother again," Isolda said. "You can't wallow in grief forever."

"Isolda!" Edana exclaimed.

"Oh, hush," Isolda said. "Father knows I'm right. It's been seven years. She's gone and that's all there is to it."

"Gone, but never forgotten," Alexander said. "We'll always have our memories of her. She lives on in our hearts."

"There you go again," Isolda said. "You're too sentimental by half."

"And you're not sentimental enough." Edana came to their father's defense. "Would it hurt you to admit that you miss her as much as we do?"

"Who are you to talk about emotions? You're an iceberg inside."

"Isolda," Alexander said.

"Well, she is," Isolda said petulantly. "Everyone knows it. She keeps everything bottled up. She always has, even before Mother died."

"That will be enough," Alexander said. "We're starting a new life in a new land. Let's not bring up old disagreements."

"Is that what you call them? But very well." Isolda looked out the window on her side. "As for this new land, I can't say I'm as entranced as she is. When you've seen one patch of dirt, you've seen them all."

Alexander sighed. He had long marveled at how unlike his daughters were. The same father, the same mother, yet they had so little in common. Edana was practical to a fault, and as her sister intimated, usually as emotionless as a rock. Isolda, on the other hand, wore her emotions on her sleeve, and was hotheaded, as well. All were traits neither he nor his wife possessed to any great degree. It mystified him how children could turn out so unlike their parents.

"What do you think of the Badlands, Father?" Edana asked.

Alexander considered a moment. "They have an unusual . . . beauty . . . about them that I find most compelling."

"Did you really just say 'beauty'?" Isolda said.

"Quit teasing him," Edana scolded. "I happen to agree."

Isolda shook her head in disbelief. "What's gotten into the two of you? Father is always all business, and you wouldn't know beauty if it bit you on the hind end."

"Isolda!" Alexander said sternly.

"Well, she wouldn't."

Alexander turned to the window. It troubled him that they seemed to have more petty arguments of late. Secretly, he blamed Isolda. His younger daughter had become too temperamental. She acted bored half the time, and was sarcastic toward everyone about nearly everything. He didn't know what to do. He hoped it was a phase and nothing more.

Moments like these, he sorely missed his wife. She knew how to relate to the girls better than he did. Whenever Isolda acted up when she was little, it was his wife who invariably calmed her down and got her to behave.

It was rough, being a man and raising two girls. He did the best he could but secretly fretted that he didn't do enough. It didn't help that he was kept so busy at his job that they hardly ever did anything outside of their work.

Troubled, Alexander gazed out at the scenery.

The vistas beyond the carriage soothed him somewhat. The many buttes, with their flat tops and sheer sides sometimes splashed deep red by the sun, were spectacular. No less so were the mesas, towering tablelands of sandstone or limestone or basalt. In addition, there were rock spires and stone monoliths of all different sizes and shapes. All of that interspersed with tracts of prairie grass and verdant valleys.

The Badlands were a fascinating riot of diversity.

Just then the driver hollered down, "About a mile to Whiskey Flats. Just over the next rise."

"Nice of him to let us know," Edana said.

"I told him to," Alexander said, and grinned. "So you two can fuss with your hair or whatever it is you do."

"What is this place like?" Isolda asked. "This Whiskey Flats?" She said the name mockingly.

"In his last letter Mr. Wells wrote that I might be pleasantly surprised," Alexander replied. "But to answer you, I'd warrant it's a typical frontier town. I only pray it has a church. Without one, vice tends to run rampant. Or so I've heard."

"Do tell," Isolda teased.

"Behave yourself," Alexander said. "Especially when we arrive. We must make a good first impression."

"Or what? People will talk about us behind our backs?"

"Isolda, please," Edana said.

"Oh, posh to you."

"The other thing I should mention," Alexander said, "is that Mr. Wells warned us to be on our guard."

"Against what?" Edana asked.

"He wasn't specific. He merely mentioned that we shouldn't expect the same civility we're accustomed to back East."

"I know," Isolda said, and grinned. "Maybe he was warning us to watch out for all that rampant vice."

"We'll find out soon enough," Alexander said.

5

Whiskey Flats wasn't what Isolda Jessup had expected. The few towns they'd passed through south of the Badlands had been little more than sleepy hamlets, and that was being charitable. The people were slovenly and unkempt, the buildings dirty and run-down. As the stage rolled into Whiskey Flats, she poked her head out, expecting more of the same, took one wondering look, and said in delight, "Oh my."

"What?" Edana stuck her head out, too, careful to put a hand over her hair to keep it from being mussed by the wind. " 'Oh my' is right."

Alexander turned and looked out. "Well, now. This isn't at all as Franklyn Wells told me it would be."

Whiskey Flats bustled with life and vitality. The main street had been lengthened, and the frame buildings that lined it stood two and in some instances three stories tall. Several saloons were slaking the thirst of those who couldn't do without liquor. A general store sat on one corner. There was a millinery with a sign written in pink letters and a blacksmith's attached to a livery stable.

"I thought Mr. Wells told you there was one saloon and not much else," Edana said.

"He did mention it had grown once the construction on the ranch started," Alexander said. "And that it would grow even more once the cattle arrived, which they have. But still."

"I like what I see," Isolda said. From the rustic population to a lot of men walking around with guns, to dogs and pigs and chickens being allowed to run about as they pleased, the place had a wild atmosphere that appealed to her.

"It's very unorganized," Edana noted.

"Isn't it, though?" Isolda said, and laughed.

The driver had to yell at a few people to get out of the way. It seemed that everyone felt they could walk down the middle of the street if they so pleased, or stand talking and force riders and wagons to go around.

"These people have no manners," Edana said.

"Now, now, sister," Isolda said. "We left culture east of the Mississippi. Out here it's life in the raw."

"Don't talk like that," Alexander said.

"Like what?"

"About things being raw. It's unseemly for a lady."

"Oh, Father," Isolda said, and laughed again.

Their stagecoach came to a stop near the livery stable. The driver jumped down and opened the door, announcing, "We've arrived, folks."

"Are you sure?" Isolda said.

"Ma'am?"

"Isolda, behave," Alexander said. He waited while they descended, then climbed out and bent his legs a few times to relieve the stiffness from sitting for so long. "Quite the town they have here."

The driver, a middle-aged man with a paunch and a trick eye that twitched a lot, nodded. "They say there's a shootin' or a knifin' at least once a month."

"Where did you hear that?"

The man shrugged. "Drivers hear all sorts of things. Whiskey Flats is part of my regular run. It ain't often someone hires a stage for private, like you done."

58

"What a wonderful idiom you use," Isolda said.

"Ma'am?" the driver said.

"Pay her no mind," Alexander said. He looked up and down the street. "I suppose our first order of business is to get word to the ranch that we've arrived so they can send someone to pick us up."

"You're bound for the Diamond B, I take it?" the driver said.

"I've been hired to run it," Alexander informed him. "How about if I hire you to ride out and have them send a wagon for us and our bags?"

"Sorry, mister. I don't have the time to spare." The driver turned to the back of the stage. "I have to get on to the next town."

"How long does it take to reach the ranch from here?" Alexander asked.

"I hear it's about three hours by wagon," the driver said. "Sooner if you ride. Find yourself a local and they'll do it for a dollar."

"I could ride out and have them send a wagon," Edana offered.

"Or we can hire a wagon and go ourselves," Isolda said.

The driver shook his head. "Not if you have a brain, you won't. Where do you reckon you are, anyhow? St. Louis?"

"How dare you talk to us like that!" Isolda bristled. She never could let an insult pass.

"All I'm sayin' is that you'd better take a look around. A good look. You see many females in the streets? You do not. But you will see a lot of cat-eyed gents who have no more respect for womanhood than they do anything else."

"Is that your way of saying they're godless ruffians?" Alexander said.

"They ain't saints." The driver started unloading.

"Colorful, isn't he?" Isolda said.

"Perhaps we should take his advice and stroll about," Alexander proposed. "Ascertain for ourselves what the place is really like."

"I could stand to stretch my legs," Edana said.

Isolda strolled slowly, amused by much of what she saw. Men spitting tobacco juice. Men scratching themselves where no man should touch in public. And the profanity. She saw a dog lift its leg at a hitch rail.

"Barbaric," Edana said.

"I agree," Alexander said. "These people are unbelievably crude. It's as if they don't care what others think of them."

"I like it," Isolda said.

"You don't mean that," Edana said.

"But I do," Isolda insisted. "When have I ever cared what anyone thought about me? I only have because Father and you made me. But this" — and she gestured at the whirl of activity — "is me."

"You're being ridiculous," Alexander said. "Your mother was always a proper lady, and so are you."

They came abreast of the Three Aces. Through the front window they could see it was packed, even though it was only the middle of the day. Boisterous babble and mirth spilled out, along with the tinkle of glasses and the tinny music of a piano.

"Who says this place doesn't have culture?" Isolda said.

Alexander was about to walk on when the batwings slammed open and out stalked three men. All three wore wide-brimmed hats and revolvers. One of them wore two with ivory grips. They hadn't shaved in days, and they were in need of baths.

The man wearing two revolvers had a scar on his left cheek. Stopping short, he leered at Edana and Isolda. "Look at this, boys. What do we have here?"

"My daughters," Alexander said coldly.

The man with the scar came off the boardwalk. He looked Edana and Isolda up and down, a lustful gleam in his eyes. "You two fillies are right pretty."

Isolda looked him up and down and imitated him, saying, "And you, you randy goat, are right ugly."

The man with the scar grinned. "I like a sassy gal. They're more fun under a blanket."

"Now, see here," Alexander said, moving between them. "I told you they're my daughters."

The man blinked as if surprised. "So?"

"So you'll treat them with respect, you obscene specimen."

"What did you just call me?"

The other two sauntered over on either side of their companion. One was lanky, with a hooked nose and big ears. The other had bulging eyes and a froglike aspect enhanced by his bulbous lips.

It was the lanky one who snickered and said, "He called you a specimen, Scar. I heard him clear as day."

"What the hell does that even mean?" said the frog.

Alexander half turned to Isolda and Edana. "Come along," he said, but before they could take a step, the man called Scar barred their way.

"You're not goin' anywhere, mister. Not until you explain what you just called me."

"I won't be treated like this," Alexander said. "Do you have any idea who I am?"

"You're mud," said the lanky one.

The frog chuckled and said, "Good one, Grat."

"Well, he is, Tuck," Grat said.

Isolda had listened to enough. She refused to be treated so shabbily. Especially by men who appeared barely intelligent enough to know their right hand from their left. Moving past her father, she poked Scar in the chest. "Now, see here. You'll leave us be and go about your own business or there will be hell to pay. You hear me?"

Scar didn't act the least bit concerned. Or mad. Instead he laughed and said, "Listen to her, boys. This gal has got a lot of spunk. I like that almost as much I like sass."

"She's a cow," Grat said. "A cow with spunk, but still."

"What did you just call her?" Alexander said.

"Let's go find the marshal," Edana proposed. "He'll put a stop to this nonsense."

The one called Tuck snorted. "Shows how dumb you are, lady. There ain't any tin stars in Whiskey Flats."

"What?" Edana said.

"There's ain't no law, you stupid woman," Tuck said.

"Don't talk to my sister like that," Isolda said. She was simmering inside. "It makes me mad."

"What will you do?" Scar said. "Take a swing at us."

He and the others laughed.

"If she doesn't, I might," Beaumont Adams said from the doorway of the Three Aces. Pushing through the batwings, he strolled out. He was dressed in his frock coat and white shirt with a string tie and a pair of polished boots. His black hat was low over his brow, shielding his eyes from the glare of the sun.

Scar scowled. "Stay out of this, gambler."

"Why, Mr. Scar Wratner, how rude of you," Beaumont said jokingly. "Would that I could, but these are my premises." He smiled at Isolda and Edana. "I was lookin' out the window and couldn't help noticing the predicament you ladies are in."

"What's a predicament?" Tuck asked.

"It means trouble," Grat said.

"Why in hell does everybody around here use big words?" Tuck said.

"It's not that our words are so big," Beaumont said. "It's that your brain is so puny."

Isolda laughed.

"You shouldn't ought to stick your nose

64

where it's not wanted," Scar Wratner warned him.

"I'll stick it where I please," Beaumont said. "You'd be well advised to light a shuck while you still can."

Scar lowered his hands to his sides so they brushed his Smith & Wessons. "Are you threatenin' us, gambler man?"

"Perish forfend," Beaumont said. "It's not me you have to worry about. It's the quick-draw artist who works for this gentleman here."

"Do I know you?" Alexander asked.

"Unless I'm mistaken, you're the new boss of the Diamond B," Beaumont said. "Mr. Jessup, isn't it? And these would be your girls. Franklyn Wells mentioned you on his last visit. He likes to stop in and wet his whistle."

"What quick-draw artist were you talkin' about?" Grat asked, his hand hanging near a nickel-plated Remington.

"You boys really ought to get the lay of the land before you go around annoyin' folks," Beaumont said. "Annoy the wrong one and he's liable to squish you."

"What the hell are you talkin' about, mister?" Tuck said. "How did squishin' get into this?"

"It's what he likes to do, I hear."

"Who?"

"Who have we been talkin' about?" Beaumont said. "The gun hand. I heard him with my own ears. He likes to squish things."

"You're makin' no kind of sense," Scar Wratner said. "Go back inside and have your fun with your customers."

"And miss the fireworks? Not on your life." Beaumont leaned against a post and folded his arms. "I might finally get to see how good he is. I've been wonderin' since I first set eyes on the gent."

"On who?" Tuck practically snarled.

"And you called this lovely lady dumb?" Beaumont said. "She has more brains in her little finger than you do between your ears."

"Don't start on my brain again," Tuck said, his jaw twitching.

"What was that about finally seein' how good this gun shark of yours is?" Grat said.

"I keep tellin' you. He's not mine. He rides for the Diamond B. He's pards with the foreman, and gossip has it he's bucked more than a few gents out, permanent, down to Texas. Neither he nor the foreman take any guff, so this should be doubly interestin'."

"What, consarn you?" Tuck said in exasperation.

"The gun battle," Beaumont said.

"We'll have one with you if you don't come clean," Scar declared.

Beaumont smiled. "That gun shark and that foreman I just told you about?" He nodded up the street. "Here they come, and they don't look any too happy. Now, why do you suppose that is?"

Isolda laughed.

6

Neal Bonner was a cattleman through and through. He'd been born on a small ranch in Texas and grown up around cows. From an early age he'd fed them, milked them, shoveled the manure of the milk cows in the barn, herded the cattle out on the range, roped them, branded them.

Anything and everything that had to do with cattle, he'd done, and learned to do it exceptionally well. Which was why, at the unheard-of age of twenty, he'd been offered the job of foreman at a neighboring ranch, the much larger Bar H. He did so superb a job there that two years later an even larger ranch, the Circle T, hired him away. He'd been there three years when Franklyn Wells came calling on behalf of the Portland Whaling Consortium and their newly created Badlands Land and Cattle Company.

Evidently Wells had gone around asking ranchers all over west Texas who they'd pick as the top three foremen, and Neal's name had been on many of the lists. But Neal liked the Diamond T. He liked the owner, he liked the men who worked under him, and he liked the land.

At first Neal had told them no. He admitted he was flattered and thanked them for their interest, but he would stay where he was.

Franklyn Wells was persistent. He wouldn't take that no for an answer. He paid repeated visits, six in a span of two months. Each time he offered Neal more money. But when Wells saw that it wasn't the money Neal loved, but the cattle, Wells shrewdly stressed the things a cowman would care about. How Neal would oversee more cattle than most foremen. How every aspect of their tending was completely in Neal's care. The ranch manager would run the ranch, but Neal, and only Neal, had oversight of the cattle.

Gradually, Wells wore Neal's resistance down. Wells's crowning argument was the challenge of it all, to make a ranch succeed where none had succeeded before, to wrest a cattle empire from the untamed wilds, as the early Texas pioneers had done.

Neal gave in and said yes, with one condition. Jericho must go with him or he wouldn't go. There was no debating the issue. It was Jericho or it was no.

Wells had been puzzled by the request. He'd assumed it was because Neal and Jericho were friends, and said as much. Neal's reply had enlightened Wells to the true nature of Westerners.

"Jericho is more than my friend. He's my pard."

Only then did Wells see that when a man called another his pard, the bond ran deeper than any except marriage. Men stuck with their pards through thick and thin.

They did everything together. They shared everything together. Their pard came before everything else, and they'd die for him if they had to.

Wells had been curious. He'd pried into how the bond between Neal and Jericho came about. And one night, over brandy in the parlor of the owner of the Circle T, Neal Bonner told a story not even the owner had heard.

Neal was at the Bar H at the time. He'd gone into the nearest town, Benton — or Benton City, as some called it — to pick up the mail. Since he had a few hours to kill before the stage arrived, he'd decided to treat himself to a drink. One and one only. He'd gone into the Longhorn and over to the bar and had no sooner taken his first sip than trouble started.

Some men were playing poker. One of them was half-drunk, and in a loud and obnoxious manner started complaining about how much he had lost, and how he wouldn't have lost it if he wasn't being cheated.

The accusation froze everyone in the saloon. It was the worst insult anyone could give, short of calling someone a horse thief.

The bartender hollered over, "That's enough out of you, Lindsey. You've had too much to drink. Go home and sleep it off."

"Like hell I will," Lindsey replied, and stood. He was a big man who liked to throw his weight around even when sober, and who had made more than a few peace-loving townsmen dance to the tune of his six-shooter. "One of you is dealin' from the bottom'," he snarled at the other cardplayers, "and I have a good idea who."

That was when Neal set eyes on Jericho for the first time.

Jericho was one of the men at that table. His head was down, but just then he'd raised it and said to Lindsey, "No one is cheatin'. If they were, I'd know."

"Who the hell are you?" Lindsey demanded.

"Jericho."

A murmur spread through the saloon. Neal overheard enough to gather that the name wasn't to be taken lightly.

Lindsey didn't seem especially impressed. "Jericho, you say? I've heard of you."

Jericho didn't say anything. In his left hand he held his cards. His right was under the table.

"I've heard you're supposed to be considerable shakes with a six-gun," Lindsey went on. "Well, I can shoot, too."

"Don't go there," Jericho said.

"I'll do what I damn well please," Lindsey said. "And I don't much appreciate you buttin' in."

"You should take the barkeep's advice."

"Who's he to tell me what to do?" Lindsey snapped. "Who are you to tell me the same?"

Neal had been surprised when Jericho set down his cards and stood.

"You're right. I shouldn't ought to stick my nose in. It's a bad habit of mine. I reckon I'm done with this game." With his left hand Jericho scooped up his money and stuck it in a pocket, then turned to go.

Lindsey stood there, staring. No one could say what made him do what he did next. Neal's best guess was that Lindsey was looking to add to his reputation as a bad man to trifle with. It was the only thing that made sense, the only thing that explained why when Jericho had taken a couple of steps, Lindsey clawed for his six-shooter.

Nor could anyone say what prompted Neal to do what he did next. He couldn't explain it himself. All his life he'd minded his own business. He never got involved when a fracas broke out. He never raised a finger to stop a shooting. But as Lindsey started to draw, Neal shouted, "Look out!"

Jericho was already in motion. He must have sensed something or seen Lindsey out of the corner of his eye because he whirled even as Neal yelled, his pearl-handled Colt seeming to leap into his hand. He fanned two shots from the hip so swiftly they sounded like one.

Lindsey was jolted onto his bootheels. "No!" he bleated, and keeled onto his back with his arms outflung. He lay gasping for air and staring at the ceiling.

No one moved. No one spoke.

Jericho came around the table. He watched Lindsey gasp, and said quietly, "You made me rush it."

"Damn, you're quick," Lindsey got out, and stopped gasping.

Jericho frowned. He'd slowly replaced the

spent cartridges, and slowly slid his Colt into its holster. "I had it to do."

"We all saw it," a cardplayer said. "We'll vouch for that with the marshal."

Jericho nodded, then did the last thing Neal expected; he walked over to the bar. "I'm obliged for the warnin'."

"Didn't seem as if you needed one," Neal said, smiling.

Jericho held out a hand. His right hand. "Jericho."

"So I heard." Neal held out his. "Neal Bonner."

"Cowhand?"

"Foreman."

"I can work cows."

"You're lookin' for work?"

"No. But if that's what you do, I can, too."

Only afterward did Neal realize this was a pivotal moment in his life. On some unconscious level he'd recognized what Jericho was offering, and on that same unconscious level he'd unhesitatingly accepted. "Come work cows for me, then."

From then on, they were inseparable.

And now, striding down Whiskey Flats's dusty main street, Neal remarked, "They've seen us."

"The gambler has sharp eyes," Jericho said.

"I don't know what it's about, but we have to avoid chuckin' lead with the womenfolk so close."

"That won't be up to me."

Neal was upset with himself. Franklyn Wells had written him that the new manager and his daughters were expected to arrive this very day, but Wells had intimated it wouldn't be until later. Neal set out from the ranch early that morning with Jericho and another hand on a buckboard, plus an extra horse, but the stage was already there when they arrived.

"Those three folks I brought in?" the driver had said when asked. "They moseyed off not two minutes ago." He'd scanned Main Street and pointed. "There they are. And say, it looks as if some hard cases have latched onto 'em."

Walking faster, Neal asked Jericho, "Do you know those three?"

"I don't recollect seein' them before, no."

"Must be new in town."

"New or not, they're trouble."

Neal girded himself. The three toughs had faced them and spread out. The one in the middle, with a scar on his face, was a rarity, a two-gun man. Usually only green kids wore two six-shooters — or the very few who were the genuine articles and could use both hands as adeptly as most used one. The man with the scar wasn't a green kid.

"Watch the one in the middle."

"The other two ain't parsons," Jericho said.

Neal hadn't paid much attention to the Jessups, but as he neared them he did. Alexander Jessup was much as Wells had described him. "Aristocratic, like one of those Roman emperors." Neal didn't know an emperor from a billy goat, but Alexander Jessup did have the air of someone who carried himself as if he were important.

The two daughters weren't at all what Neal had expected. Wells had written their names and mentioned they were "older girls," leading Neal to assume they might be fifteen or sixteen or thereabouts. But they were full-grown women, and both of them were easy on the eyes, to boot. At first glimpse, he thought the one with hair like corn silk was a shade prettier. With a shake of his head, Neal put that from his mind.

Beaumont Adams was leaning against a post, and smirking. The gambler smirked a lot, Neal had noticed, the few times he'd been in the Three Aces.

"Gentlemen," Beaumont said. "How nice

to see you again. Welcome to our street social. Permit me to make the introductions. Mr. Neal Bonner, and Jericho, I'd like you to meet three upstandin' new members of our community. Mr. Scar Wratner and his friends Bird Beak and Toad."

Isolda Jessup laughed.

The pair on either side of Scar Wratner glanced angrily at the gambler.

"What did you just call me?" said the one who did indeed resemble a frog or a toad. "My name is Tuck. And this here is Grat, not Bird Beak."

"I'm terribly sorry," Beaumont said. "They seemed to be the logical handles."

Isolda laughed once more.

"You think you're so damn funny," Tuck said. "Keep it up and I'll make you laugh out your ass."

"Hush," Scar Wratner growled. He was staring at Jericho.

Tuck hushed.

Scar went on staring. "The tinhorn over there says you're the cock of the walk in these parts."

Beaumont Adams straightened. "Hold on. I resent that, Wratner. I admit I'm not the most law-abidin' gent, but I play square at cards. Ask anyone. I never deal from the bottom."

"Good for you." Scar hadn't taken his eyes off Jericho. "Do you know what happens when there are two roosters in the same barnyard?"

"I do," Jericho said.

"How about we get to it, then?"

7

To the considerable astonishment of nearly everyone, Edana Jessup picked that moment to step between Neal Bonner and Jericho and the three hard cases. Putting her hands on her hips, she demanded of Scar Wratner, "What is the matter with you?"

"Edana, no," Alexander Jessup said. "Move out of the way."

"I will not," Edana said, glowering at Wratner. "I'll ask you again, sir. What is the matter with you?"

Scar didn't seem to know what to say or do. He looked at her and then at Jericho, who appeared equally nonplussed. "What is the matter with *me*?" he repeated. "What in hell is the matter with *you*? Listen to your pa and move or you're liable to take lead."

Beaumont Adams made a loud clucking sound. "No, no, no. You don't want to do that."

Scar glared at him. "Another word out of

you, cardsharp, and you won't like what happens."

"How about a dozen words?" Beaumont said, and paused. "Harm a hair on her head and you're as good as dead."

"Oh, I am, am I?" Scar swiveled toward him. "I'd like to see you try."

"Me?" Beaumont said in mock dismay. "It's the rest of the town you have to worry about."

"What are you jabberin' about?"

"Look around you," Beaumont said, and gestured.

All along Main Street, people had stopped what they were doing to stare. Riders, those on foot, a man in a buckboard, were so many statues, awaiting the outcome.

"You're a braver man than me, Scar Wratner," Beaumont continued. "I'd never threaten to put lead into a woman with a whole town listenin'. Not when females are so scarce west of the Mississippi and even scarcer here in the Badlands. Why, shootin' one would be worse than horse stealin'. Especially ladies as pretty as these two. Can you imagine how upset that would make the male population? It wouldn't surprise me a bit if every man in town was to haul you to the nearest tree and treat you to a strangulation jig."

Scar looked up and down the street. "Son of a bitch."

"If I was you I'd sheathe my horns," the gambler advised gravely. "Do your shootin' another time."

"Do you want I should gun him?" Grat asked Scar. "He gets on my nerves with all his prattle."

Scar shook his head. "No. He's right. This ain't the time to be slingin' lead. We'll go to the Tumbleweed and have us a drink there." He went to walk off.

"Hold on," Jericho said.

Scar looked at him.

"Let's mosey on out into the street a ways and shoo everybody off and finish this."

"I'd just as soon," Scar said.

Before either could move, Edana Jessup whirled on Neal Bonner. "Are you just going to stand there like a lump of clay?"

"What did I do?" Neal blurted, taken aback.

"Not a blessed thing, and that's the problem." Edana jabbed a finger at Jericho. "Does he or does he not work for the Diamond B?"

"He does."

"And are you or are you not the foreman at the Diamond B?"

"I am," Neal said, becoming more bewildered by the moment.

"And are you or are you not employed by the Badlands Land and Cattle Company?"

"I am." Neal liked how her cheeks flushed when she was mad.

"And is my father or is he not the ranch manager duly appointed by the aforesaid Badlands Land and Cattle Company, for whom you work?"

"The what-said?" Tuck interrupted.

"I didn't hear your answer," Edana said to Neal.

Distracted by her looks, Neal had to think before he could say "Your pa is, and I do."

Beaumont Adams got into the act. "I now pronounce you man and wife."

Isolda chortled.

"Father, tell him," Edana said. "Tell both of them."

"Tell them what, my dear?" Alexander said.

"If I hadn't heard this with my own ears," Beaumont said, "I wouldn't have believed it."

"Seriously, Father?" Edana said. "Have you lost all reason since we climbed down from that stage? Tell your foreman to tell his friend that under no circumstances is he to resort to gun play or you will fire the both of them."

"I'm right here," Neal said. "He doesn't have to tell me. If that's what you want, ma'am, that's what we'll do."

"I should think so," Edana said huffily.

"You heard the lady," Neal said to Jericho.

"With all due respect, ma'am," Jericho addressed Edana, "you're makin' a mistake. If I don't snuff his wick here and now, he might snuff one of ours later."

Edana tapped her foot in irritation. "Oh, really? Is that true — Mr. Wratner, wasn't it? Do you intend to make war on the Diamond B?"

"Hadn't planned on it, lady, no."

"Maybe we should," Tuck said, "after how they've treated us."

"I second the motion," Beaumont Adams said. "After all, there's only over sixty ranch hands, countin' all the cowboys and everyone else, and three of you. It should be a fine massacre. I believe I could sell tickets like they do at those prizefights."

"I think I hate you," Tuck said.

Scar Wratner chuckled and headed off, saying, "Gambler, you sure are a hoot. Another time."

Grat followed Scar, but Tuck fixed his bulging eyes on Beaumont Adams. "I don't like bein' called a toad. I'll remember you said that."

"It's good you can remember something," Beaumont said.

Hissing, Tuck wheeled and hastened after his friends. He looked back to holler, "You and me, tinhorn. One day soon."

Beaumont grinned. "Goodness gracious. I do believe I'm paralyzed with fear."

Isolda did more laughing, then became serious. "I doubt there's much you're scared of, handsome. Unless perhaps it's a woman with marriage on her mind."

"Enough of that kind of talk, daughter," Alexander said sternly. "You've only just met the man."

Edana uttered a hiss remarkably like Tuck's. "*Now* you speak up, Father? After that horrible scene, all you can think of to do is to scold Isolda?"

"You're a fine one to talk," Alexander said. "Your antics could have resulted in some of us being shot."

"He's right, ma'am," Jericho said, and glanced at Neal as if expecting him to say something.

Neal was tongue-tied. He'd never been all that comfortable around women he didn't know, and Edana Jessup made him doubly uneasy because she was so good-looking.

"This is a sorry start to our stay here," Edana declared.

"Oh, I don't know," Isolda said, smiling at Beaumont. "I found it quite interesting."

"My favorite word," the gambler said to her, and gave a courtly bow. "Perhaps the lady would care to take a tour of the premises? I promise to attend to your every whim."

"Listen to you," Isolda said.

"Enough!" Alexander gruffly declared. He pointed at Beaumont. "My daughter doesn't associate with questionable characters. You will stop imposing yourself on us this instant." He pointed at Edana. "Don't you ever do something like that again. Between the gambler and you, it's no wonder those three ruffians were provoked." He pointed at Neal. "As for you, Mr. Bonner, I'm severely disappointed. Frank Wells led me to believe you were the best man for the job of foreman. He praised you as capable and efficient. Instead you show up late, and when you saw we were in peril, you came to our rescue but aggravated the situation more than anything." Alexander paused. "I can't say I'm greatly impressed."

Neal felt himself grow warm in the face. He was seldom embarrassed. He seldom let himself *be* embarrassed. He was about to explain the circumstances involved but changed his mind. Jessup would only regard it as making excuses.

"If you'd like, we can collect your bags and head for the ranch."

"Must we leave so soon, Father?" Isolda asked. "We've only just arrived, and I would love to have a bite to eat."

"An excellent suggestion," Alexander said. "Some tea would calm our nerves." He turned back to Neal. "Where would you suggest? Is there a restaurant worthy of the name?"

"There's only one and for most it's good enough," Neal said.

"Lead the way."

Neal walked past them. He caught a whiff of Edana's perfume and avoided looking at her.

Alexander took the arms of both his daughters and followed.

Isolda, glancing back, grinned and winked at Beaumont Adams.

"Did you see that?" the gambler said to Jericho. "I do believe I'm in love."

"What can you tell me about Wratner?"

"I met him for the first time today, the same as you," Beaumont said. "But the name rings a bell. They say he's mighty gun wise."

"Interestin'," Jericho said, and ambled after the others.

"I'll be damned. Did you just poke fun at me?" Beaumont said.

Up ahead, Neal heard the exchange and was annoyed at himself for not asking the same thing. Scar Wratner wasn't the kind to forgive and forget. They'd braced him in the middle of Main Street, in front of God and everybody. Wratner would get back at them somehow. The man might bide his time, but sooner or later there would be a reckoning.

Neal walked past the general store and the dress shop and stopped and indicated a sign. "The eatery."

In large letters was MA'S. GOOD FOOD. CHEAP.

"How quaint," Alexander Jessup said.

Neal held the door for them. He waited for Jericho to come up and asked, "Are you hungry?"

"Not particularly."

"How about you stay outside and keep an eye on things?"

"Suits me. I don't much care for the big sugar. He looks down his nose at folks."

"He's from back East," Neal said, as if that explained it. Going in, he saw that the Jessups had already selected a table. He pulled out a chair across from Alexander and sat.

"Where's Mr. Jericho?" Edana asked.

"Keepin' watch, ma'am," Neal said. "And it's just Jericho."

"Is that his first name or his last?"

"It's the only one he uses."

"How strange."

"Everything about this place is so different from what we're used to," Isolda said. "I find it invigorating."

"You're young yet, and impressionable," Alexander said. "I've seen little to recommend this town. It's too crude by half."

"You've only just got here," Neal felt compelled to say.

"All the men with their firearms. Animals wandering where they please. The streets aren't kept clean. Franklyn Wells warned me conditions were primitive compared to those I am accustomed to, but still."

Neal was experiencing doubts. Wells had assured him that Alexander Jessup was the right man to oversee the Diamond B, but so far he hadn't seen evidence of that. "How much do you know about cows, Mr. Jessup, if you don't mind my askin'?"

"They give milk and they taste good," Alexander said. "But don't you worry. When I set my mind to something, I learn quickly. Inside of a month, I expect to have acquired most of the knowledge I'll need to run the ranch efficiently."

"That's awful optimistic," Neal observed.

"Do you doubt my father's ability?" Edana asked.

"No, ma'am. But learnin' anything in a month takes a heap of doin'. I've been workin' cattle all my life and I still learn new things from time to time."

"My father has a brilliant mind for business. It's why the consortium wanted him to manage the ranch. You should respect that."

Neal began to wonder if the whole family went around with their noses in the air. "Out here, ma'am, a man earns respect by what he does. He doesn't have it handed to him on his say-so."

"We're liars, are we?"

"I never said that, ma'am."

"Now, now," Alexander intervened. "Daughter, quit being so hard on him. He's right to be skeptical. I would be, too, were I in his boots. I don't mind having to prove myself to him or anyone else."

Neal's estimation of Jessup rose a notch. "The hands won't expect you to ride and rope. That's their job. All they'll ask is that you don't act as high and mighty as some do."

"Do you mean me?" Edana asked coolly.

89

"I was thinkin' of Scar Wratner, ma'am." Neal told the first lie he'd told in a coon's age.

"We've seen the last of him, I'm sure."

"If you say so, ma'am," Neal said, knowing full well they hadn't.

8

Isolda Jessup barely noticed the food. She was in a whirl of emotions unlike any she had ever experienced.

For starters, there was that gambler, Beaumont Adams. Something about him appealed to her. It wasn't just that he was good-looking. It was him, his personality. He reminded her of her in how he was amused by everything that went on around him. He had a keen wit, and his jests made her laugh. No man had ever done that before. Not to this degree.

The town itself, in the brief glimpse she'd had of it, appealed to her, too. Her father was right. Whiskey Flats was an untamed cauldron of violence and vice. And Lord help her, she loved that.

Isolda never had liked the life her father imposed on her. It was too reserved, too dull. He was always on her about being a proper lady, as her mother was, and never doing or saying anything that would bring scandal to the family. But as much as Isolda loved her mother — and she had loved her dearly — she wasn't her.

Her mother had been mousy and timid. Isolda liked to speak her mind. She liked to do as she pleased.

Her father was always saying how she must restrain herself and do as a lady would do. Isolda was so tired of that word she could scream. It seemed to her that forcing women to be ladies was how men kept women under their control. Why else was it that men were allowed to go to taverns and saloons but "proper ladies" weren't? And that was but one of a long list of things that ladies were forever being told was unseemly for them to do.

In a pig's eye, Isolda thought, and grinned. She'd never used that expression before. It must be her surroundings, she decided. They were bringing out the rustic in her.

Sitting back, Isolda noticed the ranch foreman was staring at her. The moment she met his gaze he looked away, which added to her amusement. There he sat, so big and strong and manly, and he was as timid as her mother. She couldn't imagine Beaumont Adams looking away. The gambler would more likely want her to sit on his lap. At that, she inadvertently giggled.

"What is so humorous?" her father asked.

"I'm excited about the new house," Isolda said. "I can't wait to unpack and settle in."

"I've brought a buckboard, ma'am," Neal Bonner said. "For your travelin' bags and such. And you and your sister can sit on the seat with the driver."

Isolda couldn't think of anything less appealing than riding on a hard seat hours on end.

"What about me, Mr. Bonner?" Alexander asked.

"I brought a horse."

"You assumed I'd ride out to the ranch?"

"You don't want to, Mr. Jessup?" Neal said.

"I'd rather not, no. The longest I've ever been on horseback in my entire life was for an hour or so, and that was years ago. Is there any chance we can rent a carriage at the livery?"

"Afraid not," Neal said. "They only have horses to rent."

"Well, that won't do. One of my first orders of business will be to acquire a carriage for the Diamond B to convey my daughters and me back and forth when necessary, and guests when we have them."

"There were a few ranches down to Texas

that had their own carriages," Neal said. "I reckon I should have thought of that. A buckboard makes for a rough ride for those not used to it."

"I'll ride in the back," Alexander said. "We can fold a blanket for me to sit on. It shouldn't be too bad."

"I have a better idea, Father," Edana said. "Why don't you ride on the seat with Isolda and the driver, and I'll go horseback?"

"I don't mind roughing it, daughter."

"I'm sure you don't," Edana said. "But I like riding, as you well know. I made it a point to ride at least once a week at Macedonia."

"Yes, you did," Alexander said. "You've always liked horses more than your sister does."

"I can't stand the stink," Isolda said.

Neal Bonner sat back as if she'd slapped him. "Of a *horse*?"

"Horses have an odor, just like everything else."

"But —" Neal stopped.

"Why do you look so flabbergasted?"

"A hog or a pig I could savvy. A chicken coop will stink to high heaven if it's not aired out. Even a dog will smell when it's been runnin' or when it's wet. But a horse has the pleasantest scent this side of a woman."

"Oh, really?" Isolda said, and was tickled when he blushed again.

Edana came to Neal's defense. "I happen to agree with him. I like how a horse smells. It's not rank or musty but rather pleasant."

"Thank you, ma'am," Neal said.

"What are you thanking her for?" Isolda asked. "You're not a horse."

Alexander cleared his throat. "I flatter myself that I understand. He's a horseman of the plains, after all, and I've heard that cowboys become quite attached to their animals."

"I'd rather be attached to a person," Isolda said, "so long as he doesn't stink." She laughed merrily.

Isolda had ordered pot pie, and had to admit it was delicious. The pieces of chicken were well done, the gravy was buttery, and the carrots and peas weren't undercooked.

But she only picked at it, thinking of Beaumont Adams, until her father caught her off guard.

"You're not eating much, Isolda. Don't you like the food? This was your idea, after all."

"Apparently I wasn't as hungry as I thought," Isolda said, justifying her disinterest. "Do we have to leave as soon as we're done? I was hoping we'd take a stroll around the town." And perhaps she'd run into the gambler again.

"I'd rather we didn't delay our departure. I want to reach the ranch well before dark, if we can." Alexander turned to Neal. "Is that possible?"

"If we leave soon it is."

"I'm curious," Alexander said. "What would you have done earlier if Scar Wratner or one of those others had resorted to their six-shooters?"

"I'd have let Jericho handle it but been ready to back his play."

"Loyalty to a friend is commendable," Alexander said, "so long as it doesn't get you killed."

"And even if it does," Neal said. "Stickin' by those we care for is the mark of a man." He caught himself and added, "Or a woman."

"That's your measure of manhood?" Isolda said derisively. "There's more to life than loyalty."

"If there is," Neal said, "I haven't made its acquaintance."

"Does that apply to wives and families?" Edana asked casually.

"If it didn't, it'd be a worthless proposition," Neal said. "A wife and young'uns deserve the best a man can give them."

"A commendable attitude," Edana said. "You have my sincere esteem."

"Lordy, ma'am."

"I beg your pardon?"

"I'm not used to all the big words you three sling around," Neal said with a good-natured smile. "Must be all that book learnin'."

"How many books have you read, Mr. Bonner?"

"Ma'am?"

"You heard me," Edana said. "I'm curious to learn how many books you've read in your lifetime."

"All the way through?"

"Is there any other way to read a book?"

"Bits and pieces," Neal said.

Isolda laughed. "Isn't he wonderful?"

"I'm waiting for an answer," Edana said. "Have you read so many that you can't count them?"

"Sort of the opposite, ma'am," Neal said. "I haven't ever read a book all the way through. The closest I've come is the Bible, but that's mostly from hearin' it spoke about a lot."

"Not one book in your entire lifetime? How is that possible?"

Neal shrugged. "In the part of Texas

where I grew up, there wasn't much schoolin'. Oh, my ma taught me to read and write, which has come in handy. But I've never owned a book in my life."

"There wasn't a schoolhouse you could attend?"

"The nearest, as I recollect, was a hundred miles away or better," Neal said. "A right far piece to go to every mornin' and make it home in time for supper."

Alexander chuckled. "I do believe our foreman has just poked a hole in your pretensions, my dear."

"What's pretentious about an education? How can he be as good at his job as they say he is if he's barely literate?"

Neal answered for himself. "The important thing is that I'm smarter than the cows. If I was dumber, I'd be worthless."

Laughing, Alexander said, "Well countered. You must be careful, my dear. I've heard that cowboy wit can be sharp."

"It's not his wit so much as you love to see us put in our place," Isolda said.

"What a terrible thing to say. When do I ever do that?"

"All the time, Father," Isolda said. "It's either your way or no way, from how we dress to how we live."

"That's not entirely true," Edana said.

"All he asks is that we comport ourselves as ladies. Beyond that, Father never imposes boundaries."

"Then why do I feel like I have shackles on my ankles?"

"Isolda!" Alexander said. "That will be quite enough. You're giving Mr. Bonner the wrong impression. Yes, I'm a taskmaster, but only at my work, not with my family."

"If you say so." Isolda had brought it up before and been treated the same way. It both amused and angered her that her sister always sided with their father. She was amused because Edana was too blinded by devotion to see her own shackles, and she was angered because it was just such blindness that kept women in the kitchen and working at drudgery all day.

Isolda was glad when the meal was over and they started back up the street. She noticed how Jericho fell into step behind them without saying a word, and how alert he was to their surroundings. His eyes were always flicking this way and that. That Colt of his gave her a strange thrill. She would very much like to have a pistol of her own. Her father might forbid it, though. Ladies shouldn't carry revolvers, after all.

As they neared the Three Aces, Isolda hoped for a glimpse of Beaumont Adams.

Fate was kind to her, for there he was, at the front window, looking out. He smiled and gave a little wave. Was it her imagination, or did he wave specifically at her and not at her sister or her father? Since her father wasn't watching, she smiled and waved back. The gambler's smile widened.

Isolda tingled with excitement. Their venture into the Wild West, as some referred to it, held more promise than she'd anticipated. She'd figured to be so bored most of the time that she couldn't stand it. But the only thing that bored her so far was Neal Bonner and his ridiculous fondness for cows. She couldn't think of anything duller than cattle. For a man to take pride in being good at handling them was about as impressive a feat as trimming one's toenails. Where was the challenge? The excitement?

No, Isolda reflected. She'd go along with this cow business for as long as she could stand it. And then, who could say?

The buckboard was parked at the side of the livery stable, the driver leaning against it with his arms folded, waiting.

"Folks, I'd like you to meet Stumpy," Neal introduced him. "He's a friend of mine from down to Texas. He can't herd cows on account of his condition, but he's right handy around a ranch at a lot of other things."

Isolda couldn't help staring. The man's "condition," as Bonner called it, was that he was missing the bottom part of his left leg and had been fitted with a wooden peg, like a pirate's.

"How do you do, folks?" Stumpy cheerfully greeted them. Short and wiry, he had gray at the temples and a beard that wasn't much of one. "I'm pleased to make your acquaintance."

Isolda shook his hand because her father and her sister did, and was struck by how leathery his skin felt. "Does it hamper you much, your leg?" she inquired, and earned a look of disapproval from her father.

"No, ma'am," Stumpy said. "I'm not much in a saddle anymore, but I can do most anything else I set my mind to."

They climbed on and got under way. Neal rode ahead, Jericho came behind. Edana, on a bay, rode alongside the buckboard.

"If you don't mind my asking," her father asked their driver as they rattled past the last of the buildings, "how did you lose your foot?"

"Rattler," Stumpy said.

"You're pulling our leg," Isolda said. "Rattlesnakes can't bite a foot off."

"Didn't say one did," Stumpy replied. "I

chopped it off myself when I was bit by one."

"You chopped off your own foot?" Alexander said, aghast.

Stumpy nodded. "Had to. I was alone, out to the line camp. It was a big un' that bit me, and I knew I was a goner. I couldn't suck out the poison on account I couldn't get my foot to my mouth. So I taken an axe to it, then stuck the stump in the fire before I bled to death."

"How appalling," Alexander said.

Not for Isolda. She found the man's story as oddly exciting as everything else in this new and wonderful land. It brimmed with possibilities. She found herself wishing that Jericho and Scar Wratner had resorted to their six-shooters back there.

She wouldn't have minded seeing some blood spilled.

9

Beaumont Adams stood at the window to his saloon for a considerable while after the Jessups went by. He was staring at the street, but he was seeing Isolda Jessup. She liked him. She was interested. He could tell.

Beaumont wouldn't have thought it. Sure, he was better-looking than most. Women told him that all the time. Sure, he was fun to be with. Women told him that, too. Fun because he hardly ever took anything seriously. Why should he, when the world and most everyone in it were plumb ridiculous?

With a toss of his head, Beaumont turned and walked to the corner table reserved for him and him alone. No sooner had he sunk into a chair than his barman, Floyd, brought him a bottle of his favorite brandy and a glass. Beaumont went through the motions of pouring, but his mind was more than a thousand miles away, in the hills of Tennessee.

Beaumont was a Southern boy, and proud of it. He'd been too young to take part in the War Between the States, but his pa and grandpa did and told him all about it. How the Yankees had pushed the South into war and then used their industrial superiority to crush the Confederacy and lay waste to everything and everyone in it. Beaumont particularly hated carpetbaggers, the Yankee vultures who swooped south of the Mason-Dixon to plunder and pillage, all legal-like.

Yankees. How Beaumont despised that word. Yet here he was, entranced by a Yankee gal. From what Beaumont had gleaned from Franklyn Wells, the Jessups were as Yankee as could be, Northern blue bloods through and through.

Yet, damn, that Isolda was an eyeful. It wasn't just her looks. There was something about her, something Beaumont couldn't put his finger on, a quality she had that stirred him, deep down. He tried telling himself that he was being ridiculous, that she was a female just like every other, but at the first contact of their eyes a shiver had rippled through him from head to toe, as if a jolt of lightning had flashed between them. And, wonder of wonders, he had a hunch she felt the same way.

"What do you know?" Beaumont said to

himself, and took a long swallow of brandy.

"What do we know about what, boss?"

Beaumont looked up. Dyson and Stimms had come up to his table without him noticing. It showed how rattled he was by the Yankee girl. No one should be able to do that. "You tell me."

"Tell you what?" Stimms said, cradling his Sharps.

Sighing, Beaumont polished off his glass and set it down. "Suppose you tell me why you've inflicted yourselves on my good nature?"

"Done what, now?" Dyson said, his hand idly resting on his Remington. "You told us to report back after we went to see Zimmerman, remember?"

"What did he say to my offer?"

Dyson glanced at Beaumont's right sleeve and hesitated. "Do you want it word for word or should I sugarcoat it?"

"Word for word will do," Beaumont said.

Dyson coughed. "Zimmerman said to tell you there's no way in hell he'd sell out to a tinhorn like you. He said it should be you who sells out to him since he aims to be top dog in this town before too long."

"Does he, now?"

"You should have heard him, boss," Stimms said. "He talked about you in front of everybody like you were dirt."

"It made me mad," Dyson said, "but we did as you told us and didn't cause trouble."

"You did right," Beaumont said. "I gave him his chance and he threw it in my face. Now no one can blame me for what comes next."

"What will that be?" Stimms asked.

"Why, we kill the son of a bitch, of course."

Edana Jessup took a lot of pride in being an independent woman. Independent in that in a world largely run by men, she could hold her own. She had a head for business, as her father liked to say. Thanks to that, and her education, she was as competent as any male born, and then some.

Edana had looked forward to the move to the West. Overseeing the dairy farms had become routine. There was no challenge to it once they had everything running smoothly. She'd needed some excitement in her life, and along came the Diamond B.

It promised to be a considerable challenge. A Western ranch wasn't anything like an Eastern dairy farm except that both relied on cows to turn a profit. But even in that regard there was a difference. It prompted her to remark, after they'd gone about a mile out of Whiskey Flats, "I shouldn't let an opportunity like this go to waste, Father."

"Opportunity?" Alexander said absently. He was engrossed in a series of bluffs to the north.

"The cattle," Edana said. "This Western breed isn't like those we're used to, or so Mr. Wells assured us. The sooner we learn all there is about them, the better we can manage the ranch."

"True."

"So if you don't mind, I'll ride with our foreman awhile and pick his brain." To further justify her request, Edana added, "Mr. Wells did say that Mr. Bonner is an expert."

"Why would I mind?" Alexander said. "I commend your diligence. Go have your talk."

Edana thanked him and jabbed her heels to take her bay up next to their foreman's buttermilk. In town she'd observed how he seemed ill at ease around her sister and her, so she sought to start things on a good footing by saying, "That's a fine animal you have there, Mr. Bonner."

Neal looked at her in surprise, then patted his mount. "Best horse I've ever ridden, ma'am. I wouldn't part with him for anything. I got him down to the Staked Plain country about, oh, seven years ago, it was."

Always the businesswoman, Edana asked, "How much does a horse cost in Texas?"

"Depends on the animal," Neal answered. "You could likely get an old swayback for ten dollars. A ridin' horse can go for anywhere from fifty or sixty to more than a hundred. A horse like mine, two hundred or better."

"Is that how much you paid? Two hundred?"

"No, ma'am. I got him for free."

"How did you accomplish that miracle? Did you steal him?" Edana joked.

"No, ma'am," Neal said. "I hanged the man who had him before me."

Edana thought he was making some kind of peculiar joke her until she saw his grim expression. "You're serious?"

"I'm always serious about hangin' folks."

"But . . ." Edana was so shocked her mind had gone numb. "Why?"

"He was a rustler, ma'am. Ed Coker was his name. He fancied himself the king of the horse thieves. Even went around braggin' about how good he was, and how he'd never been caught. Well, one day he made the mistake of stealin' a small herd from the Diamond T. I took that poorly, seein' as I was foreman, and that made them my responsibility. Jericho and me lit out on his trail. Took us pretty near ten days, as I recollect, before we caught up. Ed made a fight of it and Jericho put lead in his shoulder. Then we hanged him."

"Dear Lord."

"Ed had grit, I'll give him that. He didn't bawl or whimper like some rustlers do. He died game."

"How can you be so cavalier about it?"

"Ma'am?"

"You *hanged* him. You killed another human being. Murdered him, essentially, since he didn't have a trial and wasn't duly sentenced by a judge." Edana shook her head. "Can't you see how wrong that is?"

"Ed was a rustler, ma'am. He knew what to expect if he was caught."

"Stop calling me that. And that's not the point." Edana took a breath. "The point is that you ended another man's life without due process. Back East you would be put on trial and probably sent to prison for taking the law into your own hands."

Neal waved an arm at their surroundings. "Take a good look around us, ma'am."

Annoyed that he kept calling her that, Edana nonetheless gazed about, wondering what he was getting at. The bluffs had given way temporarily to tall spires of stone, here and there broken by the dark meanderings of shadowy ravines. In the distance a mesa reared, a world unto itself. "What am I supposed to be looking for?"

"What do you see?"

"The Badlands, what else?" Edana said. "As wild a country as anywhere on God's green earth. It's how I'd imagine the world will look after it comes to an end."

"Why, that's almost poetical, ma'am," Neal said.

"I told you to stop calling me that. Why did you ask what I saw?"

"Other than Whiskey Flats, do you see any towns hereabouts? Any homesteads or farms? Don't bother to answer. There isn't any for hundreds of miles. That's how it was down to Texas."

"That doesn't justify what you did."

"It was up to us to end the stealin'. No one else would."

"Well, there won't be any hanging of rustlers at the Diamond B. We're not barbarians. We'll live by the same laws as everyone else."

"Take another gander. Do you see any laws anywhere?"

"Now you're being facetious," Edana said. "Yes, I've read that on the frontier, men are a law unto themselves. Perhaps that applies in Texas but not here. I refuse to be a party to a hanging. Should a situation arise where you feel compelled to take the law into your own hands, you're to consult with my father or me first."

"You want me to go around shackled?"

"Don't be preposterous. I didn't say you couldn't defend yourself if you're set upon. I simply said the Diamond B won't be a party to lawlessness, even if custom is on our side in perpetrating it." Edana expected him to take exception. Instead he smiled and studied her with what she took to be a degree of admiration.

"You have some fancy notions to go with those fancy words of yours. But don't worry. I'll do as you say until you see how wrong you are."

"The nerve," Edana said, but she grinned. "Enough about that. I wanted to talk about something else. Cows."

"They're big and they moo."

Edana threw back her head and laughed. His sense of humor pleased her. In fact, his attitude toward rustling notwithstanding, nearly everything about Neal Bonner pleased her. He wasn't as handsome as, say, that gambler back in town, but he wasn't hard on the eyes, either. In fact, those eyes of his appealed to her greatly. They hinted at depths she found herself thinking she might like to explore. "I'd like to hear about these Western cattle of yours. I've always thought a cow was a cow, but Mr. Wells informed me I couldn't be more wrong. Enlighten me, if you would be so kind."

"Gladly," Neal said. "Mr. Wells has it right. Beef cattle ain't milk cows. And here's why."

Over the next hour and a half, Edana learned more about Western cattle than she'd ever had guessed was the case. For starters, the herd Neal brought up from Texas was composed mostly of longhorn stock. Longhorns were noted for their hardiness. They thrived almost anywhere: grassy prairies, brush country, even swamps. They could get by without much water better than any breed alive. They were bony, with a spread of horns that had to be seen to be believed, but for all that, Neal claimed they could weigh almost as much as a buffalo. When Edana scoffed, Neal put a hand to his chest.

"May the Good Lord strike me dead if I'm lying."

Neal went on to inform her that whereas bull buffalo could weigh two thousand pounds or more, a full-grown longhorn bull might be between fifteen to eighteen hundred pounds, and sometimes even higher. All that growing took a while. Although a longhorn was considered adult at four years, it didn't reach full maturity and size until it was eight to ten.

"Another advantage to longhorns," Neal, said, waxing passionate about his herd, "is that they don't need coddlin'. Let them loose and they can fend for themselves. All we have to do is brand them and round them up for market."

"What about the winters? They can be severe out here," Edana mentioned, and grew warm in her cheeks when he said that was a good question.

"Longhorns can take heavy snows and cold in stride, but we'll have to keep an eye on things. I was thinkin' we'd set up feed pens around the range in case a blizzard hits. Of course, gettin' out to them will be a chore, so before the cold weather hits, we might want to herd the cattle into areas that will be easier to reach. Just a thought I had," Neal finished.

"A good one," Edana said, returning his compliment.

Neal looked away, and coughed.

"What are the dangers we face? Be honest with me. How about hostiles, for instance?"

"The Indians hereabouts are pretty much whipped, ma'am," Neal replied. "The army came down on them hard after Custer." He shook his head. "No, I reckon our main worries will be those blizzards, and a drought if it goes on long enough."

"How about disease? How prone are these longhorns of yours to sickness?"

"They're your longhorns, too, ma'am," Neal said with another of his slow smiles. "I can count the sick longhorns I've seen on one hand and have fingers left over. They never come down with that blood disease that your Eastern cows get."

"Tuberculosis?"

"That's the one."

"You make it sound as if we'll have it easy."

"Not at all," Neal said. "Our worst problem will likely be rustlers."

"I hope not. But even so, remember what I said about not lynching them."

"Oh, I'll remember, ma'am. And I'll keep my rope handy for when you change your mind."

"As if that will ever happen."

"You never know," Neal Bonner said.

10

Beaumont Adams waited for the sun to go down.

In his living quarters on the second floor of the saloon, Beaumont stared at himself in the full-length mirror on his closet door. Most would call it a vanity of his, and they'd be right. For as long as he could remember, he'd liked to admire himself in a mirror.

Beaumont adjusted his hat and smoothed his frock coat. He hiked his sleeve and checked the special rig that held his derringer. It was snug in place. Sliding his hands into the pockets of his coat, he patted each of his Colt pocket pistols. The original pockets had been removed and replaced with larger leather ones so that the Colts wouldn't snag when he drew. It was an old gambler's trick that some gunnies relied on, too.

"I'm a walkin' arsenal," Beaumont said to the mirror. Chuckling, he went out and down the stairs to the saloon.

The Three Aces was doing its usual booming business. Of the three saloons in town, his was easily the most popular.

The Tumbleweed, owned by Clyde Zimmerman, did pretty brisk business, too, mainly thanks to a stable of young doves. It would do better if Zimmerman didn't water his drinks and treat everybody as if he was better than they were.

The newest saloon, called the Glass Slipper, was owned by a man named Garrison from New Orleans who liked to boast that his saloon was for a more genteel clientele.

Beaumont made for the bar. Dyson and Stimms were drinking and didn't notice him come up.

"You boys ready?"

Both turned and Stimms hastily gulped the rest of his drink, spilling some on his chin. "You bet, boss."

"Genteel as hell," Beaumont said.

"Boss?" Stimms said.

"Nothin' you would understand. Let's go see Zimmerman about acquirin' his establishment."

"Do you want we should bring more than just us?" Dyson asked. "Floyd can be spared from the bar, and Toliver and Weist are over at that table."

"They stay here to watch over things." Beaumont had added new tie-down men to his payroll as a precaution. Not that they impressed him all that much. They weren't the same quality of killer as, say, Jericho or Scar Wratner, but they'd shoot when he told them to and that was what counted. "Us three will do."

"If you say so," Dyson said uncertainly. "Zimmerman has three or four gun sharks workin' for him, in case you didn't know."

"They're not so much sharks as guppies," Beaumont said, annoyed at having his judgment questioned. "If you're scared, you can mount up and ride out and to hell with you."

"Did I say that?" Dyson said. "I just don't want you killed, is all."

"Why, Dyson," Beaumont said, "I didn't know you cared."

"Are you kiddin'?" Dyson replied. "I've never had it so good as I do workin' for you. You pay good, and you treat us decent exceptin' when you're mad, and you don't get mad much."

"I'm a regular daisy."

Beaumont made for the batwings. He liked how men stepped out of his way without being told, liked the respect he was accorded. He ate it up with a spoon.

"One more thing, boss," Dyson said. "I heard that Scar Wratner and his pards have been there all day, drinkin' heavy."

"So?" Beaumont said. He reached the batwings and stepped out into the welcome cool of night. "Wratner doesn't work for Zimmerman. He's nothin' for us to be concerned about."

"If you say so," Dyson said again. "But when he drinks a lot, he goes on the prod, and I wouldn't want him to prod us."

"You don't think you can take him?"

"Scar Wratner?" Dyson said in amazement. "I'm good but I'm not his caliber, not by a long shot."

"Do you reckon you can take him, boss?" Stimms asked.

"Easy as pie," Beaumont said. "He'd never see it comin'."

"I don't know," Stimms said. "He's cat-eyed, that one. Word is he's bucked twenty men out."

"The word is exaggerated," Beaumont said, striding along with his hands in his pockets. "I have it that he hasn't killed more than twelve."

"Oh, is that all?" Dyson said.

Beaumont laughed. "Why, Dyson, I do believe you're growin' a sense of humor. Will wonders never cease?"

"Why do you say things like that, boss? Why do you poke fun all the time?"

"I like to laugh, Dyson," Beaumont said. "I like to enjoy life. Next to pokin' a woman, laughin' is the most fun I know."

"There's drinkin'," Stimms said, "and card playin'."

"I do like cards," Beaumont admitted. "But that's more work than pleasure. What's your pleasure in life? Besides sneakin' a poke with your mule every night."

"Oh, boss," Stimms said. "Where do you come up with this stuff? I would never and you know it."

"That's not what your mule told me."

Dyson cackled.

Not many people were out and about. The wives were home where they should be. The doves were in the saloons. So was most of the male population. Nearly every hitch rail was full up. A lot of cowboys from the Diamond B were in town to wet their dry throats.

The Tumbleweed stood at the next corner. It was only one story, and longer by half than the Three Aces. The batwings had been painted red, and the front window bore the likeness of a dove in a red dress.

"That gal on the glass sure is pretty," Stimms remarked.

"Marry her, why don't you?" Beaumont said. "Your mule will send her a thank-you note."

"Oh, boss."

Beaumont looked at them. "Enough frivolity. From here on out, we're deadly serious. Stay close and cover me. Anyone goes for their hardware, and I do mean anyone, you blow them to hell and back. Do I make myself clear?"

"We have your back, boss," Dyson said.

Beaumont grunted. He knew he could count on them. They were as dull as bricks but as loyal as hound dogs. Squaring his shoulders, he sauntered inside as if he already owned the place.

Hardly anyone noticed, at first. Most every table had a card game going and the bar was lined with drinkers. The doves were mingling, as they were paid to do. At a table in the back sat Clyde Zimmerman, dressed like the Eastern dandy he was, with his three hired wolves.

Beaumont started toward their table and caught sight of Scar Wratner, Grat, and Tuck at the far end of the bar. Wratner had already spotted him. Cat-eyed was exactly right. Beaumont smiled and nodded. Scar didn't return the favor, but he did glance at Clyde Zimmerman and grin.

Beaumont wondered why. An alliance between Zimmerman and Wratner didn't bode well for his prospects. Out of the corner of his mouth he said to Stimms, "Keep an eye on Wratner. If he goes for his guns, use that cannon of yours."

"I'll try, but he's awful fast."

"I like a man with confidence," Beaumont said.

Clyde Zimmerman saw them and stiffened. He said something to the three gunnies that caused them to set down their cards and their drinks and place their hands on the edge of the table.

"I do so hate to ruin a good frock coat," Beaumont remarked to himself.

"Boss?" Dyson said.

"Remember, watch my back."

Beaumont came to within a few feet of the table and stopped. He needed to be in close. Smiling, he said to Zimmerman, "Surprised to see me, Clyde?"

"It's Mr. Zimmerman to you," Zimmerman said sourly. He had oily black hair and a black mustache, and an ample middle. "Didn't your simpleton give you my message?"

"Which simpleton?" Beaumont replied. "I have more than one in my employ."

"The nerve," Zimmerman said. "Offering

to buy me out."

Beaumont wanted to keep him talking awhile so the other three would relax their vigilance. "It was a reasonable offer, reasonably made."

"You don't fool me," Zimmerman said. "You've let it be known you intend to take this town over, lock, stock, and barrel."

"I confess I'm afflicted with a leaky mouth on occasion," Beaumont said.

"A leaky brain, too, if you expect me to sell to you. You're not the only one with ambition. I've already made overtures to Garrison, but he turned me down."

"You have to say pretty please. He's one of those sensitive souls."

"And what are you, besides a blowhard?"

"Now, now," Beaumont said, continuing with his friendly act. "Have I insulted you in any way? I have not."

"You insulted me by walking in here," Zimmerman said. "You came to threaten me to sell to you, or else."

"Why, Clyde," Beaumont said, doing his best to sound hurt, "that's not why I'm here at all."

"It isn't?"

"Goodness gracious, no. I'd never be dumb enough to threaten someone like you. Everyone knows you can't be blustered."

Zimmerman didn't hide his surprise at the compliment. "You're damn right I can't. It's smart of you to admit it."

"No, sir," Beaumont said. "You can't be blustered and you can't be bought. You are too tough for the first and too dumb for the second."

"What?"

"It takes intelligence to know when to fold. That's why really fine poker players are so rare. Simpletons hold on to a losin' hand long after they should."

"Did you just call me dumb? And a simpleton, to boot?"

"Bein' stupid is one of your more notable traits. Like that god-awful cologne you wear. And how your mouth twitches when you're mad, like it's twitchin' now. Do you have fits on occasion? I once knew a gent who twitched like you do, and he was prone to fits."

Red in the face with anger, Clyde Zimmerman rose out of his chair and leaned on the table. "How dare you?"

"You'd be surprised," Beaumont said.

"Insult me in my own place," Zimmerman fumed. "Turn around and leave or I'll have you thrown out on your ear."

"Haven't you ever heard of sticks and stones?"

Zimmerman smacked the table so hard many at surrounding tables and at the bar stopped what they were doing to stare. "Gentlemen," he said, and his three gun tippers looked at him.

It was the moment Beaumont had been waiting for. His hands had never left his pockets, and now he pointed the short-barreled Colts at two of the three and fired through his frock coat. That close up, he could hardly miss. His slugs cored their heads, splattering hair and brains. The last hired gun, and Zimmerman, had no time to react as Beaumont sent lead into each one. He shot the third gunny in the head, but he deliberately shot Zimmerman in the chest.

Clyde Zimmerman was knocked back over his chair and both crashed to the floor.

Simultaneously, Dyson's Remington cracked twice, and another of Zimmerman's leather slappers, who had rushed to help his employer, clutched at himself and pitched to the floor.

In the sudden and total silence, Zimmerman's gurgles and gasps were unnaturally loud.

Beaumont walked around the table and slid his Colts from their special pockets. "Told you that you were dumb."

A scarlet stain was spreading across Zimmerman's shirt. He was struggling to reach a Smith & Wesson, worn butt-forward on his left hip. "Bastard," he hissed, spitting blood.

"Oh, I'm that, and more," Beaumont said, grinning. "I'm now the proud owner of two saloons. When I came in here I was the proud owner of only one."

Tears of rage filled Zimmerman's eyes. "You . . . you . . ." He couldn't seem to find an insult vile enough.

"Maybe I'll change the name, though," Beaumont said. "The Tumbleweed is too ordinary. How does Zimmerman's Folly sound?"

"God!" Zimmerman practically screamed. He made a last effort to reach his six-shooter but couldn't move his arm far enough.

"Don't bring the Almighty into this," Beaumont said. "Sinners like us, we're bound for that other place. Which reminds me. Say howdy to that gent with the forked tail when you get there."

Clyde Zimmerman closed his eyes and quaked.

"Tell you what," Beaumont said. "I can be as charitable as the next gent. Do you want me to end it quick or would you rather lie there and suffer?"

"You miserable son of a bitch."

"Quick it is," Beaumont declared, and bending, he extended the Colts so the muzzles were inches from Zimmerman's face. "Thanks for the saloon," he said, and squeezed both triggers.

Beaumont turned to the onlookers. Some were in shock. Most looked as if they didn't know what to do. Beaming, he called out, "Ladies and gentlemen, the Tumbleweed is under new management. In honor of the occasion, all drinks for the next hour are on me."

Glances were exchanged, whispers broke out, and then someone let out a hearty cheer. Others followed suit, and there was a rush for the bar.

"So much for the dear departed," Beaumont said, and chuckled. "Ain't life grand, boys? Ain't it truly and wonderfully grand?"

"If you say so, boss," Stimms said. "I've always thought it was kind of confusin' myself."

Beaumont Adams laughed for joy.

11

Alexander Jessup was pleased.

Alexander liked order more than anything. It was the key to his success in business. He imposed efficiency where there was inefficiency. Always with a view to increasing income. He was never ruthless or stupid about it. Some businessmen cut expenses to the bare bones to reap more profit. That often led to an inferior product, which resulted in a drop in sales and invariably brought their businesses to ruin.

Alexander used a different approach. The dairy farms were a good example. He'd been hired to take scores of individuals' farms and create a dairy empire, as it were. He'd succeeded by imposing order. By having the farms conform to standards and practices that made everything run smoothly.

From what he could tell on his buckboard ride to the ranch house, Neal Bonner shared his philosophy.

Alexander was impressed by how the herds were maintained. Herds, plural. Good graze was scattered over the Diamond B. The huge herd brought up from Texas had been broken into smaller herds, which in turn were driven to where they would best flourish. As hardy as longhorns were, they still needed graze and some water. With his knowledge of their habits and how much forage they needed to thrive, Neal Bonner wisely made sure that they were placed where conditions were ideal.

Stumpy, their driver, told Alexander all about it. Stumpy proved to be a revelation. Once Alexander got him talking, he couldn't shut Stumpy up.

Stumpy told him that Neal had learned about cattle at an early age. That Neal had been taught the ranching business from top to bottom by some of the best foremen in all of Texas. He noted how Neal only hired hands who would be loyal to the brand, treated everyone fairly, and was friendly but firm.

"He's a good one." Stumpy summed up his evaluation. "Me and the boys would do anything for him."

Stumpy went on to inform Alexander that with Neal running things, all Alexander had to do was sit back in the ranch house and take life easy.

Alexander assured him that wouldn't be the case. That he liked to become involved in every aspect of every business he ran. "I like to keep my hands on things," was how he put it.

"Be careful where you put those hands on a longhorn," Stumpy replied, chuckling. "Some of them don't take kindly to bein' touched, and will gore you as quick as anything."

They encountered some of the Diamond B hands as they crossed the range. Again, Alexander was impressed. To a man, they had an air of competence about them. They all "knew cows from horns to hock," as Stumpy put it.

"Neal wouldn't hire no coffee coolers, nor empty heads," Stumpy cheerfully assured him.

"No what?"

"Layabouts, nor those who don't know diddly about cattle. Neal only takes on those who are cow savvy and like to work."

The land impressed Alexander, too. When he'd first set eyes on the Badlands back on the stage, he was struck by how alien everything looked. The towering buttes, the sheer bluffs, the sweep of rock in a myriad of shapes, seemed like a landscape from another world. But the more he saw of the countryside, the more he grew to like its bizarre beauty. On a prairie, there would be league after league of flat and grass. In the mountains, mile after mile of forested slopes. Much of it all the same. But not here in the Badlands. Here, nothing was the same. Every square mile was different from the square mile before it. Every part was unique.

At one point on their trip, Alexander turned and looked past Stumpy at Isolda. "Are you all right, daughter? You've hardly uttered a word the whole way."

Her elbow on her leg and her chin in her hands, Isolda answered without much enthusiasm, "Why wouldn't I be all right?"

"Magnificent scenery, don't you think?"

"If you say so."

"What the matter with you?"

"Nothing," Isolda said. "I was just hoping we'd stay in town a little longer. I could have used the rest after that long stage ride getting there."

"You'll have plenty of time to rest at the ranch."

At last she showed some interest, and sat up. "What will I be doing there, exactly? You haven't said."

"Helping me, as always."

"But helping you how? From what I gather, you're going to have Edana work closely with the foreman, overseeing the cow end. But what will I be doing? Feeding the chickens?"

Stumpy chortled. "Sorry. I couldn't help overhearin'."

"You'll assist me with the bookkeeping, as you did with the dairy farms," Alexander informed her. "Plus, you'll have other duties."

"It doesn't sound very exciting," Isolda said.

Alexander was surprised by her statement. "Since when does excitement enter into what we do? Unless you mean the excitement of running things smoothly and turning a tidy profit."

"Yes, Father, that's exactly what I mean," Isolda said in a tone that suggested it definitely was not.

Alexander wondered what had gotten into her. He attributed her lackluster interest to fatigue. "You'll feel better about things once you're rested. Personally, I can't wait to get started."

"You love being a businessman, Father. It's what you do."

"Well, of course," Alexander said. "It's

what we all do."

Isolda looked at him. "When were we given the choice to do anything else? You trained us from childhood to be your helpers. You never asked us if we wanted to help. You took it for granted we did."

Surprised, Alexander said, "You've never once objected in all the years we've been doing this."

"I never saw anything else that interested me."

"Are you saying that now you have?" Alexander asked, puzzled by what on earth it could be.

"No, Father," Isolda said. "I was just making conversation." She bent and put her elbow on her leg again and her chin in her hand.

"Give yourself some time, ma'am," Stumpy interjected. "You'll like this life. It grows on you to where you wouldn't do anything else."

"If you say so," Isolda said.

"I know one thing," Stumpy said, and grinned. "That sister of yours has taken a shine to Neal. They've been jawin' and jokin' and smilin' like they're the best of friends."

"Edana has a way with people," Alexander said proudly. "She's good at getting them to open up."

"Well, she's sure opened Neal. I don't reckon I've ever seen him jabber so much."

Alexander glanced over his shoulder. "It's too bad Mr. Jericho has to ride back there by himself. He might like to join in the conversation."

Stumpy snorted. "Mister, that gal of yours couldn't open him up with a can opener. Jericho ain't like normal folks." He quickly added, "Don't get me wrong. He's a top hand when it comes to cattle."

Alexander regarded the driver a few moments. "I'd like to ask you something and I want you to be honest with me."

Stumpy's mouth curled in what might be annoyance. "No need to insult me, Mr. Jessup."

"I did no such thing."

"You sure as blazes did," Stumpy insisted. "You just said I might lie to you when I'd never do any such thing."

"I didn't mean it that way," Alexander said. "It was a figure of speech, nothing more." He paused. "I'd like to ask you about Mr. Jericho. In your opinion, would you say he's an asset or a detriment to the Diamond B?"

"A detri-what?" Stumpy said.

"Is it good or bad to have him work for

me?" Alexander made it as plain as he could.

"What could be bad about having Jericho ridin' for your brand?" Stumpy rejoined. "That's plumb ridiculous."

Now it was Alexander whose mouth curled. "Hear me out. And keep in mind I'm from the East. My sensibilities are undoubtedly different in certain respects than yours and the rest of the punchers. But I would very much like to know something, and I believe you can enlighten me."

"I'll try," Stumpy said, "but I ain't ever enlightened anybody before."

On the other side of him, Isolda laughed.

"It's about Mr. Jericho," Alexander said. "Even before I arrived, I was told about his reputation. That he's a gun shark, I believe you call it."

"He's that and then some."

"So my question is this." Alexander paused. "Is it wise to have a man like that working for the Diamond B?"

"Didn't what happened with Scar Wratner teach you anything?"

"I'm sure if it had come to blows, others would have come to our assistance," Alexander said.

"Blows?" Stumpy repeated, and snorted. "Mister, Scar Wratner doesn't hit folks. He shoots them."

"But I was unarmed."

"Doesn't matter. Heeled or not, if he takes a dislike to somebody, he'll gun him without battin' an eye."

Alexander considered that. "Let's say that Mr. Wratner is as callous as you assert. Doesn't having a man like Mr. Jericho on my payroll practically ensure that there will be more trouble?"

"If there is, it won't be Jericho who starts it. It'll be Scar Wratner."

"But do you see my point? I did some asking around, and I know that many ranches do perfectly fine without someone like him on their payroll. Which makes me question why I should keep him on."

"You need Jericho for two reasons," Stumpy said. "First, if you cut him loose, you lose Neal, too. They're pards."

"That's what Franklyn Wells told me."

"That little feller in the bowler? He was right. Pards stick. What one does, the other does. If one goes, the other goes."

"I admire their sense of friendship, but still."

"You're not payin' attention," Stumpy said. "Neal and Jericho ain't friends. They're *pards*."

"I'm afraid I don't see the distinction," Alexander admitted.

Stumpy flicked the reins. "How can I explain this? Do you have any really good friends, Mr. Jessup?"

"Who doesn't?" Alexander said. "There are a dozen or so, I suppose, I'd put in that category."

"Would you do anything for them if they asked you?"

"Within reason."

"Meanin' there are things you'd do and things you wouldn't?"

"I'm not about to break the law for them. Or violate my own morals and ethics, no matter how good a friend they are."

"That's the difference, right there. Friends have limits. Pards don't."

"That's carrying friendship a bit far, don't you think?" Alexander said. "There's such a thing as common sense. But very well. I'll give this pard business more thought. In the meantime, what is the second reason I should keep Mr. Jericho on?"

"To keep you and your gals safe. These here Badlands aren't as tame as you're used to. It's not like back East where folks don't pack hardware and there's tin stars everywhere. Here it's wild and wicked, and havin' a gun-wise gent like Jericho to back your play is just some of that common sense you were talkin' about."

Alexander sat back and thoughtfully regarded the Diamond B's foreman, who was in conversation with Edana. She was the more animated of the pair, which mystified him. Normally she was reserved around men. "I'll take your advice under advisement," he said to the driver. "But I'll also be honest and say I don't see the great necessity you do."

"A gun is a needful thing in these parts," Stumpy replied. "More so a gent who can use one."

"Everyone can shoot. It's not that difficult. I've fired a rifle on a few occasions myself, back when I dabbled in pheasant hunting in my younger days. I must have gone out twenty to thirty times."

Stumpy tittered. "Did you, now? We don't have pheasants where I come from, but I hear tell they're big birds that hide in the high grass and you have to flush 'em. Is that how it works?"

"Dropping a pheasant on the wing is considered great sport, yes."

"And how many of those pheasants did you drop?"

"It was over twenty years ago."

"How many?"

"They're incredibly fast when flushed," Alexander said. "It's not uncommon for a hunter to miss more than he hits."

"Why, Mr. Jessup, I do declare. You're ashamed to say."

Alexander took umbrage. "I am not. I just don't see where it's relevant. For your information, though, I seem to remember bagging three or four."

"Three or four out of twenty to thirty tries," Stumpy said, and whistled. "Well, that's another reason you need Jericho."

"How so?"

"You miss too much," Stumpy said. "He doesn't."

12

Edana Jessup had never had three hours fly by so fast in her life. It seemed to her she'd barely begun talking to Neal Bonner, and they arrived at their destination. She was genuinely surprised when he rose in his stirrups, peered head, and declared, "There's your new home, ma'am."

"You don't need to keep calling me that," Edana said for what had to be the tenth time. She gazed up ahead. Somehow she'd gotten it into her head that there would be a house and a few outbuildings and that would be it. She couldn't have been more wrong.

The ranch house itself was a sprawling three-story structure with a porch that ran around the entire bottom and a balcony on the second floor at the front. The architecture involved a lot of peaks and sloped roofs that made Edana think of the houses she'd seen in Germantown, near Philadelphia. It was painted white with black trim around the windows and doors. An acre of yard was surrounded by a whitewashed picket fence.

Another dozen buildings were arrayed around the house. The stable was obvious and had an attached corral. She wasn't sure about the purpose of the other structures, so she asked Neal.

There was a bunkhouse for the hands. Long and low, it had been fashioned from logs. There was the cookhouse, which Neal joked was the most popular place on the ranch. There was a shop for the ranch blacksmith, and a smaller shop for the man who did carpentry work. There was a chicken coop and a hog pen. There was a building for the buckboard and the cook's wagon when he was out with the hands. There was a woodshed and a toolshed and sheds for other purposes. There was a windmill near the house, the vanes slowly spinning. There were outhouses. There were several corrals, not just the one by the stable.

Men were everywhere, involved in a variety of tasks. A cowboy was working a horse in a corral. The blacksmith was hammering at something on his anvil. Another man worked a pump to draw water.

"Why, it's a like a small town," Edana

said, stirred by the picturesque scene.

"There's more to runnin' a ranch than most folks think about," Neal said in that slow Texas drawl of his.

"There will certainly be a lot for me to learn," Edana admitted. "I'd appreciate all the help you can give me."

"Anything you need, ma'am, anything at all, you just say the word."

Edana felt her cheeks grow warm. It annoyed her. She kept reacting to him in ways she shouldn't. She told herself it was because he was so rugged-looking and so virile. That last insight upset her. She shouldn't be thinking about him that way. Theirs was a business relationship, nothing more. She was acting like a smitten little girl, something she'd never done before.

Neal drew rein and Edana followed suit.

"So you can drink it in," he said.

Stumpy brought the buckboard to a stop alongside them, and her father stood up in the seat.

"Mr. Bonner, I'm impressed. I truly am. Mr. Wells told me that he'd left the building of the ranch up to you, but I had no idea."

"Were you expectin' a soddy and some lean-tos?" Neal joked.

"I wasn't expecting anything this remarkable."

"Shucks. With enough money you can do most anything, and those consortium fellers said to spare no expense. I took them at their word." Neal swept at arm at the bustling ranch grounds. "This here is pretty much like the ranches I worked at down to Texas, only grander. Mr. Wells said he wanted everything ready to go when you got here, and we had to work like the dickens to get ready."

"You've done fine, truly fine." Alexander sat back down. "I'm eager to get started. Edana, as soon as we unpack, you and your sister will accompany me on a tour. I want to meet everyone and get a feel for the place. Mr. Bonner, be at the house in half an hour, if you would. Stumpy, let's go."

The buckboard rattled on, and Edana went with it. She was tempted to look back at their foreman but didn't. She had a ranch to assist her father in running and must start acting the part.

Neal Bonner leaned on his saddle horn and watched the buckboard, and Edana Jessup, move off. He was thinking that he'd never spent a pleasanter time in his life than his ride out with Edana. The clomp of a hoof as a horse came up next to his reminded him he wasn't alone.

"Well," Jericho said.

" 'Well,' yourself," Neal said.

"I don't believe I've ever seen you jaw so much."

"Don't start."

"You think you know a fella, and he turns out to have a leaky mouth."

"I was bein' polite."

"Is that what they call it these days?"

"I swear," Neal said, and gigged his buttermilk.

Chuckling, Jericho clucked to his zebra dun. "Is it me, pard, or are you a mite prickly today?"

"You can go to hell."

Jericho laughed.

"She's the boss's daughter. I had to fill her in on things."

"She's easy on the eyes, too. If she takes to you, you might have found your runnin' mate."

"We've hardly just met and you have me married off."

"All I'm sayin' is that for a long-haired partner, you could do worse."

"Says the expert. When you've said 'I do,' then you can talk. Until then, I'll thank you to keep your matrimonial insights to yourself."

"You haven't been around her half a day

and already you're talkin' like she does."

"I swear," Neal said, but he grinned.

They made for the stable.

"What do you make of the other one?" Jericho asked.

"Why?" Neal saw a chance to tease him back. "Are you interested?"

"You know better. Didn't you see her on the way out? She doesn't seem all that happy."

"Maybe she'd rather be back East. It's a big step, comin' out here. Give her a while. The ranch will grow on her."

"Someone might."

"Meanin'?"

"The looks she was givin' that gambler and the looks he was givin' her."

Neal shook his head in amusement. "First you have me practically hitched, and now you have Isolda and Beaumont Adams makin' cow eyes at each other. You should give up throwin' a rope for a livin' and become a parson so you can marry folks off to your heart's content."

"If parsons wore a gun I could be one," Jericho said. "But there's somethin' eatin' at that gal. Watch her close and you'll see."

"I have too much work to do to indulge in your romances. Besides, she's a grown woman. She can do as she pleases."

Neal thought he might spend the half hour treating himself to a cup of coffee. But the blacksmith came to let him know they were running low on horseshoe nails. The cook reported that he could use molasses and flour the next time someone went into Whiskey Flats. Then the bronc buster ambled over to inform him that three new horses had been broken and added to the string.

Before Neal knew it, the half hour was almost up. He spent a few minutes out in back of the bunkhouse, sprucing up. After taking off his hat, he filled the basin with water, dipped his face in, then scrubbed dry with a towel that had already seen considerable use. He combed his hair, slapped dust from his clothes, and was ready.

Alexander Jessup and his daughters were waiting on the front porch, the women in rocking chairs, Jessup pacing.

"There you are. We were ready sooner than I expected, but no matter. We're eager to have you show us around."

Neal saw Isolda stifle a yawn. He began to wonder if Jericho might be onto something but put it from his mind for the time being. The sun was roosting on the horizon and he'd like to complete the tour before they lost the light.

Alexander and Edana listened to everything he said with intent interest. Isolda, not so much.

Neal explained that the most important essential for a ranch to thrive was water. So far the Diamond B had two workings wells; he hoped to eventually have four. In reply to a question from Edana, he related why it was a benefit to a ranch that size to have its own blacksmith. "Otherwise the ranch has to have all its smithin' done by a town blacksmith, which takes up a lot of time goin' back and forth, and those town smiths don't work cheap."

Alexander wanted to know how many horses the ranch owned and was shocked by Neal's answer of "Pretty near five hundred."

"Why in the world do we have so many?"

"Necessity," Neal said, using the word to impress Edana. "Especially during the roundups." He went on to enlighten them to the fact that each cowboy was allotted a string of eight horses. The cowboy rode the animals in turns so that he always had a fresh mount. He also was expected to become familiar with the strengths and weaknesses of each particular horse, and use them accordingly. A good circler, for instance, was mainly put to that job. A horse that had a knack for the demands of roping became the cowhand's chief roper. And so on.

"The hands take pride in their animals," Neal mentioned. "No one is allowed to ride another puncher's horses or they're liable to come to blows."

"Is it possible I can select one for myself?" Edana said. "I like to ride, and I'm sure I'll be doing a lot more of it than ever before."

"You can do what you want, ma'am. I'll help you pick one out my own self," Neal offered.

"I'd be ever so grateful."

Alexander raised his voice a little. "Let's continue with the tour, shall we?"

Neal would swear he blushed, but he hid his embarrassment and led them to the stable to show them the Diamond B's prize bull. A gorgeous golden brown, the bull stood five feet high at the shoulders. His horns measured over eighty inches from tip to tip and swept up on either side, increasing his height by another two and a half feet.

"My word," Alexander blurted when they stopped at the stall. "Where did we acquire that monster?"

"The same place we got the rest of the herd. Texas. His name is Bocephus. He's two thousand pounds of bovine magnificence."

Isolda, who had hardly said a word since they began, rolled her eyes and remarked, "Honestly, now. A cow is a lot of things, but that isn't one of them."

"Bocephus is a bull, ma'am," Neal corrected her. "And he'll do more for our herd than all of us put together."

Alexander boldly stepped to the rail. "Why is he in here instead of out on the range with the rest of the longhorns?"

"We let him loose, he'll turn wild. Every time we want him to sire with a cow, we'll have to find him and rope him and tame him down."

"Better herd management, in other words," Alexander said, nodding in approval.

Isolda still wasn't impressed, apparently. "What difference does it make which cows he mates with?"

"Cows are like people," Neal said. "No two are the same. Some have good qualities. Good coats, good horns, a gentle disposition, and the like. Others are too skittish or they'll try to gore you if you go near their young or they have some other trait we'd like to weed out of the herd."

"So you play matchmaker?" Edana said

with a grin.

"Daughter, please," Alexander said.

This time Neal didn't blush, but he noticed that Edana's cheeks flared a nice shade of pink. Isolda, on the other hand, still appeared bored. As they left the stable he sought to remedy that by asking, "What part of ranchin' interests you the most, ma'am? You haven't said."

"Probably because there isn't any," Isolda replied.

Alexander turned on her. "All right. That's enough. I don't know why you're being so ill-mannered, but it stops here and now. Is that understood?"

"Whatever you say, Father," Isolda said. "Now, if you'll excuse me, I'm not feeling all that well." She veered off toward the ranch house.

"What in the world has gotten into her?" Alexander said.

"It's been a long trip," Edana replied. "She's tired, is all."

"You were at her side the entire way," Alexander said, "yet I don't see you acting so atrociously."

"Give her time," Edana urged. "Once she's had a good night's sleep she'll be her usual self again."

"I hope so," Alexander said. "I'll be

entirely too busy to pander to her womanly tantrums."

"That's not fair, Father," Edana said. "She's always done her share of the work without complaint. Give her time and she'll come around."

"What do you think, Mr. Bonner?" Alexander asked.

"I think I'd have to be addlepated to stick my nose into your family business," Neal said. "Ask me about the cattle or ask me about the hands or ask me about most anything except your girls."

"We're women, not girls," Edana said.

Alexander sighed. "I only hope that from here on out things go smoothly."

13

Beaumont Adams woke up at his usual time, noon. He went through his usual ablutions, dressed, and stepped to his full-length mirror. The sight of the holes in his frock coat brought a frown. He made sure he'd reloaded both of his pocket Colts after the affray in the Tumbleweed, and that his derringer was in place up his sleeve. Then, tilting his hat brim, he left his living quarters.

Dyson and Stimms were waiting at the bar.

"We're here as you told us to be." The former stated the obvious.

Beaumont grunted and had Floyd pour him a brandy. He didn't feel entirely awake until he had his first of the day. He sipped and smiled and said, "Ahhh."

"That sure was somethin' last night," Stimms remarked, "how you bucked those fellers out in blood."

"What a wonderful reminder to start my

day with," Beaumont said.

Stimms always confused easily, and said, "What's wrong, boss? You killed them slicker than a greased hog."

"And you can't get any slicker than that." Beaumont drained his glass, shuddered slightly, and smacked the glass down. "Let's go. I have errands. Watch my back at all times."

"That's what you pay us for," Dyson said.

"By the way, you did good last night, shootin' that one."

"Just doin' what you pay me to do."

Stimms looked downcast. "I didn't get to shoot anybody. No one would try anything with me pointin' my Sharps at them."

"That's because most people are intelligent enough not to want to be blown in half," Beaumont said, and strode for the batwings.

Whiskey Flats was bustling, as it nearly always was these days. Word had spread of the shooting, and a lot of fingers were pointed in Beaumont's directions and a lot of whispering went on.

Some men would be pleased. Some shootists would drink in the notoriety as Beaumont had just drunk the brandy. But Beaumont didn't see himself as a gunman, and he could do without being talked about. The last thing he wanted was a reputation as a killer. He was a gambler and a businessman. That he sometimes had to shoot those who tried to cheat him at cards or didn't see things his way when it came to business was merely part of his profession, like always having an unopened deck on him or ordering liquor for his saloon.

Saloons, Beaumont reminded himself, and smiled. Two were better than one and three would trump the two. But first he had something else to do.

That time of the day, the general store had mainly female customers buying food and dry goods and whatnot. A lot of looks were cast Beaumont's way as he walked up the main aisle to the counter.

A transplanted Ohioan by the name of Guthrie ran the store for Beaumont. He always wore a white apron and always tied the knot at the front instead of the back, which Beaumont thought was peculiar.

"Mr. Adams!" Guthrie declared, beaming. "What a surprise. You haven't been in here in the past week or more."

"Why should I have to come by so long as you run things like I want?" Beaumont said.

"Yes, well." Guthrie coughed. "What can I do for you?"

"Where's that mail-order catalogue of

153

yours?" Beaumont asked. "I need a new one of these." He touched his frock coat.

"I have several catalogues," Guthrie said, reaching under the counter. "The one you want is the latest from Montgomery Ward. They have quite a collection of men's clothing." He brought up a catalogue with a bluish green cover and flipped the pages.

"Here we go. Men's and Boys' Wear." He bent to read.

Beaumont had to submit to being measured with his frock coat off, which he didn't like. It put his pistols out of reach. It also bothered him that Guthrie had to measure the length of his arms and the rest of him twice, as if the man didn't trust he had done it right the first time. Finally he shrugged back into his frock coat and asked, "How soon will the new one be here?"

"Oh, it shouldn't take longer than a month. Possibly six weeks."

Beaumont looked up from adjusting his coat. "That long?"

"It's not like we're in Chicago or Kansas City where the mail service is efficient and delivery is quick," Guthrie said. "We're in the Badlands."

"No foolin'."

"I only meant that our mail service is erratic and slow. Sometimes things come on time, but too often there are delays. Perhaps you'll be lucky and it will show up as soon as two weeks from now."

"That's still too long for me to go around with holes in my clothes."

Guthrie glanced at the bullet holes and swallowed. "Might I make a suggestion, sir?"

"So long as it doesn't involve you usin' that tape measure."

"No, I was going to suggest the new seamstress lady who has opened a shop on Second Street. She maybe can patch the holes for you until your new frock coat gets here."

"Second Street, you say?"

"Yes, sir. Right next to the bakery."

"That just might do. I'm obliged."

"Always glad to be of help."

Beaumont wheeled and left. He dearly wanted to go see the seamstress, but it had taken too long in the store and he had other business to attend to.

The Glass Slipper stood at the end of the next block. A newer building, it had been painted a shade of blue. Instead of the usual batwings, these were in the shape of butterflies. Beaumont had never seen the like. There was a small chandelier in the middle of the room, and the poker tables were covered with green cloth. The bar was polished mahogany.

Only a few drinkers were present, and a man at a table playing solitaire. Short and rotund, he was dapperly dressed and what little hair he had was neatly combed.

He showed no alarm as Beaumont approached, and went on laying out cards. "Mr. Adams," he said, his drawl almost as pronounced as Beaumont's. "To what do I owe this honor?"

"Garrison," Beaumont said. He took a chair without being asked and crinkled his nose. It was like sitting next to a flower garden. Garrison even had a flower in his lapel. A pink rose.

"I hope you're not here to give me the same treatment you gave poor Zimmerman."

"That depends," Beaumont said. "I want to buy you out."

Garrison stopped laying cards. "And if I don't want to sell?"

"Zimmerman didn't, either."

"I must say, this is terribly abrupt," Garrison said, but without any resentment. "Not that I didn't expect it."

"I'll pay you a fair price."

"Couldn't we reach some other arrangement?"

"I don't see how." Beaumont placed his

forearms on the table. He deliberately thunked his hidden derringer on the wood. He liked doing that. It always got people's attention.

"Why are you out to eliminate your competition?" Garrison asked.

"It's not that so much," Beaumont said. "Whiskey Flats is growin'. Thanks to the Diamond B, the town has become downright prosperous. A savvy gent could become rich, if he plays his cards right." Beaumont grinned at his little joke.

"That savvy gentleman bein' you?"

"I aim to rule the roost," Beaumont admitted. "The saloons are just the start. Before I'm done, I'll own this town and everybody in it."

"I see," Garrison said. "You crave power."

"Power, hell," Beaumont said. "I want to have more money than I know what to do with. Like that Midas."

"Ah. I assume you'll have all the business owners contribute a share of their proceeds to let you live in the style to which you'll become accustomed?"

"I like how you put that," Beaumont said.

"I read, sir. Voraciously."

"And yes," Beaumont said. "I'll get around to that. But I won't be greedy about it. Ten percent should do me."

"I see," Garrison said again, and thoughtfully drummed his fingers. "Since you're being so reasonable, perhaps you could extend me the same courtesy."

"I'm listenin'."

"I don't want to sell out," Garrison said. "I don't want to be dead, either. So what I propose is this." He paused. "I sign my saloon over to you and you let me go on running it and I pay you twenty percent of the take."

"If I get rid of you, I'll have one hundred percent," Beaumont said.

"True. But with three saloons and all your other interests, you won't have much time to run things personally. It would help to have someone do it for you. Someone who knows the business."

"Someone like you."

"Exactly."

Beaumont sat back. "The problem I have with that is more holes."

"I beg your pardon?"

"You didn't see the holes in my coat?"

"I did, in fact, but I didn't deem it polite to mention them."

"Polite?" Beaumont said, and laughed.

"Civility, Mr. Adams, counts for everything with me. There's so little of it in the world today. I was raised in the cultured society of New Orleans, in a part of the city some call the Garden District. My parents have a fine mansion, servants, you name it. They sent me to the best schools."

Beaumont became curious. "I have to ask, then. What in hell happened that you ended up here?"

Garrison gazed rather sadly at the batwings in the shape of butterflies, and then sniffed his pink rose. "That's rather personal. Suffice it to say I became the black sheep of my family. An outcast, if you will."

"Did you kill somebody?"

"Far worse than that, at least in their eyes." Garrison frowned. "My mother had a breakdown. My father called me into his den, offered me a cigar and some Scotch, and informed me that he never wanted to see me again. He went on to say that if I ever stepped foot over his threshold, he'd have me drawn and quartered."

"That still doesn't explain your saloon."

Garrison brightened and looked about them. "It's my oasis of culture in the sea of ignorance and violence we call life."

"You sure don't sound like a back-shooter," Beaumont said.

"Whatever do you mean?"

"Those holes I was talkin' about," Beaumont said. "I take over your saloon, I'll have

159

to be lookin' over my shoulder all the time, never knowin' when you might open up on me."

"I've never harmed a soul in my life," Garrison said.

"There's always a first time."

Garrison seemed to consider his next words carefully. "I don't rightly know what to say. Yes, I'll resent it. I'd have to be an idiot not to. But I'm not idiot enough to buck you, like the late Mr. Zimmerman did. I've made it as plain as I can that I want to go on living. I also realize you must make a tough decision. Do you trust me not to back-shoot you someday or do you snuff my wick here and now?"

"That pretty much sums it up," Beaumont said. "Even if I let you ride out, I'd never know but when you'd come back."

"I don't envy you your decision."

"You don't envy *me?"* Beaumont said, and snorted. "Mister, you plumb beat all. But damn me if I haven't taken a shine to you."

"Does that mean we have a deal?"

"If the deal is that I take over the Glass Slipper and you go on runnin' it and pay me thirty percent of the take. You're to bring in a few doves, too. I hear tell you don't have any."

"Must I?" Garrison asked.

"Doves bring in more customers, and more customers means more money. Why wouldn't you want to?"

"They're women."

"That's the whole point. What do you have against females?"

Garrison sighed and held out his hand. "I agree, if you do. Thirty percent after expenses, the whores, the works."

"Thirty percent *before* expenses," Beaumont corrected him. "I might be feelin' generous but not that generous." He stood. "I hope I'm not makin' the worst mistake of my life. But in case I am." He half turned. "Dyson. Stimms."

The pair had been standing a respectful distance back but now straightened and came forward.

"Boss?" Dyson said.

Beaumont pointed at Garrison. "If he ever kills me, you're to kill him. I'm givin' two hundred dollars to my lawyer to hold on to in case you ever have to, as payment."

Stimms patted his Sharps. "Hell, boss, I'd splatter his brains all over this floor for half that."

"You heard him," Beaumont said.

"Nicely played, sir," Garrison said. "Nicely played, indeed."

Beaumont grinned and walked out. Shoving through the butterfly batwings, he stopped abruptly.

Three men barred his way, one on the boardwalk and two to either side at the edge of the street: Scar Wratner, Grat, and Tuck.

"Gentlemen," Beaumont said, hiding his unease. It occurred to him that maybe Garrison had been stringing him along, that it could be Garrison had hired Scar Wratner to do him in. "To what do I owe this unexpected honor?"

His thumbs hooked in his gun belt, Scar Wratner smiled a smile as cold as ice. "I've been lookin' for you, card slick."

14

Isolda Jessup was bored. She'd been at the Diamond B less than twenty-four hours, and she was so restless she couldn't stand it. Despite being so tired from their long journey that she could barely keep her eyes open the night before, she'd slept fitfully. Twice, she'd woken up and just lain there in her bed, feeling ill at ease.

Isolda hadn't wanted to come west. When her father first mentioned the position he'd been offered, she didn't expect him to take it. Ranching was a far cry from running dairy farms. She'd assumed he'd decline. To her amazement, he didn't.

Her sister's eagerness wasn't nearly as surprising. Edana loved a challenge. For as long as Isolda could remember, her older sister threw herself into everything she did with the determination she would succeed no matter what. Long hours, tedious work, Edana never minded so long as she got the job done.

Not Isolda. She was their bookkeeper, and a duller job would be hard to imagine.

Sure, she had a head for business, but she found it much less exciting than Edana did. Truth was, over the past year or so, she'd begun to wonder if she shouldn't do something else with her life. Something she liked. Something that would be as exciting for her as running a dairy farm, or now a ranch, was for her sister. But the big question was: what?

Isolda mused about it all morning. She went through the motion of eating breakfast, even though she wasn't all that hungry, and spent the morning going through a pile of receipts the foreman had saved for her.

"Mr. Wells told me to, ma'am," Neal Bonner let her know.

Isolda didn't like Bonner. She wasn't entirely sure why. He was nice enough. Almost too nice, in that simpleminded cowboy way of his. Always calling her "ma'am." Always treating her and her sister with the utmost respect. Why, he would hardly look her in the eye, he was so shy around women. He wasn't at all like Beaumont Adams.

Beaumont Adams. Now, there was a fine figure of a man, Isolda reflected. A man who would not only look her in the eye, but let his own wander over her body as if she were a piece of pie he wanted to take a bite out of. And Lord help her, she liked that. She'd never had a man regard her with such . . . hunger . . . before. It excited her.

She tried to tell herself it shouldn't. She reminded herself that her father expected her to behave like a lady, and tried to put the gambler's handsome features from her mind. But as she worked on the receipts she kept seeing him instead of the bill she was looking at.

Isolda found herself wishing she could see him again. Soon.

Her father and sister returned at midday for a quick bite to eat. Isolda joined them since if she didn't, her father would raise a stink. She said very little, but neither noticed. They were too excited about the work ahead.

"I must confess," Alexander said halfway through the meal, "running the Diamond B will be more of a challenge than running those dairy farms ever were. There's so much to learn."

"Is there ever!" Edana said. "I spent the morning with Neal. Mr. Wells was right about him. Neal's knowledge of cattle is incredible."

Isolda smothered a laugh.

"Neal, is it?" their father said. "I prefer you call him Mr. Bonner, both when you're around him and when you're not."

"Yes, Father," Edana said.

"What about you?" Alexander said to Isolda. "What have you been doing all morning?"

"Accounts," Isolda answered, and had an inspiration. "Which reminds me. Our incredible foreman did a wonderful job of stocking the ranch with everything that has to do with cows —"

"Don't tease your sister," Alexander said.

"But I'm afraid no one told him that a bookkeeper can't do all the sums in her head. I need a lot more paper and I'm short on ink. I could stand to buy a few ledgers, too." Isolda put as innocent a look on her face as she could manage. "So I was wondering if it would be all right if I went into town tomorrow morning to buy what I can find and order what I can't."

"I have a lot to do here, but I can go with you, I suppose," her father said.

Isolda seized the opening. "Why bother? I'll have Stumpy drive me. If we leave early I can be back by nightfall."

"Edana should go, too," Alexander said.

"Whatever for?" Isolda countered. "She

166

has plenty to do, what with learning about cattle from her good friend Neal."

"Stop that, you hear?" Edana said.

"I'll be perfectly fine, Father," Isolda said. "If you're truly worried, send a couple of your cowboys along. I understand they're reputed to be perfect gentlemen around women." She threw that last in as icing on her argument.

"I don't like the idea of you going alone," Alexander said, setting down his soupspoon. "Not after all the tales we've heard about hostiles and outlaws and the like. These are the Badlands, after all. I don't feel it's safe and there's no one I trust to —" He glanced out the kitchen window and suddenly stopped.

"Father?" Isolda said when he just sat there.

"Why not?" Alexander said.

"Why not what?"

Alexander turned to Edana. "Would you agree that Mr. Bonner's judgment is of the very highest order?"

"I couldn't agree more, yes."

"Then I should rely on that judgment, shouldn't I? Since we'll be working so closely with him."

"That goes without saying," Edana said.

Alexander faced Isolda. "Very well, daughter. You get to go into town tomorrow. Leave at sunrise. I'll inform Stumpy he's driving. And I'll take your advice and send one of our cowboys along."

"Just one?" Isolda said.

"From what we hear," her father said, "this one will be more than enough."

Beaumont Adams lowered his hands to his pockets and started to slide them in, saying, "You have, have you?"

Scar Wratner glanced at Beaumont's pockets and laughed. "No need for your hideouts, gambler man. If I was out to bed you down permanent, you'd already be lyin' there with holes in your head."

"Then what?" Beaumont said in puzzlement. He'd had little to do with the notorious leather slapper since Wratner showed up, and was at a loss to guess what they had to talk about.

"How about if we take a stroll?" Scar Wratner said, and without waiting for a reply, he turned and sauntered along the boardwalk, saying over his shoulder to Grat and Tuck, "You two hang back. This is between him and me."

Beaumont gestured to indicate that Dyson and Stimms should do the same. Falling into step with Wratner, he said, "If this is about me pokin' fun when you braced Alexander Jessup yesterday . . ."

"The rancher? I couldn't care less about him. He riled me, is all, callin' me a specimen. I still don't know what the hell that is."

Beaumont kept quiet.

"No, I wanted to talk about somethin' else. I want to offer you somethin'."

"Your scar? No, thanks. I like to look at myself in the mirror."

Scar's scar twitched. "Don't start up again, damn you. Save your funny remarks for that gal you were oglin'."

"I have no idea what you're talkin' about."

"Sure you don't," Scar said. "But I'm not here to talk about the filly, either."

"Than what do you want to talk about?"

"If you'd shut the hell up for two minutes, I'd tell you," Scar said in mild annoyance. "What you did last night was damn slick. It took grit to get in close like you did to blow out their wicks. You were the talk of the Tumbleweed the rest of the night. It got me to thinkin'."

"Oh?"

"I asked around, and there wasn't any bad blood between you two. You didn't kill him on account of some grudge. It appears to me that the only reason you did it was to help yourself to his saloon. Yet you already have one of your own that does real well, from what I saw when I've been in there."

"You figured that out all by yourself."

Scar stopped and swung around, his hands at his sides. "Poke fun at me one more time. I goddamn dare you."

"Force of habit," Beaumont said. "Go on."

Scowling, Scar resumed walking. "It hit me that if I was right, you might be out to rule the roost hereabouts. You'd likely help yourself to Garrison's, too, and who knows what else?"

"Now I *am* impressed," Beaumont said. "I figured it would be a while before anyone caught on." He'd intended to go about taking over as quietly and secretly as possible. Less trouble that way.

"I'm not as dumb as some folks seem to think," Scar said, and touched his scar. "It's this thing," he said bitterly. "It makes me look dumber than I am."

Beaumont smothered another retort.

"I'm not just fast with pistols. I have a brain," Scar said. "But it's my pistols I'd like to put to work for you."

Beaumont came to a halt. It was turning into a day of surprises. First Garrison, now this. "What makes you think I'd want to take you on?"

"Common sense," Scar said. "You, by yourself, might be able to pull it off. You're not afraid to kill. Everybody saw that last night. But there's still bound to be some who will raise a ruckus about you takin' over. And you won't be able to take them by surprise like you did Zimmerman."

"What's your point?"

"Do I really have to spell it out?" Scar said. "You hire me and my pistols to back your play."

"I already have Dyson and Stimms."

"Small-fry. So are Grat and Tuck, for that matter." Scar grinned. "But me and these?" He patted his Smith & Wessons. "I'm not small-fry, and everyone knows it. My reputation can work for you. If someone has to go through me to get to you, they'll think twice. Taking over will go a lot smoother."

Beaumont had to admit he had a point. With the notorious gun shark on his payroll, he'd be far less likely to have anyone stand up to him. But it created an important question. "I'd imagine you don't come free."

"Not hardly," Scar said.

"How much do you reckon your services are worth? I pay Dyson and Stimms a hundred a month."

"Don't insult me. I wouldn't be on your payroll, not the same as them. You and me would be partners."

"Uh-oh," Beaumont said.

"What's the matter? You don't think I'd be worth it?"

"You said it yourself. I aim to rule the roost. Not share the roost with someone else."

"Who said you have to? I've got no interest in runnin' things. I'll leave all that up to you." Scar paused. "I was thinkin' more like a fifth of what you make. In return, I'd keep you safe and kill anybody who needs killin'."

"A fifth is a lot."

"You still get the other three-fourths," Scar said, "which will be more money than you know what to do with. And it's not as if I'll stick around forever. Sooner or later Whiskey Flats will tame down. Towns always do. And I don't like tame towns."

"I'm not fond of them myself."

"Tame towns have law dogs, and tin stars are always quick to raise a stink when I gun someone."

"I've met a few marshals who were less than friendly to gamblers in my travels," Beaumont remarked.

"Gamblers and shooters aren't well liked," Scar said. "Decent folks look down their noses at us. Some towns get so tame they outlaw guns and cards, both. Like it is back

East. There's those who say the West will be the same one day. I sure as hell hope I'm not around to see that."

"Me, either."

"So you see?" Scar grinned. "We have a lot in common. What do you say to my offer? I'll stick for as long as you need me. Then I'll mosey on to wilder pastures and leave you to have it all."

"I need to think on it some," Beaumont said. He half expected Wratner would get mad and was glad he had his hands in his pockets. He was under no delusions about being able to outdraw him. But the surprises kept coming.

"That's only fair, I reckon," Scar said. "Take as long as you need to. I'll be around." Hooking his thumbs in his gun belt, he ambled off.

Grat and Tuck hastened to catch up to him.

"Well, now," Beaumont said.

"Is there a problem we should know about, boss?" Dyson asked as he and Stimms came up.

"No problem at all, boys," Beaumont said. "Fact is, life is treatin' me nice for once. It makes me suspicious."

"Of what?" Stimms asked.

"Of when it's goin' to jump up and kick me in the teeth."

15

Isolda could hardly sleep, she was so excited. What she was doing was so bold, so audacious, it would scandalize her father. If he found out, he might punish her by restricting her to the ranch. She didn't want that. She must be clever. She must outsmart him.

Isolda was up an hour and a half before dawn. She'd taken a bath the night before and done her hair to perfection so that all it needed now was ten minutes of brushing to make it shine. She realized she might be wasting her time. Three hours in the buckboard with the wind and the dust might make a mess of it. But that's why shawls were invented.

In order not to make her father suspicious, Isolda had to forgo her most revealing dress, the one she wore to dances and on other special occasions, in favor of a plainer one. She chose a dress that clung to her where a man was liable to appreciate clinging the most. She also wore her smallest shoes. They tended to hurt her feet after a while, but she wasn't walking to town, so it shouldn't be a problem.

Now came the important part. Her face. Isolda knew men found her naturally attractive. She wasn't above helping things along, though. The year before she'd gotten hold of some Crème Celeste and fallen in love with it. A mix of almond oil, rosewater, white wax, and that oily substance they took out of a whale's head, it was, in her estimation, simply wonderful. It not only smelled nice and kept her skin from becoming too dry, but it hid wrinkles, too. Today it would keep her looking fresh until she got to Whiskey Flats.

Isolda also dabbed a little castor oil onto her eyelashes and eyebrows. The sheen was alluring. Then there was the pomade, made from beeswax, for her lips. She had to be careful to apply it lightly or it made her lips sticky, and she hated that. Finally she had a carmine dye she liked to rub into her cheeks. She'd been told it was made from dead insects, but she didn't care. She liked the luster it gave her.

Finally done, Isolda admired her reflection in the mirror of her portable toilet table. It was made of rosewood with a velvet lining, able to hold all her toiletries and then some, and she never went anywhere without it.

With a shawl over her shoulders and a handbag in hand, Isolda ventured down to the kitchen. Her father and sister were already there. Her father believed that breakfast was the most important meal of the day and insisted they eat with him, even though she had made it plain countless times that she was never hungry early on and much preferred to save her big meal for supper.

Alexander stopped chewing long enough to ask, "Are you ready to go?"

"Yes, Father," Isolda said dutifully. She forced herself to eat some toast and picked at an egg to please him.

Edana was looking at her and grinning. "Your hair looks nice today," she remarked.

"Why, thank you," Isolda said, thrown off guard by the praise. Her sister rarely complimented her on her appearance.

"And your cheeks are the very pink of health," Edana said.

Isolda realized her sister was aware of the extra effort she'd gone to, and was teasing her. "How observant you are today."

"I feel very much alive," Edana said.

"Here we are, starting a new life. Think of all the new experiences we'll have."

Isolda made the mistake of saying, "A cow is a cow."

Alexander smacked his fork onto his plate. "Here we go again. Thinking like that annoys me, daughter. You couldn't be more wrong. A longhorn isn't a dairy cow, and this ranch is nothing like those dairy farms. So what if you mainly handle our bookkeeping? I expect you to familiarize yourself with all aspects of ranching life as you did with the dairy profession."

"Yes, Father," Isolda said while thinking there were few things that interested her less.

"Personally, I'm looking forward to all the new things I need to learn," Edana said. "And not just about the cattle. At my request, Neal is going to teach me how to use a rope one day soon."

"So you can throw a loop over him?" Isolda said.

Edana looked down at her food.

"What will you be doing, Father?" Isolda pretended to care.

"Mr. Bonner is taking us out on the range," Alexander answered. "I want to see some of these longhorns up close."

"Be careful you don't get too close,"

Isolda said. "They call them 'longhorns' for a reason."

They all heard the clatter of the buckboard as it came around the house, and Stumpy saying, "Get along there, you lazy so-and-sos."

"Oh my," Isolda said, rising. "Time for me to leave."

"I'll walk you out," her father said.

"No need. Finish your meal."

"I insist."

Isolda was in too good a mood to argue. She'd gotten the better of her sister, and she would soon see Beaumont Adams again. Humming to herself, she hurried down the hall and out the front door onto the porch. The buckboard and Stumpy were waiting. So was someone else. At the sight of him, she stopped in consternation. "What's *he* doing here?"

"I told you I was sending someone along to watch over you," Alexander said, moving to the rail. "Mr. Bonner assured me that you're in perfectly safe hands with Mr. Jericho along."

"Mornin', ma'am," Jericho said. His black hat was low over his brow, hiding his eyes. In the growing daylight, the white of the pearl handles on his Colt contrasted sharply with the black of his leather vest. Isolda was fit to spit nails. "I hate to put Mr. Jericho to any special bother," she said in the vain hope her father would take the hint.

"He works for me, my dear," Alexander said. "It's no bother at all, is it, Mr. Jericho?"

"I ride for the brand," Jericho said. "What you want, I do."

"Excellent," Alexander said with a broad smile. "Heed me closely." He nodded at Isolda. "I don't want anything to happen to her. Although Mr. Bonner deems it unlikely, should you encounter any hostiles, you're to protect my daughter with your life."

"That goes without sayin'," Jericho said.

Stumpy piped up with "Same here. I'm not about to let redskins get their hands on a white gal."

"When you get to town," Alexander said, still only addressing Jericho, "you're not to let anyone near her who doesn't have any business doing so. That especially goes for — what was his name? Scar Wratner."

Isolda was relieved he hadn't mentioned Beaumont Adams. But her relief was short-lived.

"It also applies to that gambler. Edana tells me he was too free with his eyes, and I won't have a man like that around my girls. Do you understand?"

"I savvy," Jericho said.

Stumpy interrupted again. "Just so I know, Mr. Jessup. How far are you willin' for Jericho to take it?"

"I don't get your meaning."

"Let's say we run into that gambler feller or Wratner and they say somethin' they shouldn't to Miss Jessup and Jericho tells them to back off and they won't. Can he shoot them with your blessin'?"

"I'd rather it didn't come to that," Alexander said.

"What's he to do, then? Say 'pretty please' and if they laugh in his face, tuck tail?"

"I don't tuck," Jericho said.

"You're making more of this than I think is war ranted," Alexander said to Stumpy. "Despite what every one keeps telling me, I can't see Adams or Scar Wratner resorting to firearms without being provoked, and you're not under any circumstances to provoke them."

"What about if they do the provokin'?"

"I leave it to your best judgment," Alexander said. "The important thing is that no harm comes to my daughter."

Isolda saw Stumpy give Jericho a troubled look. She couldn't tell what Jericho was thinking, because his face seemed to be made of stone and that black hat covered his eyes. "Don't worry, Father," she said. "I'm sure we'll be just fine."

"I hope so," Alexander said. "It would devastate me if anything were to happen to you or your sister." He took hold of her arm. "Here. Let me help you up."

Isolda settled in the seat and carefully slid the shawl up over her head to protect her hair. "Whenever you're ready," she said to Stumpy.

"We're ready now, ma'am."

Isolda was jostled slightly as the buckboard lurched into motion. She didn't look back. Her father probably expected her to, but she wasn't feeling particularly sentimental at the moment. Not that she ever did normally, anyway.

Glad to be finally under way, Isolda sat back and smiled. The sun hadn't fully risen yet, and a brisk breeze was blowing. She shivered slightly.

Stumpy noticed and said, "I've got a blanket in the back if you need it, ma'am. Brought it just for you."

"That was thoughtful," Isolda felt obligated to mention. "But I don't need it right now."

"Suit yourself," Stumpy said. "And if you don't mind my sayin', you might want to turn a bit and watch to the east. Sunsets out here are downright pretty."

Isolda had seen the sun rise before. But she had nothing else to do, so she humored him and shifted.

Jericho was following behind, and touched a finger to his hat brim.

Isolda nodded, even though she resented his being there. Or, rather, she resented that her father had made him come along. She gazed past him at the horizon, and received a surprise. Stumpy was right. The sunrise was spectacular. The sun seemed larger somehow. It reminded her of nothing so much as a great circular furnace, shimmering with molten fires, suspended on edge. From it radiated bands of red, orange, and yellow. She had never seen a sunrise so dazzling. By some freak effect of the atmosphere, she had the illusion she could reach out and touch it. "It truly is wonderful."

"Told you, ma'am," Stumpy crowed. "The sunsets can be just as pretty, but I'm partial to sunrise myself. It makes me start off the day in a good mood."

"I've never enjoyed nature as much as my sister does, but I agree with you about your sunrises."

"Thank you kindly."

After that, not a word out of him. Isolda had the sense that as friendly as Stumpy had been, he wasn't entirely comfortable around her. Or perhaps he wasn't comfortable around females, period.

Neal Bonner had told Edana not to be offended if the hands acted shy around them. Cowboys, by and large, held a high respect for womanhood but were so unaccustomed to their company that when circumstances conspired to throw them together, the average cowboy's tongue became tied in knots.

Isolda thought that was silly.

It was bad enough, in her estimation, that a lot of men put women on pedestals. Churchgoing ladies and married ladies in particular. But then don a woman in a tight dress and have her prance around a saloon, and suddenly she wasn't deserving of a pedestal anymore.

Isolda had always thought that was hypocritical. As far as she was concerned, she shouldn't be treated any differently than a man treated another man. That Stumpy plainly did brought her old peeve to the surface. Just once she'd like a man to regard her as just another person. As no better, or worse, than he was.

For now she put it from her mind and gave some regard to the scenery. In the spreading glow of the new dawn, the Badlands acquired a rosy tint that made them less stark, less foreboding. The colors in the rock strata stood out, and many cliffs and buttes were golden with reflected light.

After about an hour, the charm of the landscape wore off. The sun was all the way up and the temperature climbed.

Isolda wasn't looking forward to two more hours of just sitting there doing nothing. Turning to Stumpy, she asked, "What would you like to talk about?"

"Ma'am?"

"All this time on our hands, we should make conversation. Pick a subject and we'll talk about it."

Stumpy shifted uncomfortably. "The only things I know much about, Miss Jessup, are horses and cows. How about you pick which it should be?"

"Neither," Isolda said. "I have no interest in horses and even less in cows." She had an idea. "I know. Why don't you tell me about yourself?"

"Me, ma'am?"

"Where were you born? Where did you grow up? Do you have family? Those sorts of things."

"Well, let's see. I was born in Illinois but my pa moved all of us to what's now called Wyomin' Territory when I was a sprout. Ma and him died a few years back. He went first and she didn't want to live anymore and went soon after. I've got a sister in Colorado, but I don't see her much." Stumpy shrugged. "That's all there is to me, I reckon."

"Well, that was entertaining," Isolda said.

"Ma'am?"

"I was hoping there was more to you." Isolda glanced over her shoulder. "I know, I'll ask Mr. Jericho."

"I'd think twice about that, ma'am. He won't take kindly to you pryin' into his personal life."

"Oh, really?" Isolda said, and raising her arm to get her bodyguard's attention, she called out, "Mr. Jericho! If you would be so kind, come up here and join us. I have some questions to ask you."

"Oh Lordy," Stumpy said.

16

Solomon Corinthians Jericho was born to a deeply religious woman on a cold and blustery winter's morning in North Carolina. Esther Jericho loved her Bible. She never went anywhere without it. She attended church not once but three times a week, and sang in the choir. She was devoted to the Lord, and to Scripture. So when her first child came into the world, she showed her devotion by naming him after her favorite person from the Old Testament and her favorite book from the New.

Her husband, Abe, didn't mind. He wasn't as religious himself. He only went to church because she made him. It wasn't that he didn't believe. He'd just rather be off hunting or fishing or just about be doing anything other than listen to a sermon.

Solomon didn't mind his name, although he didn't like that a lot of the kids called him "Sol" for short. It sounded too much like "Sal," which was short for Sally, and a girl's name besides.

Then he turned fourteen, and something happened that not only changed his name forever after, but changed his life, as well.

Sol had been raised to treat everyone fairly and decently, to do unto others as he'd like them to do to him. He never bullied anyone and didn't like it when others did.

He didn't like liars and cheats, either. His mother was always reminding him to be a good boy, and he took that to heart.

He got into trouble a few times when he saw someone being picked on and stuck up for them. Tempers flared, and tempers often led to blows. His mother always sat him down afterward and explained how he must turn the other cheek. Solomon tried. He honestly tried. But by the age of twelve he knew he wasn't a cheek turner. It just wasn't in him.

Then came his fourteenth year and he took the family wagon into town. A neighbor boy he knew was being picked on by several young men, strangers who were passing through, and who'd had a lot to drink. Sol tried his mother's way. He tried to get the boy away from them without violence, but one of the men started pushing him and calling him names, and when he couldn't take it anymore and slugged him, the man pulled a knife.

All three strangers jumped him, and it was plain to Sol that they aimed to kill him if they could. But he was strong for his age, and quick. Everyone was always saying how quick he was. He broke one's nose and smashed another's teeth, and then he and the last boy scuffled and somehow the boy stabbed himself with his own knife, cried out, and died.

Solomon panicked. The sheriff in those parts liked to boast that there hadn't been a killer he hadn't had hanged. Solomon didn't want to hang. So he ran.

Looking back years later, he regretted being so rash. It had been self-defense. A jury might have let him off. But he didn't know that then, and he fled all the way to New Orleans by taking a job hauling for a freighting outfit. He didn't stay in New Orleans long. The city was too big for his tastes, and too refined. He had little in common with all the fancy folk with their elegant clothes and carriages, and even less with the river rats who swarmed the docks. He was a plain country boy, and he drifted in search of a place where he'd feel more at home.

It took him a while. Three years of roaming. But he found the heaven he was looking for.

They called it "Texas."

Solomon took to the Lone Star State like a duck to water. Most of the people were down-to-earth, and he liked that. They were friendly, and he liked that. And they didn't pry into what others had done in the past, and he especially liked that.

Out of worry there still might be a warrant out for his arrest, he changed his name by dropping Solomon and Corinthians and calling himself Jericho. When anyone asked if that was his first or his last, he always told them it was his only and let it go at that.

Jericho took a job at a ranch. It was his introduction to cattle and to six-shooters. He bought his first Colt the day he turned eighteen, never suspecting that less than a month later, he'd kill two men with it.

His employer was squabbling with another rancher over water rights. The other rancher had a bigger spread, and more hands, and two of them were toughs who reminded Jericho of those bullies from his younger days.

On a sunny summer morning, Jericho went into Jeffersonville with his boss to pick up supplies. Mr. Hamilton — that was his boss's name — told him to wait with the wagon while he went down the street. As

Hamilton passed the saloon, who should stroll out but the two toughs, and they were on the prod. They insulted Hamilton and dared him to go for his six-gun, but he refused. Hamilton was no gun hand, and he was pushing fifty, besides. One of them knocked him down.

That was when Jericho stepped in. He'd felt oddly calm. He didn't shout or curse or do any of the usual things men did when they were about to come to blows. He walked up and told them to light a shuck, or else.

They picked the "or else."

Jericho relived that moment many times over the days and years ahead. He'd been practicing with his Colt to where he could draw and hit a bottle at ten paces about eight times out of ten. The toughs were closer than ten paces. They clawed for their hardware and he drew and shot both in the chest before either cleared leather. He was as surprised as Mr. Hamilton and the other onlookers at how quick he was.

That was the day his life changed. He was no longer just a cowboy. He was a gun shark, a quick-trigger man, a killer. Men talked about him. They pointed at him, and whispered.

Jericho hadn't wanted it, but there it was.

He heard that the other rancher was bringing in someone to deal with him, and he practiced harder with his Colt, every spare moment he had, until he could hit bottles ten times out of ten.

Over six weeks went by, and just when Jericho figured the rumors were false, he was in Jeffersonville one afternoon with several punchers and a man came down the street and loudly proclaimed that his name was Luke Spicer, and he was there to kill him.

Jericho was amazed at how open and loud the man was about it. Later, he learned that this Spicer was a bad man who hired his gun out and had killed a lot of others. Spicer always made it a point to provoke the other man into going for his six-shooter first. He tried it with Jericho, but Jericho never let name-calling anger him. That he didn't rise to Spicer's insults made Spicer mad, and easier for Jericho to return the favor. Jericho told Spicer that he heard a cur yapping somewhere, and Spicer glowered. Jericho sniffed a few times and asked Spicer if there was an outhouse nearby or was it him, and Spicer turned red. Then Jericho asked if Spicer's ma was proud of giving birth to such a miserable son of a bitch, and Spicer went for his pearl-handled, nickel-plated Colt.

Jericho's hand flashed and his own Colt boomed and bucked, and Luke Spicer ended up spread-eagle in the street with a hole between his eyes. The pearl-handled Colt had fallen at Spicer's feet, and Jericho went over and helped himself to it. He felt he was entitled.

The shooting had some unforeseen consequences. He went from being whispered about to being practically famous. Texans took their shootists seriously. Killers were talked about as much as the weather.

The second consequence was that the sheriff looked him up to tell him that no, the sheriff wasn't going to arrest him, and yes, the sheriff knew that Luke Spicer had come looking for trouble, and Jericho might like to know that as contemptible as Spicer was, Spicer had a few equally contemptible friends who might come looking for Jericho, and the sheriff would take it kindly if Jericho wasn't in his jurisdiction when they caught up to him.

Jericho would have stuck for Mr. Hamilton's sake, but the rancher sat him down and told him that things were getting out of hand, and Mrs. Hamilton was worried they would escalate even more. They both agreed it might be best if Jericho moved on.

Jericho did. His next years were spent

drifting. He mostly worked cattle. Once he briefly hired on as a deputy with a friendly marshal who got blown to hell by buckshot when they went to arrest a man accused of horse stealing. The marshal had no chance. The man came to his door loaded for bear, or lawmen, as the case was, and at the marshal's knock, threw the door wide and cut loose. The marshal took a barrel full in the chest. Then the horse thief swung on Jericho, but Jericho already had his Colt out and put two slugs through the man's heart. That was it for law work.

The incident was written up in the local newspaper, and his reputation grew. It got so he rarely mentioned his name so he wouldn't be recognized.

It was strange how life worked out sometimes. Growing up back in the hills, he'd never have imagined that one day he'd be regarded as a killer of other men. His ma would be horrified if she knew. She'd raised him to be better than that. Some nights, when he lay thinking of her, it filled him with shame. But he always shrugged it off. A man did what he had to, and had no more control over his fate than he did over the weather.

Jericho was drifting again when he stopped in Benton City. He'd reckoned to play some poker, have a drink or two, and turn in. A nice, quiet night. Then Lindsey accused someone of cheating who wasn't, and tried to back-shoot him. He'd had his head half-turned and was watching the no-account out of the corner of his eye when Lindsey made his play. It surprised him when the big cowboy shouted a warning. He'd gone over to shake the cowpoke's hand, and now it was seven years later and they were still together.

Pards for life was how Jericho like to think of it. Or until a filly came along to sweep one or the other away.

Jericho could tell Edana Jessup was interested in Neal almost from the moment he'd met her. It showed in her eyes. She probably wasn't even aware that she gave it away.

Jericho could also tell that Neal liked her. Liked her more than any women they'd come across. He had to face the fact that, even though they'd only just met, it could be that Edana was the one for his pard. Time would tell.

As for the other sister, Jericho hadn't cottoned to her. She had cold eyes, aloof eyes, eyes that said she looked down her nose at most of the world and everyone in it. Jericho would as soon have nothing to do with her. But his pard, Neal, wanted him to watch over her, so here he was, escorting the buckboard into Whiskey Flats when he'd rather be at the Diamond B.

Jericho didn't pay much attention to the talk she was having with Stumpy. Just so much chatter, as far as he was concerned. Then she twisted in the seat and beckoned, saying she had some questions to ask, so he gigged his zebra dun alongside the buckboard. "Ma'am?"

Isolda had that looking-down-her-nose look. "I want to ask you a few questions," she said again.

"About what, ma'am?"

"You."

Jericho looked at Stumpy.

"It's not my doin'," the older hand said.

"Call it womanly curiosity," Isolda said. "Plus, I'm bored. But I'd like to hear all about you. Where you grew up. How you ended up a shootist, or whatever it is they call you. Everything."

"No, ma'am," Jericho said.

"I beg your pardon?"

"I reckon I won't."

Those cold eyes of Isolda's narrowed. "I'm your boss's daughter. For that matter, since the consortium hired the three of us to run the ranch, I'm as much your boss as my father is. Do you agree?"

"If you say so."

"Then you'll do as I want."

"No, ma'am."

Isolda sat up and bunched her small fists. "How dare you refuse? It was a reasonable request. Your presumption is uncalled for. I demand you tell me what I want to know."

Jericho didn't respond. He'd already told her no twice, which was one more time than he should have to say it.

"Say something, blast you. You can't just ignore me. That's rude. I'll speak to my father about you."

"You do that, ma'am."

"I'll have you disciplined, or even fired."

"If you say so, ma'am."

"You don't believe I will?" Isolda said, her voice rising. "I'll show you. I won't stand for impertinence. Stumpy here will be my witness that you've treated me with rank contempt."

"I will?" Stumpy said.

"You and that Neal Bonner," Isolda said to Jericho. "Father and my sister think the world of him, but I don't. You think he'll protect you from being fired, but he won't. He's only the foreman."

"I wouldn't ask him to protect me, ma'am."

"Quit being so polite. I'm mad at you,

damn it."

"I can see that, ma'am."

Isolda uttered a strangled snarl of baffled resentment. "Do you think you're being cute? Is that it?"

"Not in a million years, ma'am."

"Ohhhh, you make me so mad."

Jericho rose in the stirrups and peered to the northwest. "You might want to hold off on takin' out your bile on me."

"Why should I?" Isolda demanded.

Jericho nodded at riders in the distance. "Because some Injuns are comin' our way."

17

Edana Jessup had seldom looked forward to anything as much as a ride around the Diamond B with its foreman. She could hardly sleep the night before for thinking about it. When she eventually did doze off, she only slept a couple of hours and woke up again and thought about it some more.

She told herself that she was excited about seeing the ranch. That she was also looking forward to spending more time with Neal Bonner she attributed to a flight of fancy that would soon pass. So what if he was ruggedly good-looking and competent? It wasn't as if she hadn't been around men before.

Edana resented her sister teasing her about the rope business. Isolda was a fine one to talk. Edana suspected her sister was keenly interested in the gambler they'd met, Beaumont Adams.

But there sure was *something* about Neal

Bonner.

Edana felt it was that competence of his. Competence was a trait she admired above all others. Her father had a lot to do with that, since from childhood she'd been in awe of his. Her father always knew exactly what to do and never let anything stand in the way of his doing it. She had a sense that Neal Bonner was the same, especially when it came to cattle.

For their ride, Edana donned the outfit she always wore back East. It consisted of a long-sleeved blouse with large buttons down the front, a flared skirt that allowed for free use of her legs, and a high top hat with a narrow brim popular with Eastern ladies, tilted slightly. On her feet she wore riding boots with over a dozen eyelets and red laces.

Alexander was on the porch, and smiled as she emerged. He wore a hat similar to hers, along with a coat open at the front, a white shirt and white vest, and pantaloons with tassels at the knees. His boots were made from calf leather and had straps at the top to make them easier to pull on. "I daresay we present quite the sight, wouldn't you say?" He held out his elbow for her to take. "Let's dazzle the locals, shall we?"

Edana laughed. Her father was usually so

serious about things. It was rare for him to joke. She attributed it to the raw atmosphere of the Badlands. "I'd wager they've never seen anyone dressed like we are."

She proved to be right on that score.

Neal Bonner had their horses saddled and ready at the stable. He wasn't alone. Four hands were already mounted, apparently waiting to go along. Neal turned on hearing them come up, and his mouth fell.

The four cowboys looked flabbergasted.

To his credit, Neal recovered quickly. "Mr. Jessup. Miss Jessup," he said. "You're all set, I see."

"I'm looking forward to this," Alexander said. "A tour of my new domain, as it were."

To be polite, Edana smiled at the cowboys. "Gentlemen," she said.

"Lord Almighty," a young hand on a sorrel exclaimed. He had a mop of corn-colored hair and wore a brown shirt and a brown bandanna. Like all of them he also had a Colt high on his hip.

"Hush, Billy," Neal said.

"Is something the matter?" Alexander asked. "They look as if they've just swallowed flies."

"It's your clothes," Neal replied.

"What about them?"

"Nothin'," Neal said. "But it probably

201

wouldn't hurt, the next time you're in town, to buy some new ones."

"That's no answer." Alexander turned to Billy. "How about you, young man? Why were you so shocked?"

Billy had an easy grin. "Shucks, Mr. Jessup. I didn't mean nothin'. I just ain't used to folks goin' around dressed like peacocks, is all."

"Billy, consarn you," Neal said.

"Peacocks?" Alexander repeated.

"You know, those birds with the pretty feathers on their hind ends," Billy said. "I saw one once, over to Kansas City. You sort of remind me of them."

Now it was Edana's turn. "Peacocks?" She saw that the other cowhands were trying not to grin or laugh, and looked down at herself. "I've ridden in an outfit like this for years."

"Don't pay him no mind, ma'am," Neal said. "You're dressed different than ladies out here dress, is all, and to some folks, different is the same as peculiar." He gave Billy a pointed look.

Billy squirmed in his saddle and said to Alexander, "I'm plumb sorry, Big Sugar. It won't happen again."

"What did you just call me?"

" 'Big sugar' is what punchers call the

owner," Neal translated.

"It's the consortium that owns the Dia-mond B," Alexander said. "I merely run it for them."

"We can call you Little Sugar," Billy said, and laughed.

Edana almost laughed, too, at her father's expression.

"I'm not sure if I'll ever become ac-customed to their vernacular," Alexander said. "There's no rhyme or reason to it."

"Verna — what?" Billy said.

Neal stepped to the sorrel and put a finger to his lips.

"Oh," Billy said. "Sure."

A middle-aged hand with a bulge in his cheek from a wad of chewing tobacco spat on the ground, wiped his mouth with his sleeve, and chuckled. "That boy never has learned when to keep quiet." He wore a tan hat and larger spurs than the other hands. And a Smith & Wesson revolver instead of the usual Colt.

"Don't you start, Yeager," Neal said.

"How about if we get under way?" Edana proposed. The same bay she had ridden out from town was tied to the rail, and she undid the reins and swung up without ask-ing for assistance. She noticed the cowboys looking at her strangely. "You've never seen a woman climb on a horse before?"

"How did that hat not fall off?" Billy asked. "It's sittin' cockeyed."

"Hairpins," Edana said, enlightening him. "You might try using them sometime."

Billy blushed, the other hands cackled, and Neal gave her one of his warm smiles.

"Can we get under way sometime today?" Alexander said.

The Diamond B was too large to tour in a week, let alone a day. Neal's intention was to take them on a sweep of the nearby range and show them a few of the areas within easy riding distance where the graze was good.

Edana rode on one side of him, her father on the other. She sat her saddle straight and flattered herself that she rode as well as any of the men.

The countryside fascinated her. The mix of bluffs and buttes and the many rock formations made her think of a sculptor gone wild. That the rock came in so many colors surprised her. She'd always thought of rock as bland. But there were reds and browns and yellows and places where the rock was almost white. Interspersed were green valleys and small plains.

They had been at it a couple of hours when Edana remarked, "You know, I do so love this country. It has a beauty about it that's hard to describe."

Neal looked at her. "A heap of beauty," he said.

Edana hoped she didn't blush. "A person could get so enamored of the beauty, I'd imagine he'd want to live here forever."

Alexander harrumphed. "Let's not romanticize, shall we? New York is just as picturesque in its own way, and a lot greener."

Edana disagreed but held her tongue.

"I will confess that when you travel about in New York, it's always more of the same," Alexander said. "Out there, go a few miles and the terrain changes."

They came on a lot of cattle. In groups large and small, and sometimes singly. Most of the longhorns merely stared, but some melted away.

The longhorns fascinated Edana as much as the landscape. They were different from dairy cattle, larger and rangier and deadly-looking with those long horns of theirs. She made a comment to that effect.

Neal stared at the same bunch she was looking at. "They do tend to get wild when they've been off in the brush a spell, but they're right tame the rest of the time. I never saw anybody gored in all the years I worked longhorns down to Texas, although there was a bull or two who tried."

"What I'm most interested in is the money they'll bring," Alexander said. "The expense-to-profit ratio."

"That's where longhorns have other cattle beat," Neal said. "They don't need much upkeep. You let them loose on the range and they fend for themselves until roundup time."

"That is a definite advantage," Alexander said. "Dairy cows require a lot of upkeep."

They talked business awhile, and Edana was pleased at how Neal held his own. She would never have guessed to look at him that he could calculate costs per pound and other factors so readily in his head. She found herself warming to him more and more.

They crested a ridge and drew rein. Below spread a small valley, lush with graze. Here and there were longhorns, and a stand of oaks.

Edana unslung her canteen and treated herself to a few sips. "I have to say, Mr. Bonner, that the Diamond B is everything I'd hoped it would be, and more."

"I'm mighty pleased to hear you say that, ma'am."

"Wresting a working ranch from the wilderness will be quite the enterprise,"

Edana commented. When Neal didn't answer, she looked over and saw that he had risen in his stirrups and was staring intently down into the valley. She looked, and stiffened. "Is that a dead longhorn?"

The hands had seen it, too, and Billy said, "Want us to go have a look-see, Neal?"

"We'll all go," Neal said.

Edana capped her canteen and had to hurry to catch up. At the bottom they brought their horses to a trot. That the cowboys were so concerned over a single longhorn puzzled her. She imagined that, given the nature of the Badlands, some died all the time. She posed that to Neal.

"It's not all that common, ma'am, no," he answered. "Longhorns are hard to die, as we say in Texas. They don't get many diseases and most are shipped off to market in their prime, so not many live to old age."

"What about wolves and other predators?"

"Longhorns can give them quite a scrape and more often than not come out on top."

The dead one lay on its side, the head and most of the body intact. Only a haunch was missing. The body had started to bloat and a few flies buzzed. There was no evidence scavengers had been at it yet.

Yeager dismounted. His spurs jingling, he walked in a circle around the dead animal, then hunkered by the head and pointed. "Bullet hole."

Neal scowled. "Saw that."

Yeager moved to the hind end and hunkered again. He put a finger to the hide where the haunch had been. "This was cut off."

Neal grunted.

"Someone shot one of our steers and took some of the meat?" Alexander said. "Indians, do you think?"

"Give a search," Neal said to the hands, and joined them as they gigged their horses around about the carcass.

"They look so grim," Alexander remarked.

"They take their cattle seriously," Edana said. "I like that."

"So do I, but you'd think it was one of them who was lying there."

In a while Neal and the cowboys returned. "Not a lick of sign anywhere," he reported.

"So I was right about it being Indians," Alexander said. "I've heard they're quite adept at hiding their tracks."

"Could have been," Neal said, although he didn't sound convinced. "And if it's hostiles on the warpath, they'll be out to kill more than just cattle."

"You don't mean they'd try to do us harm, as well?" Edana said.

"That's what 'warpath' means." Neal regarded the dead longhorn. "My instincts tell me it's not Injuns, though."

"How so?" Alexander asked.

"Injuns kill animals for food. They're not like some whites who shoot buffalo for the sport of it and then leave the carcasses to rot. To an Injun, that's a terrible waste. They can't savvy thinkin' like that."

"You've never heard of them slaughtering cows for the fun of it?" Alexander said.

"No," Neal replied. "That's the point. For them it wouldn't be fun. They'd see it as a terrible waste." He nodded at the dead longhorn. "Which is why I don't think Injuns are to blame here."

"Because they took just part of the meat and left the rest?"

"Injuns would never do that."

"I see," Alexander said thoughtfully. "But if not Indians, then who? Would one of the hands have done it?"

The cowboys, Neal included, glanced sharply at him.

"I suppose not," Alexander said.

"What does that leave us?" Edana said. "Someone happened by, a white man, evidently, and decided to shoot one of our cattle for his evening meal?"

"A haunch would last a lot of meals," Neal

said. "But yes, that's pretty much what it leaves us."

"Would a white man do that, though?" Edana asked.

"Not if he had a lick of sense, no," Neal said.

"Then we're back to Indians?"

"So it would appear. We'll spread word for the punchers to keep their eyes peeled. I could be wrong, and there might well be some Injuns hereabouts."

Young Billy patted his six-shooter. "If there are, and they're lookin' for trouble, we'll give them plenty."

18

Isolda was so mad at Jericho that it took a few moments for what he'd just said to sink in. She gazed in the direction he was staring and beheld three riders, far off. "How can you tell they're Indians?" she demanded. She couldn't make out any of their features.

Stumpy half rose out of the seat. "I can't tell what they are," he said, "but if Jericho says they are, they are. He's got hawk's eyes."

Jericho gigged his zebra dun to where he was between the buckboard and the riders, and drew rein. He waited with his hand on his hip, close to his pearl-handled Colt. "If there's shootin'," he said without looking back, "get her in the bed of the buckboard and stay down low."

"Will do," Stumpy said. He shifted his holster on his belt so he could reach it easily. "You heard him, ma'am?"

"I'm sitting right here," Isolda said a trifle

indignantly. She didn't like being treated as if she were helpless. "I still don't see that they're even Indians."

"Give it a minute, ma'am," Stumpy said.

The stick figures gradually grew. Two of the riders were men, behind them a woman. The men rode pintos, the woman a sorrel that appeared to be dragging something behind it.

"I still . . ." Isolda started to repeat herself, and stopped. The men wore leggings and moccasins and one had what appeared to be feathers in his hair. The woman wore a doeskin dress. As they came closer she remarked, "Why, they're all old. And what is that thing the woman is hauling?"

"A travois, ma'am," Stumpy said. "Injuns stretch a hide between a couple of long poles and use it to cart things around."

"What are they doing *here*?" Isolda said.

"It's the Badlands, ma'am," Stumpy said. "Injuns roam about out here from time to time."

"I mean what are they doing on the Diamond B?" Isolda amended. She almost added, "You simpleton."

"They don't know this is a ranch, ma'am. To them it's just country they're crossin' to get wherever they're goin'."

"We should post signs to keep them out."

212

"Around the whole ranch?" Stumpy said, incredulous. "It wouldn't do much good. Not many Injuns can read the white tongue."

"We call that English," Isolda said drolly.

The Indians drew rein. The one with the feathers in his gray hair held a hand in front of him with his first and second fingers pointed at the sky and the rest closed, then raised it head-high.

"What is he doing?" Isolda asked.

"That's sign language, ma'am," Stumpy replied. "He's sayin' they're friendly."

The old Indian launched into a talk in his own tongue, with a lot of gesturing and pointing. He stopped when Jericho moved his hands in a series of gestures.

"What now?" Isolda said.

"The old buck was tryin' to tell us somethin', but Jericho let him know we don't speak Sioux."

"Is that who they are?"

"Dakotas, ma'am, yes. Minniconjous, I'm thinkin', although what they're doin' in these parts I can't say, unless they're on their way to visit kin in another band."

The old warrior used his hands again. Jericho responded in kind, and the old one smiled and grunted and flicked his reins, leading the others around the buckboard and on off to the south.

Isolda glanced at the travois as it went past. Several bundles wrapped in fur had been tied on, along with blankets and a folded buffalo hide.

Jericho reined his zebra dun around. "They were peaceable. We can be on our way."

"Sign language is one of your many talents, I take it?" Isolda said.

"I know enough to say howdy," Jericho said. "Learned it from a fella who used to scout for the army. I played cards with him now and then in Texas. He rode the finest Ovaro I ever saw."

"You don't say," Isolda said. She couldn't be less interested.

"We should mosey on," Stumpy suggested.

Isolda agreed and motioned for him to do so. She was still mad at Jericho for refusing to impart his past, but she decided to let it drop. What did she care? She was interested in Beaumont Adams.

Stumpy didn't say a word the rest of the way, which suited Isolda just fine. Jericho rode behind them, as taciturn as ever.

When Whiskey Flats sprouted on the horizon, Isolda sat up and slid her shawl off. She fluffed at her hair and smoothed her dress and wiped dust from her shoes with a handkerchief from her handbag.

"You gals sure do a lot of preenin'," Stumpy commented with a grin.

"Did I ask you?" Isolda rejoined.

"I was just sayin', ma'am."

"Don't." Isolda supposed she shouldn't be so abrupt with him, but she was tired of being treated as if her gender were peculiar.

Presently they entered the town. It was the middle of the morning and the streets were busy with shoppers and strollers and the like.

Isolda was eager for sight of the Three Aces. When Stumpy brought the buckboard to a halt in front of the general store, she absently said, "What's this? Why did you stop?"

"You came in for paper and ink, didn't you?" Stumpy said. "Where else would we get any?"

Isolda felt foolish. She went to climb down and suddenly Jericho was there, offering his arm.

"Ma'am," he said.

Isolda almost slapped his arm away. "Thank you," she said, and alighted. "I'll be busy for the next couple of hours, so you two do as you please." She extracted her hand and stepped on the boardwalk.

"I'm not supposed to let you out of my sight, Miss Jessup," Jericho reminded her. "Remember?"

"My father said no such thing, and I won't have you underfoot while I shop. Stay out here and wait for me. I shan't be long." Isolda marched inside before he could argue, and peeked out the window.

Jericho, looking unhappy, leaned against the buckboard.

Isolda grinned. Outsmarting the cowboy was child's play. But then, he'd never suspect what she was about to do.

The proprietor, who introduced himself as Guthrie, was at the counter, flipping through a catalogue. Isolda told him who she was and Guthrie mentioned that he'd heard about her father coming to run the Diamond B. He informed her that he carried ink and paper and would set some aside but he'd sold out of ledgers a while ago and hadn't bothered to order more because hardly anyone ever used them. She told him to order half a dozen for the Diamond B, then glanced at the front door and said, "By the way, is there a back way out?"

"The back door," Thomas Guthrie said. "But why use that when you can go out the front?"

Isolda had her lie prepared. "My father

sent a couple of punchers along and one of them has talked me to death the whole way here. I'd like to slip away and have some quiet time to myself."

"I'll be happy to help," Guthrie said. He indicated a doorway at the rear. "Go out there and follow the hall. But what do I tell the cowpokes if they ask where you got to?"

"Say you were busy and didn't notice."

"I hate to lie, Miss Jessup."

"Even if it's for a good cause like my ears?" Isolda asked.

Guthrie laughed. "All right. I suppose a little white lie won't hurt."

"You're a dear," Isolda said to flatter him, and whisked to the hallway. She was pleased at how easy he'd made it.

Although she'd only been indoors a short while, the bright glare of the sun hurt her eyes. Squinting, she went past the backs of several buildings and up an alley to Main Street.

Jericho was still leaning against the buckboard, his head down as if he were pondering. There was no sign of Stumpy.

"Good," Isolda said. She waited until several women came up the street and stepped in front of them so Jericho wouldn't see her. Keeping the women between them, she hurried down the street. She didn't have far to go. The general store wasn't more than a block from the Three Aces.

At the batwings, Isolda paused. She'd heard that it was improper, if not outright indecent, for a woman to enter a saloon. But few in town knew who she was, and she had her mind set on seeing the gambler. Pushing through, she took several steps and drew up short.

The whole place had frozen. The card-players, the drinkers, the men standing around, the bartenders, every last one had stopped what they were doing to stare.

Some wore comical expressions of astonishment. One man's cigar fell out and he fumbled in catching it and it hit the floor.

A beady-eyed weasel in seedy clothes was the first to recover. "What do we have here?" he asked with a lecherous twinkle, and sauntered toward her like a cat sneaking toward prey.

"I'm looking for someone," Isolda said.

"And you've found him, honey," the seedy man said. "How about I treat you to a drink and we get better acquainted?"

"How about if someone tells me where I can find Beaumont Adams?" Isolda said.

Suddenly two other men pushed the lecher aside. One was as thin as a broom handle and wore his holster on the front of his belt instead of on his hip like most men. The other had a beard and carried a big rifle in the crook of his arm. The pair from the other day.

"Miss Jessup, ain't it?" the thin one said. "I'm Dyson and this here is Stimms. We work for Mr. Adams. He's in the back. It's a little early for him to be up and about, but I'll go tell him you're here."

"I'd be ever so grateful," Isolda said.

Dyson indicated an empty table. "Why don't you have a seat? Stimms here will watch over you until I get back."

"I don't need watching over."

"In here you do."

Stimms patted his rifle. "Anybody looks at this gal crosswise, I'll blow their heads off."

"That would be a little extreme, don't you think?" Isolda said.

"For them it would," Stimms said. "It's hard to get around without a head."

"I can't dispute that," Isolda admitted.

Dyson touched his hat brim. "It shouldn't be too many minutes, ma'am. Make yourself comfortable."

Isolda did.

Beaumont was having the most wonderful dream. He was on a picnic with the vision of loveliness he couldn't get out of his head.

Seated on a blanket in a field of clover and flowers, she was spoon-feeding him chocolate pudding, his favorite. He was about to kiss her when a loud thumping intruded. His dream faded and he was back in the land of the living, only to find that someone was pounding on his door. "Who the hell is it?"

"Dyson, boss."

Beaumont rolled over. One look at his window shade told him something must be wrong. "It's not noon yet." He had a standing rule he wasn't to be awakened before then unless there was a crisis.

"I know that, boss," Dyson said. "But this is important."

Beaumont shook his head to try and clear the cobwebs. "Is someone actin' up? Maybe pulled a knife or a gun?"

"No and no," Dyson said. "It's her."

"Who?" Beaumont said, thinking he must be referring to one of the doves. "Darietta? Clarabelle? Miranda? Has one of them come down with somethin' or found out they're pregnant?"

"It's not any of the painted cats, boss," Dyson said. "It's that other lady."

Beaumont was annoyed at having his dream interrupted, and vented his irritation with "What lady, you damn nuisance?"

"That Eastern gal."

"What?"

"That one who laughed a lot and called you handsome. You said how pretty she was. Don't you recollect?"

"What?" Beaumont said again. He wasn't sure he was hearing right.

"She's here, boss. In the saloon. She said she came to see you. I have her waitin' out at a table. Stimms is standin' guard over her."

"What?" Beaumont blurted again, feeling foolish doing so. "I must still be dreamin'."

"If you are, that'd make me part of your dream, and since I've been up awhile I must be real — unless you dreamed of me eatin' eggs and bacon and goin' to the outhouse."

"Stop talkin' a minute." Beaumont slid out of bed. He couldn't get his brain to work. The whole thing seemed unreal. Padding to his door, he opened it.

"God Almighty!" Dyson exclaimed, and averted his eyes. "Put some clothes on, will you?"

"I need to be clear," Beaumont said. "Miss Jessup is in the Three Aces right this moment?"

The back of Dyson's head bobbed. "She marched right in as bold as you please and asked for you."

"For me personally?"

Still not looking at him, Dyson said, "Boss, are you awake or not? Why do I have to say everything twice? Yes, she asked for you. Stood up to Rinson, too, when he got fresh with her."

Beaumont started to say, "What?" and caught himself. His blood set to boiling, and just like that, his head cleared. "What did Rinson do?"

"He made some remark about gettin' better acquainted. You know how he is. Thinks he's candy for the ladies. He'd only be candy if they like ugly."

"Two things," Beaumont said. "Inform Miss Jessup that I'll be there shortly. Ask her if there is anything she wants, anything at all, and get it for her."

"The other thing?" Dyson said when Beaumont didn't go on.

"Rinson. He's not to go anywhere."

"He won't."

Beaumont closed the door and moved to his washbasin. As he filled it, his head was awhirl with what Miss Jessup's visit might mean. That she'd specifically asked for him made it all the more wondrous. Especially since they hadn't been formally introduced, and a high-bred lady like her wouldn't think of approaching a man like him unless it was deemed proper to do so. Hurriedly washing, he stepped to his closet for his best shirt and pants. As eager as he was to find out why she was there, he took extra time at the mirror. "Whatever can she want?" he asked his reflection.

Then, shrugging into his frock coat and donning his black hat, and with his derringer up his sleeve and his pistols in their pockets, Beaumont went out to meet the woman from his dream.

19

Alexander Jessup was delighted. He'd only been at the Diamond B a short while and already he could tell he was going to love his new work. Secretly he'd been a little worried it might not be a good fit. What did he know about the West and cattle, after all? But he'd always been a fast learner, and his knack for business management inevitably served him in good stead.

And, too, a ranch wasn't all that different from a dairy farm in certain respects. Both had similar expenses in the form of employees on the payroll and for the upkeep of the stock. Dairy cows, it turned out, required more. Longhorns were practically self-sustaining. The cost of fattening them for market was so low that the profits to be made were considerable. He could see why the consortium had been interested in the venture. The investors stood to reap huge returns on their investment.

Truth to tell, Alexander also found himself warming to the endlessly fascinating landscapes in the Badlands. They possessed a natural beauty that had to be seen to be appreciated.

It was the middle of the afternoon when Neal Bonner brought them back from their tour of the range. Bonner immediately went to spread word about the dead longhorn. It was only one of the many thousands the Diamond B owned, yet as the foreman remarked, "Losin' a single one isn't somethin' we should take lightly."

Alexander liked that. It showed that Neal Bonner had his priorities straight. The cattle came before all else.

Alexander wasn't so fond of the fact that his older daughter showed signs of being smitten. He'd noticed some of the looks she gave Bonner, and her tone when she talked to him sometimes, a tone Alexander never heard before.

He'd always known it would happen, eventually. Human nature being what it was, sooner or later his girls were bound to grow up. He wasn't an expert on females by any stretch, but there came a point in many a woman's life where she cast about for someone to share that life with. He hadn't expected it to happen here, of all places, and certainly not now, of all times.

Not that there was anything wrong with Neal Bonner, Alexander decided. The foreman seemed to be an upstanding young man. He inspired respect in the cowboys, which said a lot for his character right there.

As for the cowboys themselves, Alexander was intrigued. They were so unlike the workers at the dairy farms. It was like comparing the dairy cows to longhorns. The former were so tame they went through life eating and giving milk and that was it. The latter had a wild streak and were unpredictable.

Alexander's initial assessment of the punchers was that they were as self-reliant as the longhorns they rode herd over. Their colorful talk, the way they dressed — it was like being in a different country. They were well-mannered, though, and respectful of womanhood.

And then there were their pistols.

Alexander had been told a lot of Westerners wore sidearms, but it hadn't really sunk in. The reality of so many men going around with guns had been a little startling.

That incident in town, with the man called Wratner, had demonstrated that some of them would resort to a revolver at the drop of a feather, and they'd drop the feather.

Which brought Alexander's train of thought around to Jericho. The man was an enigma. That he was deadly was indisputable. But Alexander still wasn't certain he wanted someone like that on his payroll. If he were being honest with himself, he'd let Jericho go. But if he did that, he'd lose Neal Bonner, too. So for the time being the status quo would continue.

Now, having cleaned up after hours in the saddle, Alexander stood on the porch surveying the ranch. Smoke rose from the cookhouse chimney, and at the blacksmith shop, the smith was forging a horseshoe. A puncher was carrying tack into the stable, and another man was painting a shed. Over at a corral, their bronc buster was at work.

The screen door squeaked and Edana joined him. She had changed from her riding outfit into a dress and, rare for her, put on a bonnet. "What did you think of our excursion, Father?"

"Instructive," Alexander said. "You?"

"I find myself falling in love with the place," Edana said, "which is preposterous, I know, given how short a time we've been here."

"Not preposterous at all, daughter," Alexander said. "I find myself feeling the same."

"You do?"

"You sound surprised."

Edana leaned on the rail. "Why do you suppose we like it so much? Because it's new and different?"

"There's an intangible quality I can't quite put my finger on. It's not just the cowboys and the cattle. It's the land itself. Something about it seeps into you, changes you."

"Yes," Edana said, nodding, "I've felt that, too, and felt silly for doing so."

Alexander chuckled. "I've heard some people say that the West gets into the blood and changes a person. I always scoffed at the idea, but now I'm not so sure they weren't right."

"I like Neal Bonner. He'll be a fine foreman."

"Oh?"

"Why do you say it like that?"

"Do you remember Tim Burbank, our dairy farm overseer?"

"Of course. He was good at his job, too."

"He wasn't at all like Mr. Bonner. Sort of scrawny, and skinny, and that Adam's apple of his was so big he looked like a turkey buzzard."

"What are you saying? That I'm impressed by Neal more because of his looks than his competence?"

"I wouldn't go that far. He's quite excellent at what he does. But his looks might be a factor in another regard."

"I'm sure I have no idea what you're talking about."

Alexander grinned and put his arm around her shoulders. "I trust your judgment. You've always had a good head on your shoulders. Especially when it comes to business. Your sister, on the other hand, can be a bit flighty. She doesn't invest herself in her work as fully as you do."

"Don't expect me to speak ill of her. We're as close as two sisters can be."

"Are you? I hope so," Alexander said. "You don't bicker much, like some sisters do. It would please me greatly if you two continue to get along, even after I'm gone."

"You're not going anywhere," Edana said. "You're young yet."

"Oh, I have a few decades left," Alexander said, smiling. He nodded toward the corral. "What do you say we go watch our horse tamer at work? I understand it's a popular sport."

"Why not?" Edana said.

They went down the steps.

"I hope your sister gets back soon," Alexander remarked. "I worry about her being off by herself."

"Jericho and Stumpy are with her. Neal

says she'll be perfectly fine."

"Well, if Mr. Bonner says it . . . ," Alexander said, and laughed.

"Oh, Father," Edana said, but she laughed, too.

The world was a funny place. That was a conclusion Isolda had come to years ago. She had looked around her one day and seen how silly people were and had been amused by their antics ever since.

Most people worked at jobs they hated, for a pittance. They went through each day doing the exact same thing they'd done the day before. They ate the same food and wore the same clothes.

If that wasn't silly, Isolda didn't know what was.

The men in the Three Aces were certainly silly. Since she'd come in, they moved as if on eggshells and spoke only in low tones. There was no coarse behavior, no crude jokes or gruff laughter or even any swearing. It was as if a saint had walked into their lives, not a flesh-and-blood female. They accorded her the respect they'd give a nun.

It amused Isolda no end.

When Dyson returned and informed her that Beaumont Adams would join her in a few minutes, she thanked him. Dyson whispered to Stimms and Stimms went over to the bar and said something to the weasel who had approached her earlier. The weasel reacted as if he'd been kicked and kept glancing at the hallway to the back and nervously licking his lips.

Dyson then asked if there was anything she wanted, anything at all.

Out of sheer contrariness, and to add to her amusement, Isolda nodded and said, "I could really go for some milk right about now."

"Milk, ma'am?"

"If you would be so kind."

"But this is a saloon, ma'am."

Isolda smiled sweetly. "What's your point?"

Coughing, Dyson replied, "Nothin', ma'am. If it's milk you want, it's milk you'll have." He turned to the bar. "Floyd, get over here."

Wiping his hands on his apron, the barkeep joined them. "What would the lady like?" he asked genially. "Brandy? Or wine maybe? We have a few bottles. Or I could fix one of those new drinks ladies back East like."

Dyson enlightened him. "She's hankerin' for milk."

"This is a saloon."

"I told her that. She'd like milk anyway." Dyson held up a hand when Floyd when to speak. "The boss says to give her anything she wants. So either find her some or send someone to fetch some or you can tell the boss your own self that you couldn't do it."

"No, thank you," Floyd said. "Milk it is." He made for the batwings.

"Hold on," Isolda said. Her little joke had gone far enough. "I've changed my mind. What I'd really like is a glass of water."

"Now, that we have," Floyd said in relief.

"Then why are you standin' there?" Dyson said.

Isolda smothered a laugh. These two were comical. She liked how they were willing to wait on her hand and foot. All because Beaumont Adams said so. And speak of the devil.

The gambler came out of the back like a sleek mountain cat coming out of its den. He stopped and stared, and Isolda had the impression he was drinking the sight of her in as he would drink fine whiskey.

"Mr. Adams. What a pleasure to see you again." Isolda offered her hand.

Beaumont clasped it and gently squeezed, his forefinger rubbing her palm. "I confess to bein' taken aback," he said politely. "We were never introduced yesterday."

"Let's not stand on ceremony." Isolda motioned at the onlookers. "And I apologize for disrupting your establishment. Half the men have stopped drinking."

Beaumont gazed about them and laughed that easy laugh of his. "Why, so they have. Females spook them, I reckon."

"Unless the female wears a tight dress and has a saucy sway to her hips."

"Doves aren't like ordinary gals," Beaumont remarked. "A man doesn't have to put on airs around them."

"I'd rather they didn't put on airs around me, either," Isolda said. She was going to invite him to sit, but just then he glanced over at the bar and his face hardened.

"Will you excuse me a minute? There's somethin' I need to do." Sliding his hands into the pockets of his frock coat, Beaumont walked over to the man who had accosted her. "Rinson," he said.

Rinson seemed to be trying to shrivel into the floor. "You're up early today."

"I hear tell you've appointed yourself the welcomin' committee," the gambler said.

"What? No. Where did you hear that?"

"I've heard you invite folks to become better acquainted with you," Beaumont said. "Which sounds to me like a good idea."

"It does?" Rinson said dubiously.

"Sure. If you'd been better acquainted with me, you wouldn't have made the mistake you did." Beaumont's right hand flashed out, holding a pistol. With an oath, he slammed it against Rinson's jaw and Rinson fell where he stood. Still conscious, Rinson tried to rise and Beaumont kicked him in the ribs.

Rinson yelped and flipped onto his side. "I'm sorry," he cried.

Beaumont hit him again and again, raining blows until Rinson lay unmoving with gashes on his forehead and temple. Isolda thought the gambler would kill him, but Beaumont stepped back, breathing heavily. "Stimms, drag this pile of manure out of here." He came back to her table, the Colt at his side, blood dripping from the barrel.

"I guess you taught him," Isolda said.

Beaumont inhaled and steadied himself. "I apologize. I know most ladies would find that distasteful."

"I'm not most ladies," Isolda said. It hadn't sickened or disgusted her; quite the contrary. She patted the chair next to hers. "Have a seat so *we* can become better acquainted."

"Is that why you're here?"

"Can you think of a better reason?"

"I do believe, ma'am," Beaumont said,

grinning, "that I'm in danger of fallin' for you."

"I certainly hope so," Isolda said.

20

Neal Bonner had a lot on his mind.

There was his new boss, for starters. Alexander Jessup was proving easy to get along with. Jessup didn't act as if he were the Almighty, as some bosses did, and the man seemed genuinely eager to learn all there was about raising cattle so he could do his job that much better. Neal liked that.

There was the boss's older daughter. When it came to the ranch, she was as devoted as her father. Her enthusiasm was a joy to behold. So was she. The more Neal was with her, he wanted to be around her even more. Neal liked that, too.

Isolda was the wild card in the family's deck. Neal wasn't sure what to make of her. The little he'd seen, she didn't act as if she cared one whit about the Diamond B or learning the ins and outs of the cattle trade. She didn't seem interested in much besides herself. Neal didn't like that, but it was her life and she could do as she pleased.

Neal was glad he'd sent Jericho to watch over her. He had unbounded faith in his pard. It felt peculiar, though, going around without Jericho at his side. They were together so much that Neal felt as if a part of him were missing.

Neal was thinking of that when he emerged from the stable and saw Alexander and Edana making for a corral. He hastened over. Edana heard his spurs jingling and looked around with a wide smile.

"Mr. Bonner. What a delight to see you again so soon."

"Honestly," Alexander said. "Have you no shame?"

"Sir?" Neal said uncertainly. "What are you two up to, if you don't mind my askin'?"

"I've never seen a bronc buster work," Alexander said, "and since I must acquaint myself with every aspect of ranch life, there's no time like the present."

The bronc buster's handle was Hollander, but the punchers called him Holland for short. He limped when he walked, a legacy of the time a horse kicked him and shattered his shinbone. It didn't hamper him any.

Holland had a mustang tied to a snubbing post. The horse stood, legs splayed, watching Holland approach with a bridle. Holland tried to slip it on and the mustang jerked away. Holland persisted. The mustang finally let him but didn't like the feel and kept tossing its head. When it stopped, Holland brought a saddle blanket over. The horse stared at it suspiciously and, when Holland flapped it, tried to rear. When it subsided, Holland tried again.

"Why is he shaking the blanket like that?" Edana wanted to know.

"To get the critter used to it so it won't run off out on the range when a puncher saddles up."

"Are all the wild ones so skittish?" Alexander asked.

"Some take a heap of breakin'," Neal said.

The mustang stopped rearing, but it trembled as Holland placed the saddle blanket over its back. He fetched the saddle next, and no sooner had he started to swing it on than the mustang bucked and kicked. Holland had to dart back. Undaunted, the buster took hold of the rope with one hand to keep the mustang still, and swung the saddle on with the other. The mustang nearly pulled free and Holland nearly lost his footing. Hanging on, he let the horse quiet down before he did the cinch.

The mustang snorted and pawed the ground.

"Now comes the tricky part," Neal said.

Holland carefully slid the rope off the mustang. Before the horse could bolt, he grabbed an ear and twisted. The pain held the mustang still for the few seconds it took Holland to fork leather. Once he was in the saddle, all hell erupted.

The mustang arched its back and tried to reach the sky. Legs straight, it came down with jarring force. Holland stayed on. The horse whirled one way and then another. Holland wasn't thrown. The mustang carried on until it was tired and stood panting with its head hung low.

"He did it," Edana exclaimed.

"Not quite yet," Neal said,

Another puncher hopped off the top rail and carried a slicker over to Holland, then quickly got out of there.

Holland held the slicker close to the mustang's face and flapped it as he had the blanket. The horse launched itself straight up, then bucked and whirled as if there'd be no tomorrow.

Edana was mesmerized. "How can he stay on like that?" she asked in awe. "If it was me, I'd have been thrown by now."

"Holland has been bustin' broncs since he

was knee-high to a calf," Neal said. "I can't recollect the last time he was tossed."

"It must be hard on his body," Alexander observed. "The pounding he takes."

"Most peelers quit young, while they still have bones left."

"Which is it? Busters or peelers?" Alexander asked.

"Either will do," Neal said. "We also call them scratchers and squeezers on occasion."

"My word. Can't they make up their minds?" Alexander said. "I think I'll call him my horse tamer and let it go at that."

In the corral, the mustang stopped bucking and Holland rode in circles while continuing to flap the slicker.

"Look at that," Edana said. "He's tamed him."

"The mustang ain't full broke yet, ma'am," Neal said. "Holland will work with it some more before we add it to the string. Some ranches aren't as particular, and that creates trouble for the punchers. There's nothin' worse than tryin' to herd cattle on a horse that doesn't want to herd."

"I'd like to ride that animal," Alexander declared.

"As soon as Holland is done with him in a few days, I'll get word to you," Neal said.

"I'd like to ride it now."

Both Neal and Edana said, "What?" at the same time.

"To see what it's like to ride a horse like that," Alexander said.

"I'd rather you didn't," Edana said.

"There's no need, Mr. Jessup," Neal said. "Even the punchers wouldn't. It's askin' for trouble."

"Nonsense. Call Mr. Holland over here."

Against his better judgment, Neal hollered and beckoned.

The bronc buster dismounted, handed the reins to his helper, and limped over, swatting dust from his shirt and pants. "What can I do for you, Neal?"

"You can do it for me," Alexander said. "I'd like to ride that horse you just broke."

"Mr. Jessup?"

"You heard me," Alexander said. "I want to show the men I'm not afraid to get my hands dirty. A couple of times around the corral should do it."

"You're the big sugar," Holland said. "You don't have to prove nothin' to nobody."

"He's right, Mr. Jessup," Neal said. "The punchers won't think poorly of you if you don't do all the things they do. You have different responsibilities than the rest of us."

"I'd like for them to respect me," Alexander insisted, and turned to Holland. "I appeal to you as our expert. A couple of turns is all I'm asking. Is it safe or not?"

"Safe enough," Holland said, "but it would please me considerable if you changed your mind."

"I'm determined to do it and I won't be denied." Alexander moved toward the gate. "Tell them how I am, daughter, so they'll understand."

Edana moved after him, saying quietly to Neal, "I'll try to talk him out of it."

"What do I do?" Holland asked.

Neal, for one of the few times in his life, hesitated. Were it up to him, he'd flat-out say no. But Jessup was his boss. And if he made a fuss over it, Jessup might think he was being coddled. "You stay next to the horse," he directed. "Tell him it's a bucker and you don't want him thrown. Say it's not all the way broke yet and you'd blame yourself if somethin' happened to him."

"I'd do that anyhow," Holland said, and hurried back.

Alexander had gone over to where the helper was holding the mustang. The horse was exhausted from its efforts to throw Holland, and stood still when Alexander patted it.

Neal took that as a good sign.

"I'm ready," Alexander said as Holland came up.

"I'll hold him steady," Holland offered, gripping the bridle. "Go nice and slow so as not to spook him."

"I doubt he has any fight left," Alexander said.

More cowboys were coming from every direction as word spread.

Neal climbed to the top rail, frowning. He saw Edana talking in a low voice to her pa.

Alexander shook his head.

"What's goin' on, Neal?" Billy asked.

"We heard the boss is fixin' to ride that mustang," Yeager said, and spat tobacco juice. "What the hell for?"

"To show us he can," Neal said.

"Well, that's silly," Billy said. "If I was runnin' things, I'd sit around takin' it easy and let the rest of you get your necks busted."

No one laughed.

Alexander was walking around the mustang with his hands behind his back.

"What's he doin'?" Billy asked. "Tryin' to figure out which side to climb on?"

"Hush, you infant," Yeager said.

Neal decided to go in. If he didn't like how things were unfolding, he'd put his boot down and end it. Trying to act casual, he climbed over and went to Edana. She gave him a worried glance.

"I tried to get him not to. He won't listen."

"I heard that, daughter," Alexander said. "I want all of you to stop treating me as if I'm worthless. I resent it." Turning, he gripped the saddle horn. The other puncher moved to help him, but Alexander angrily motioned him away and climbed on.

Holland handed him the reins.

All the mustang did was twitch an ear. Its head was still down, and it was slick with sweat.

"Are you ready, Mr. Jessup?" Holland asked.

"Doesn't it look like I'm ready?" Alexander said. "Release him."

Holland let go of the bridle. "Easy does it, sir."

"I know how to ride a damn horse," Alexander said. He flicked the reins and said, "Get on, there."

The mustang tiredly obeyed.

Neal had to admit that the horse looked about as fierce as a half-drowned kitten. He moved back to give it room, and Edana followed his example.

Holland stayed close to the mustang.

"Please be careful, Father," Edana said.

"I won't be coddled, daughter," Alexander said. "Not even by you."

"At least he's not wearin' spurs," Neal said for Edana's ears only. Jessup might jab too hard and set the mustang off.

Apparently unconscious that she was doing so, Edana gripped his arm. "I never would have expected him to try anything like this."

It was pride, Neal reckoned. Jessup wanted to prove he was worthy to be their boss. Neal just hoped the man wasn't overreaching.

The mustang plodded in a circle, Jessup holding the reins higher than he should but otherwise seeming relaxed and confident.

"That should do it," Holland said as the horse drew close. "You've gone around once."

"I'll go around twice," Jessup said. "This animal is tamer than some I've ridden back East."

"You can't really trust a horse until it's been on the string awhile," Holland replied. "Breakin' is only the first step."

"Be that as it may," Jessup said, and went past them.

"He can be so stubborn," Edana said.

Neal only had eyes for the mustang. So far it showed no signs of being agitated. When Holland broke a horse, it usually stayed broke.

"I hope to heaven he doesn't do anything like this again," Edana said. "I'll be worried sick that he might."

"Men will be men, ma'am," Holland said.

"There's such a thing as common sense," Edana replied. "As you pointed out, he has nothing to prove to anyone."

Alexander was holding his head high and nodding at some of the punchers lining the rails.

"If my sister were here, she wouldn't have let him," Edana said. "She's much more outspoken than I am. I indulge him too much."

"What was there to indulge, ma'am?" Neal asked. Dairy farms didn't strike him as particularly dangerous.

Alexander was coming around toward them again. "See?" he said. "I told you there was nothing to worry about." He rode past and over near the snubbing post. "How about that?" he said to the onlooking cowboys. "Two whole times and I'm still alive."

Some of the punchers chuckled and grinned.

"Do you want to help me down now, daughter?" Alexander continued his little act. "Maybe hold my hand while you're at it?"

There was laughter, and Edana turned red.

Holland limped toward the mustang.

Neal let out a breath of relief. It was over. He'd escort the Jessups out and come back to tell the bronc buster that under no circumstances was Alexander to do that again without his say-so, boss or no boss.

That was when Neal saw the yellow jacket.

21

It took Beaumont Adams a while to figure Isolda Jessup out. Here she was, considered to be a lady in every sense of the word, yet she'd brazenly walked into his saloon and asked for him as if it were the most natural thing in the world for her to do. Which, clearly, it wasn't. A few minutes of talking and he learned she'd never been west of the Mississippi River until she came to the Diamond B, and that she'd never been in a saloon in her life. Why now, then? And why him?

He was pondering that when she said out of the blue, "You're not one to look a gift horse in the mouth, are you?"

"Ma'am?"

"Call me Isolda or I swear I'll walk out and you'll never see me again."

"I wouldn't want that," Beaumont said, "Isolda."

"You've been deep in thought. You're trying to put a reason to this, aren't you?" Isolda said, flicking a finger at him and at herself.

"You should get one of those crystal balls and set yourself up as a mind reader like the Gypsies do," Beaumont said.

"Let's clear the air. What is it about my visit that puzzles you so much?"

"Your visit," Beaumont said.

"I see. I hardly know you. I'm an Easterner, and the daughter of the new manager of what promises to be the largest ranch in the Badlands. And my coming to see you is unseemly, according to most people." Isolda paused. "Is there anything I've missed?"

"That pretty much covers it," Beaumont admitted. "Not that I don't like havin' you come. I took a likin' to you at first sight when I saw you out in the street."

"And I to you," Isolda said. She sighed and gazed about the saloon. "I'll be honest with you. I'm sick to death of what I do. Mainly I've been my father's bookkeeper. I write in ledgers all day. Compile receipts. Catalog expenses. It's tedious. I've reached the point where it bores me so much I can't stand to do it anymore. I've wanted something different for a long time. Not just in my work, but in my life."

"Different how?"

"All my life, I've done what my father wanted me to. It was his idea I go to school, his idea I take business courses, his idea I work for him. I went along with it because, quite frankly, I had no idea what *I* wanted. It gave me something to do. And it was easy." Isolda pinched her lips together. "But when my mother died, I began to see things differently. I realized I could spend my whole life doing something that didn't mean anything to me. And I grew to hate it."

"Ah," Beaumont said. He thought he saw where this was going. "So you came west for excitement and adventure."

"No. That might have been at the back of my mind, but I came because my father and sister were coming and they took it for granted I'd work with them as I always have. That it could be an adventure didn't occur to me until we arrived in Whiskey Flats and encountered Scar Wratner, and then I saw you."

"Since you're bein' so frank," Beaumont said, "what is it you want of me? To take you on picnics? Go on moonlit rides together?"

Isolda laughed. "I'm far more practical than that. Tell me. What are your plans? To run this saloon for the rest of your days?"

"I aim to take this town over lock, stock,

and barrel," Beaumont revealed. "To become so rich and powerful I can do whatever I want."

"*That's* your life's ambition?"

"I admit it's not one a churchgoer would
approve of," Beaumont said. "But I live by
my wits and my cards and my guns. I've
lucked into somethin' here. I'm in the right
place at the right time to set myself up as a
king, and I'd be a fool not to seize the
crown."

"I like how you put that," Isolda said, and
smirked. "Every king needs a queen, and
I'm interested in being yours. With my head
for business wedded to your guns and cards,
you'd be unstoppable."

"What about your pa and your sister?
They might not take kindly to you associat-
in' with a no-account like me."

"You're hardly that, and I don't care what
they think. I'd like to see more of you. If
things work out, fine. If you decide you want
nothing to do with me, well, I can't say I
didn't try to interest you."

Beaumont sat back and whistled softly.

"What?"

"You're the most remarkable gal I've ever
met."

"Because I know what I want and I go
after it?" Isolda grinned. "I get that trait

from my father." She looked toward the batwings and her grin died. "Oh, damn. I forgot about him."

"Who?" Beaumont said, turning.

Jericho had just walked in.

Neal Bonner was going to shout a warning to Alexander Jessup, but once again he hesitated.

Yellow jackets were common most everywhere. They were a type of wasp, not a bee, as some thought. They nested in great numbers and could be a nuisance when people ate outdoors. The females were prickly and prone to sting.

This particular one flew past Alexander and down around the mustang's rear legs. The horse wasn't moving, and it appeared to Neal that the yellow jacket would fly on. Then it did the last thing he wanted it to; it landed high on one leg. The mustang flicked its tail to swish it off, and all hell erupted.

The yellow jacket must have stung it, because the mustang let out with a whinny and kicked with both legs. A hoof caught the puncher who had been helping Holland, and Neal heard the sharp crack of a rib breaking. The puncher cried out and fell, clutching himself, and the mustang arched its back and launched itself at the sky.

"Father!" Edana cried.

Alexander Jessup clutched at the saddle horn and somehow managed to stay on. "Whoa, horse, whoa!" he shouted.

Neal and Holland closed in to help. Holland lunged at the bridle, but a sweep of the mustang's head sent him sprawling. Neal leaped, grabbed hold, and was lifted off his feet and whirled as if he were weightless. The mustang was in a panic.

Neal dug his boots into the ground in an effort to hold the horse still so Jessup could dismount. "Get off!" he shouted.

Alexander nodded and unhooked a foot from a stirrup. He pressed both hands to the saddle, about to push off and jump down.

Neal could never say what made the mustang do what it did next. The sting couldn't have been that painful. He'd warned Jessup that the horse wasn't entirely broken yet, but Jessup didn't listen. And now, without any warning, it lowered its front shoulders and slammed into the snubbing post in an effort to be shed of Jessup.

Edana screamed.

Alexander was swinging his other leg over the saddle and in another moment would have leaped clear. The sudden pitching threw him off balance. He fell between the mustang and the post, and this time the crack of bones was even louder.

Neal let go of the bridle to try and grab Jessup and pull him out of there, but the mustang whipped around, knocking him down. He scrambled up again as cowboys hollered and vaulted over the corral. Holland tried to grab the bridle and was again sent tumbling.

"Father! Father!" Edana rushed in and a leg clipped her and she was knocked away, staggering.

Neal spied an arm sticking out. Darting around the mustang, he saw that Alexander Jessup was on his side, evidently unconscious, blood trickling from his mouth and nose. Gripping the man's wrist, Neal sought to drag him out of there before the horse could do more harm. But the mustang reared, kicking at Billy and Yeager and others trying to gain control, and a front hoof came down on Alexander's hip. Neal was sure he heard a crunch.

Beside herself, Edana screamed and pushed at the mustang and was bowled over.

Billy drew his six-shooter, but Holland yelled, "No!"

Springing forward, Neal got his hands under Alexander's arms. As he pulled, the mustang wheeled and its hindquarter struck his shoulder. He nearly lost his hold. Pulling for all he was worth, he dragged Jessup out. But he'd only taken a couple more steps when the mustang plowed into him. He cartwheeled, the sky and the ground changing places. The next he knew, he was on his back and the world was spinning. Tides of pain washed through him, but he made it to his knees.

Bedlam reigned. A dozen or more punchers were trying to lay hold of the plunging, kicking mustang, and having no success whatsoever. Several were down, one man spitting blood.

Edana was trying to reach her father. She went to dash past the mustang and the horse reared yet again, its hooves above her head. Edana raised her arms in a vain bid to protect herself. She would be borne down, crushed, trampled.

Neal wasn't aware of drawing his Colt. Suddenly it was in his hand, and he thumbed back the hammer and fired. He was pointing it at the mustang's head, but he could well miss; he wasn't Jericho.

At the blast, a hole appeared near the mustang's eye, and the mustang whinnied stridently and folded in on itself, missing Edana as it crashed to earth. It kicked once and was still.

Shock turned the punchers to stone. Shooting a horse for any reason was rarely done.

Neal heaved up and reached Alexander at the same moment Edana did. Sobbing, Edana cradled her father's head. "Look at him."

Blood continued to ooze from Alexander's mouth and nose. His one arm was bent at an unnatural angle and his clothes were torn and caked with dust.

"Get him to the house," Neal barked at Yeager. "Find a board or somethin' to carry him on."

Punchers scrambled to obey.

Edana clasped Alexander's hand and stroked his brow. "Father, can you hear me?"

Neal put his hand on her shoulder. "I don't reckon he can," he said. "We have to get him inside." He was going to add, "And send for the sawbones," but there wasn't one. Whiskey Flats didn't have a doctor yet. They were entirely on their own.

"Oh, Neal," Edana said in despair. "What will I do if I lose him?"

"Don't talk like that," Neal said. But they just might. It depended on how busted up Jessup was inside. Neal wasn't feeling so good himself. He'd taken a couple of hard hits, and his shoulder wouldn't stop hurting. "Are you all right?"

"What?" Edana tore her gaze from her father. "I'm sure I'm bruised but I'll be fine. You look bad off yourself. Someone should check you over."

"After your pa is tended to."

A lot of commotion preceded four cowboys arriving with a long plank. It wasn't that wide, but with a puncher at either end and on both sides to prevent Alexander from falling off, they hurried from the corral and crossed to the house. Edana bid them carry him to his bedroom and place him on the bed. It was done as gently as possible, but Alexander groaned a lot and continued to bleed badly.

Neal issued commands. For water to be put on the stove and heated. For towels to be brought. For the mustang to be disposed of.

In the middle of everyone hustling about, the cook showed up. His name was Kantor and he had some medical experience in that he'd driven ambulance wagons during the Civil War and sometimes had to assist the doctors and nurses. After the war he'd found a job as a cook's helper at an eatery in St. Louis and stayed long enough to learn the essentials. City life hadn't appealed to him, though, and when he'd heard of a ranch that was looking for a cook, he signed on. Other ranches and nearly twenty years later, here he was. He favored a stovepipe hat and had a big belly. "I came as soon as I heard, Neal. What can I do?"

"Have a look at Mr. Jessup." Neal put an arm around Edana and tried to pull her off the edge of the bed, where she was sitting, but she resisted.

"Let me be. I'm not leaving his side."

"We need to let Kantor examine him," Neal said, "and he can't do it with us in the way." He was struck speechless when Edana buried her face in his shoulder and sobbed. Awkwardly patting her, he said, "There, there."

"He's not going to make it."

"We don't know that yet," Neal said. He drew her away, then motioned at the cowboys in the room and the hall. "Everybody doesn't need to see this."

Nodding, Yeager commenced to shoo the rest out.

Kantor had taken Alexander's left wrist and was feeling for a pulse. "It's awful weak," he announced, and when Edana sobbed, he looked at Neal as if to say he was sorry for being so careless.

Yeager got the last of the hands from the

bedroom and shut the door behind them, saying as he closed it, "We'll wait outside for word."

"Maybe I should go with them," Neal said.

"No!" Edana virtually shouted it, and clutched his shirt. "I'd like you with me. You're the only friend I have here."

Kantor set to removing Alexander's clothes, slowly, carefully, piece by piece, and setting them aside. When he unbuttoned Alexander's shirt and parted it, he inadvertently recoiled.

"What is it?" Edana asked.

"You don't want to see, ma'am," Kantor said.

Edana pulled loose from Neal and looked over the cook's shoulder. "Lord, no," she gasped.

22

The entire saloon fell silent.

Isolda met Jericho's gaze as he came toward their table. She refused to act embarrassed, refused to behave as if she'd done anything wrong. She was a grown woman. She could do as she pleased.

Men playing cards at another table got up and moved back. Others who were close by did the same. The bartender put his hands under the bar and kept them there.

Dyson and Stimms had been at one end and now started toward the table but stopped at a gesture from Beaumont Adams.

Smiling, Isolda said, "Look who is here."

Jericho stopped about six feet out. "You snuck off on me, ma'am."

"That I did," Isolda admitted.

"I wish you hadn't," Jericho said. "Your pa gave me orders."

"Which is why I did it," Isolda said. "I

knew you'd have objected if I'd told you I wanted to come here. You might even have tried to prevent me."

"You need to leave now, ma'am," Jericho said.

Isolda barely contained a surge of temper. "What will you do if I refuse? Sling me over your shoulder and carry me out."

"If it comes to that."

Beaumont Adams had been listening intently. "Hold on," he said. "What's this about orders?"

"Her pa doesn't want her to talk to you," Jericho said.

"What did I do to deserve that?" Beaumont asked in surprise.

"There was mention of your eyes bein' too free," Jericho said.

"Well, hell," Beaumont said.

"I don't care what my father thinks or wants," Isolda said. "No one is going to stop me from talking to whomever I desire."

"I have it to do, ma'am," Jericho said. "I'll take you out whether you like it or not. It'd be best if you come along peaceable. If you don't, there's liable to be blood spilled."

"What will you do? Hit me?"

"It won't be your blood, ma'am."

Isolda was furious that he refused to do as she wanted. "You would resort to violence?

Is this more of that riding-for-the-brand nonsense?"

"It is, ma'am."

"Quit being so polite. Can't you see I'm mad? What *will* you do? Grab me by my arm and drag me out?"

"If it comes to that," Jericho said again.

Isolda looked at Beaumont. "I'm sorry about this intrusion. These cowboys take their jobs much too seriously. I refuse to be intimidated. I'll stay and talk to you for as long as I want."

Jericho, too, looked at Beaumont. "Tell her what will happen if she does. Tell her how it is."

"Tell me how what is?" Isolda said. She noticed that Dyson and Stimms stood poised as if ready to resort to their pistol and rifle, respectively, and that Floyd appeared to be holding something behind the bar.

"He's been quite frank with you, my dear," Beaumont said. "He doesn't have any choice in the matter. He'll try to take you out and I'll try to stop him and that's when the blood will be spilled."

"There are more of you than there are of him," Isolda said. "Surely he won't dare defy all of you."

"Oh, he'll dare hell itself to do as your

father wants," Beaumont said. "It'll be him or us, and I wouldn't bet money on us bein' a sure thing. I've heard tell that Jericho here is mighty quick on the shoot."

"I am that," Jericho said.

"Listen to him boast," Isolda said in disgust. "You're saying you can't beat him?"

"It would be a close thing," Beaumont said, "and, even if I tied him, he's not apt to miss at this range."

"This is intolerable," Isolda said. "I'm being treated as if I'm a child and have no say in my own life."

"Ma'am," Jericho said. "You'd best get up now."

"I'll be damned if I will. You'll just have to drag me out."

"Oh, ma'am," Jericho said. "What you've done." He took a step but stopped when Beaumont Adams started to straighten. "Don't," he said.

The gambler grinned. "I'm afraid I don't have much choice, either."

"You try to point that arm with the hideout up your sleeve, I draw," Jericho said. "You reach for either pocket, I draw."

Over at the bar, Dyson said, "Boss? What do you want us to do?"

"Say the word," Stimms said.

Floyd's mouth was twitching. "To hell

with this. Who does he think he is, actin' so high and mighty?" Glowering at Jericho, he declared, "I want you out of this saloon, mister, right this minute."

"Floyd, don't," Beaumont said.

Either Floyd didn't hear him or he ignored him, because when Jericho didn't move, Floyd snarled, "I will by God blow you in half." With that, he jerked a scattergun up, cocking a hammer as he did.

Jericho shot him.

There was the flash of nickel plating and pearl, and the boom of the Colt, thunderous in the confines of the room. A hole appeared in the middle of Floyd's forehead even as the back of his head exploded, showering hair and blood and brains on the mirror. For a few moments Floyd swayed. Then the scattergun fell from fingers gone limp and Floyd followed it to the floor with a loud crash.

Jericho twirled the Colt into his holster so blindingly fast the revolver was a blur.

"God Almighty," someone said.

Someone else whistled.

Facing the table, Jericho said to Beaumont, "There doesn't have to be any more. She might listen to you."

Isolda was struck speechless. She'd never seen anyone killed before. The brutality of it should horrify her, but it didn't. She watched a gob of brain slide down the mirror, leaving a trail of goo in its wake, and wasn't the least bit appalled. She didn't feel sick to her stomach. She didn't feel anything except a strong sense of excitement.

"You can see how it is," Beaumont said.

"What?" Isolda tore her eyes from the gore.

"There will be more shootin' unless you go with him," Beaumont said. "Not that I want you to, you understand. You are a delight to be with."

Isolda yearned to spend the rest of the day and into the night in the gambler's company. She found him fascinating. That she was being forced to leave was an outrage. Then and there she hated the man called Jericho as she had never hated anyone or anything in her entire life. "I'll go, but only because it would upset me greatly were you or any of these others to come to harm on my account." She glared at her new hate.

"I'm only doin' my job, ma'am."

Isolda went to rise, but Beaumont beat her to it and pulled out her chair for her.

"Thank you," she said. "At least someone here is a gentleman."

"I hope to see you again," Beaumont said, "under more favorable circumstances."

"Count on it." Holding her head high and her back stiff, Isolda marched out. Jericho backed up, staying at her side but never taking his eyes off the others. He sought to push a batwing for her, but she swatted his hand aside and did it herself.

Blinking in the bright glare of the Badlands sun, Isolda headed for the buckboard. She refused to so much as glance at her second shadow.

"I'm right sorry, ma'am."

"No, you're not," Isolda said scathingly.

"I hired on to nursemaid cattle for the Diamond B, not to nursemaid a filly like you. Truth is, I didn't like havin' to shoot that hombre. One shootin' always leads to another, and I can do without that." Jericho paused. "Then there's the fact that your personal life is none of my business. I honest to heaven don't care who you hanker after. But I have your pa to answer to."

He sounded so sincere that Isolda halted and regarded him with slightly less venom. "Do you mean that?"

"If I didn't, I wouldn't have said it."

"Then you can do me a great favor by not mentioning any of this when we get back to the ranch."

"I'm no chatterbox. But folks love to gossip, especially about a shootin'. Your pa is bound to hear about it, and that you were there."

"Let me worry about that," Isolda said. "In the meantime, not a word to anyone when we get back. Not even to your friend, Mr. Bonner."

"I don't keep secrets from Neal, ma'am. He's my pard."

It exasperated Isolda no end, how obtuse the man could be. "Then at least ask Mr. Bonner not to say anything to my father. Explain that this is between my father and me. Can you do that much?"

"I can," Jericho said.

Isolda marched on. The trip hadn't turned out as she'd wanted, but she held hope for the days and weeks to come. She'd shown Beaumont Adams that she was interested and he clearly reciprocated.

Perhaps her stay in the Badlands would turn out to be more rewarding than she could possibly have imagined.

Neal Bonner had never felt so heavy of heart. He was miserable to his core, and he had only himself to blame. He should never have let Alexander Jessup ride the mustang.

Long ago, Neal had learned to trust his instincts. A man couldn't always rely on what went on in his head. He had to rely on his gut, too, on those occasions when a feeling came over him that something or other shouldn't be done or should be avoided. He'd gone against his instincts with regards to the mustang, and look at what happened.

Now, pacing the front porch, he prayed that his mistake wouldn't cost his new boss his life. Kantor was up there doing what he could, with Edana helping. Neal had felt useless just standing there, so he'd come out for a breath of fresh air.

Over a score of cowhands and ranch workers were waiting for word, as well.

Billy, Yeager, and Holland were on the porch with him, leaning against the rail, equally downcast.

Clearing his throat, Billy said, "You'll wear a rut in those boards if you don't stop walkin' back and forth."

"This is no time for your jokes," Neal said.

"Who's jokin'?" Billy said.

Neal went on pacing. He needed a release for his tension. He had half a mind to disperse the men and tell them to get back to work, but they were as concerned as he was, even though they hardly knew the man lying in the bed upstairs.

This was a bad omen, this accident, Neal reflected. Some might call it superstition, some might call it downright silly, but a thing like this could set tongues to wagging. A new ranch starts, and one of the first things that happens is the new manager is busted to pieces.

Neal stopped and turned to the front door. It was all he could do not to barge on in and go up to find out how things were going.

"I blame myself for this," Holland remarked miserably. "I shouldn't have let him climb on."

"What were you to do?" Yeager said. "He's the boss."

"What happens if he doesn't make it?" Billy asked.

"Don't talk like that, boy," Yeager said. "You'll jinx it."

"I'm only wonderin'," Billy said. "You saw the shape he was in, the same as me. Will those cock-a-doodle-doos back East hire somebody else to take his place? Or will they maybe let Neal be the big augur?"

"How would we know?" Yeager said.

Neal was jarred by a thought. If Jessup did pass on and the consortium did hire a new manager, where did that leave Edana? She'd have to pack up and go, along with her sister.

"What's the matter?" Billy asked. "You look sickly all of a sudden."

"Quit lookin' at me," Neal said.

The front door opened and out came the cook. Kantor had blood on his hands and was holding a towel, but he made no attempt to wipe the blood off. "I did the best I knew how," he said wearily.

"And?" Neal prompted.

Kantor shook his head. "I doubt the best sawbones alive could save him, as broken up as he is." He motioned. "You should go on up. She wants to see you." Kantor stepped aside and slumped against the wall, his head bowed. "I am plumb tuckered out."

Entering, Neal closed the door behind him. He took the stairs three at a stride. The bedroom door was closed. Cracking it, he peered in.

Alexander Jessup was on his back, propped on pillows, the bedspread pulled to his chin. His eyes were closed and he was breathing raggedly.

Edana was perched on the edge, holding her father's hand in both of hers. Wet tracks glistened on her cheeks and her eyes brimmed, but she wasn't sobbing or wailing. She'd either heard him or sensed him because she glanced over. "Neal? Is that you?"

Swallowing, Neal went in. He took off his hat and stayed by the door. "I'm awful sorry," was all he could think of to say.

More tears trickled and Edana said, "Come on over, if you would."

They were the longest three steps Neal ever took. His mouth had gone as dry as a desert, and he had to will his legs to move. When she looked up at him in abject sorrow, he yearned to crush her to his chest and tell her he was there for her.

"He won't make it," Edana said forlornly.

Neal felt his own eyes moistening and fought the impulse.

"Your cook did everything he could."

Neal coughed.

Edana turned and placed a hand on her father's brow. "Oh, Neal. Whatever will I do without him?"

Neal didn't know what to say, so he said nothing.

"We had such plans, he and I," Edana said fondly. "We were going to build the Diamond B into one of the most profitable ranches anywhere. Isolda would help, but it would mainly have been on our shoulders. He was looking forward to the challenge." She tenderly stroked her father's forehead. "And now this."

Alexander groaned. His eyelids fluttered, and opened, and he looked about in confusion. "Where?" he said. "What?"

"Father!" Edana exclaimed, and slid closer. "We didn't think you'd come around. Lie still. You've been hurt."

"Daughter?" Alexander gritted his teeth and quaked. "I feel so strange. I can't seem to collect my thoughts."

"Don't try," Edana said. "Just rest."

"Daughter?" Alexander said again. He gazed at the ceiling and smiled. "Why, there's your mother. She's come to meet me." A peaceful look came over him and he tried to raise his arm as if he were reaching for someone when suddenly he went limp, his eyes closed, and his head sagged to one side.

"Oh, Father," Edana said, and lowering her face to the spread, she burst into loud sobs.

23

The buckboard got back early. It was still light, the sun not quite set, when it clattered and rattled over the last low rise and before them stretched the home ranch with its many buildings and corrals.

Jericho was riding beside them and almost immediately announced, "Somethin's wrong."

"Eh?" Stumpy said, looking up.

Isolda was annoyed with him. He hadn't been as friendly on the way back as he had on the way out. Not that she cared whether he liked her or not. "I don't see anything the matter," she said. It was as boringly picturesque as before.

"Where is everybody?" Stumpy said.

Only then did Isolda realize hardly any of the hands were out and about. There should be men working at various tasks, but the only sign of life was smoke rising from the cookhouse chimney and a single puncher lounging in front of the bunkhouse.

"I see Neal," Jericho said.

Isolda was about to ask where when she spotted the foreman seated in a rocking chair on the front porch of the ranch house. Although "seated" wasn't quite the right word. Slumped would have been better, as if he had collapsed into it.

"Somethin' has happened," Stumpy said. "Somethin' awful bad."

"You're just guessing," Isolda said.

"No, ma'am," Stumpy said. "I can feel it in my bones."

Isolda was tempted to tell him what he could do with his old bones. But she sat up and held her bag in her lap and grew a little anxious as Stumpy brought the buckboard up to the house and held his hand out to help her climb down. She refused the offer and clambered from the seat on her own, her legs stiff from the long ride.

Jericho had dismounted and was approaching the steps. "Pard?" he said.

Neal Bonner rose from the rocking chair with the air of someone going to his own grave. He came to the steps and stared sorrowfully at Isolda. "I'm sorry for your loss, ma'am."

Isolda was taken aback. "What loss?"

"You'd best go right in," Neal said. "Your

sister is upstairs in your pa's bedroom. She wanted to be alone with him."

A terrible dread filled Isolda. She rushed up the steps and was inside and on the second floor before she regained control of her emotions. Moving to the doorway, she halted. Her father lay as one dead in his bed. Her sister had her face buried in the covers and an arm partly over him. "Edana?"

Edana jerked up and turned. Her eyes moistening, she startled Isolda by dashing over and throwing her arms around her. "Oh, sister. I wish you had been here. I've felt so alone."

Isolda stared over her shoulder at the bed. She could feel her blood draining from her face, and a light-headedness came over her. "Is Father . . . ?"

"Dead? Yes," Edana said, stepping back. Tears flowed, and she sniffled. "He insisted on riding a mustang and was thrown. Our cook did all he could, but there was nothing anyone could have done."

Isolda was too shocked to dwell on the absurdity of the cook playing at being a doctor. Going over, she sat on the bed and studied the pale face that for years had been both her comfort and her trial. She'd loved her father. She truly did. But he'd annoyed her no end with his insistence that she help in the family business. It had been his idea she take up bookkeeping. She'd have quit it long ago if something better had come along. "Oh, Father," was all she said.

Edana joined her and clasped her hand. "I was with him at the end. He said he saw Mother."

"Delirium," Isolda said.

"You don't know that," Edana said. "It could very well have been her in her spirit form."

"Don't start with that again," Isolda said. A long-running point of contention between them, one of many, was her refusal to believe in the fairy tale of life after death. Her sister did, though, and so had her father.

"I can't think of a better time," Edana said. "Father has gone to his reward. We must give him a proper burial so his soul can rest in peace."

"I agree about the funeral, but the rest is so much doggerel."

Edana shook her head in reproach. "I will never understand how you can't have faith."

"I'll never understand how you do."

"There's the Bible, for one thing," Edana said. "God and Jesus and . . ."

Isolda held up a hand. "Let's not quarrel.

Not here. Not now. I'll go along with whatever you want, but don't impose the other on me."

Edana looked at her strangely.

"What?"

"It just occurred to me," Edana said, "you're not crying. I fell apart when he passed on, yet there you sit, as cool and collected as can be."

"Why, so I am," Isolda said. She was mildly shocked at her lack of emotion. But then, she always did keep a tight rein on her feelings, except for her flares of temper. She'd held everything in for so long that there were days when she'd thought she would burst. "I'll weep for him later. Right now we should see about having a coffin made and arrange for his body to be shipped back."

"No," Edana said. "We'll bury him here. It's fitting."

"It's insane," Isolda said. "This isn't our property. We're only running this ranch. We must take him back and bury him in the family plot at the cemetery, where he'd want to be buried."

"In what state?"

"New York, of course."

"I was referring to his physical state," Edana said. "Decomposition will have set in long before we can get him there. He'll bloat and decay unless he's embalmed, and who is there to do the embalming? We're hundreds of miles from any funeral home."

Isolda hadn't thought of that.

"It would take a week and a half by wagon, if not longer, to get him to one," Edana continued, "and by then the smell would be horrendous. The rot would be so advanced that preserving his remains would be out of the question."

"We can fill the coffin with salt."

"From where? We don't have nearly enough." Edana placed her hand on their father's chest. "I'd like to bury him next to Mother, too. But circumstances have conspired against us. And now that I know they're together again in the hereafter, it's not really necessary."

Isolda bit off a sharp retort. "Let me think about it. There has to be a way."

"For your sake I'll talk to Neal. Perhaps he knows of a method." Edana had stopped crying but dabbed at an eye. "The other big question is what will become of us."

"Us?" Isolda said.

"What do we do for a living now that Father is gone? Move back East? I, for one, would rather not. The men who hired Father to run the Diamond B will need someone to replace him. I'm sending word to Franklyn Wells, and he'll probably get here as quickly as he can, but it will still take him weeks to arrive."

Isolda hadn't thought of that, either. What would she like to do? she asked herself. She was no longer bound to her father, and his bookkeeping. She could do whatever she wanted, and she knew just what that was.

"This is the end of our life as we knew it," Edana said sorrowfully.

"Yes, it is," Isolda agreed, and inwardly she bubbled with excitement.

Beaumont Adams left Dyson and Stimms at the Three Aces. If he showed up with them at his back, it might give the impression he had a yellow streak. He kept his hands in his specially lined pockets, though, so he could resort to his pistols if he had to.

He wasn't stupid.

The man he was seeking had taken a shine to the Tumbleweed and could be found there most anytime after sunset. Beaumont figured it was because the Tumbleweed attracted the coarser element. A hard case like Scar Wratner fit right in.

The stars were out and a brisk breeze whirled dust in tiny eddies as Beaumont strode down Main Street.

It had been an interesting day, to say the least. Isolda Jessup's visit had started things off. He still couldn't get over how brazen she'd been. For a decent woman to go into a saloon was unthinkable. In some towns she would be ostracized by her more upstanding sisters.

Beaumont told himself that part of Isolda's audacity must stem from her being from back East. Eastern ladies must not be as snobbish as the Western variety. But then, most Western ladies came from back East, so that explanation didn't hold water.

No, Isolda Jessup was a rarity in that she apparently didn't give a good damn what other women thought. She would do as she pleased and the rest of the world could go to hell.

Beaumont liked her outlook. He liked even more that she'd made a special trip to town to see him. She had made her interest plain. Now it was up to him to do something about it.

Beaumont must tread carefully. Isolda wasn't a saloon tart to be dallied with when he was in the mood and otherwise forgotten. She wasn't Darietta. She had wit, intelligence, beauty. With a woman like her at his side, a man could accomplish just about anything. Beaumont must cultivate her with care.

It had rankled him, having to let her walk out with that Texas-bred gun slick. Not that Beaumont had anything against Jericho. The man was only doing his job. But it had left the impression, in Beaumont's own mind, anyway, that he lacked grit. It didn't help that Floyd went and got his brains blown out, and he hadn't done anything about it.

Well, he was doing something now.

Beaumont strolled into the Tumbleweed as if he didn't have a care in the world. Smiling good-naturedly, he nodded at a few cardplayers he knew.

At the far end of the bar stood the gent he sought with an arm around a young dove. Wratner was nuzzling her neck and she was squealing and playfully pushing against him, but not too hard.

Grat and Tuck were at a nearby table. Both came to their feet when Beaumont strode up and he nodded at them, too.

"If you're hungry, Ma's is still open," Beaumont said.

Scar Wratner raised his head and chuckled. "Well, look who it is, darlin'. Your new boss."

The young dove regarded Beaumont with awe. "I saw you shoot Mr. Zimmerman and

281

those others. It was something."

"Go mingle with the other customers," Beaumont said. "I have business to discuss with Mr. Wratner here."

She giggled and nodded and scampered off, but not before Wratner gave her a loud smack on her fanny.

"I've been expectin' you, gambler-man."

"Oh?" Beaumont caught the bartender's attention and pointed at a bottle. The barkeep promptly brought it and a glass and set them in front of him.

Scar Wratner slid his empty glass over. "Fill mine while you're at it." Leering after the dove, he nodded and said, "I heard about your visitor. Hell, the whole town has heard by now."

"So?"

"So everyone is sayin' as how Jericho waltzed into your place and took that Eastern gal right out from under your nose."

"That wasn't how it was," Beaumont said in irritation as he poured.

Scar Wratner shrugged. "The important thing is that it showed you I was right. You need me. That's why you're here. To take me up on my offer."

"You're awful sure of yourself."

"Show me anyone else in this two-bit town who can hold a candle to me besides you and Jericho."

"Thanks for includin' me at the top," Beaumont said dryly.

"I've seen you at work," Scar said. "With me to back you, inside of a month this town will be yours."

"It will be mine anyway," Beaumont declared.

"Then why are you here if not to hire me?"

Beaumont mustn't appear too eager. He stalled by raising his glass and taking a couple of slow swallows. "You have me pegged," he admitted. "I've given it a lot of thought and I'd like you on my payroll." He took another swallow. "But not at a fifth of all my earnin's."

"How much, then?"

Beaumont leaned on the bar. "In return for your six-shooters bein' at my beck and call, you can run the Tumbleweed for me and keep half of the profits. That's more than fair, if you ask me."

Scar looked at the drinkers lining the bar and the cardplayers, and frowned. "What the hell do I know about runnin' a saloon?"

"That will be the easy part," Beaumont said. "A man of mine by the name of Deitch will do the actual busywork, keepin' the books and orderin' the liquor and such. All you have to do is show up and drink and fondle the gals to your heart's content."

"I don't know," Scar said uncertainly, although it was obvious the idea appealed to him.

"You'd be the cock of the walk," Beaumont said, laying it on. "Deitch will answer to you as he will to me. Anything you want, within reason, you can do."

"My own saloon. That would beat all."

"Don't forget fifty percent of the proceeds. We're talkin' hundreds a night if you don't take to killin' folks and scarin' everybody off."

"My own saloon," Scar said again.

"Under me," Beaumont amended, and thrust out his hand. "Do we have a deal or not?"

Scar Wratner laughed and thrust out his. "We do. Let me know when you want someone's wick snuffed, and he's as good as gone."

24

Edana Jessup didn't think things could get any worse.

The father she had loved and adored and looked up to had died under horrible circumstances, casting her and her sister adrift on the turbulent sea of life. They had no jobs of their own and would no doubt be asked to pack up and leave. The consortium would hire a new manager, and that would be that.

She spent a sleepless night tossing and turning and was up before the rooster crowed. Dressing, she made her way to the kitchen and put coffee on the stove. It was still dark out and she wasn't expecting company, which was why she jumped when someone knocked lightly on the back door. Going over, she parted the small curtain and peeked out. "Neal!" she exclaimed in delight, and wasted no time in throwing the bolt and working the latch.

The foreman had his hat in hand and wore a sheepish expression. "Sorry to bother you so early, ma'am, but I saw the light and figured one of you must be up and about."

"Come in, come in," Edana said eagerly, pulling on his arm. "You have no idea how auspicious your timing is."

"Shucks," Neal said. "I don't reckon I know what auspicious even is."

Edana ushered him to a chair and bid him sit. "Coffee will be ready in a while. In the meantime, how about if I prepare eggs and bacon? How hungry are you?"

"Not hungry at all," Neal admitted. "I've been too worried to pay much mind to food."

"Worried about the ranch and the transition, no doubt," Edana said, sitting across from him.

"No, ma'am," Neal said. "Worried about you."

"Oh."

"About what will happen now that your pa is gone. Will you and your sister light a shuck?"

"We'll probably be asked to," Edana said. "But I'd rather not go if it can be avoided." She bent toward him. "I have a plan. Whether it succeeds depends on your help. If it does, I might be able to stay. If not . . ."

286

She didn't finish.

"I'd do anything in the world for you," Neal said.

Edana swore her ears were burning. "The only way I will get to stay is if I can convince the men who hired my father that I can do the job every bit as competently as he could."

"What would you need from me?"

"An education in ranching," Edana said. "You've already shared a lot, but now I need to know everything that has a bearing on making the Diamond B a success. And by everything, I mean every detail, no matter how piddling."

"I can do that," Neal assured her.

"We'll have to be together from daybreak until sunset for days on end." Edana grinned self-consciously. "Can you stand that much of my company?"

"That and more, I reckon."

"I apologize for imposing myself on you in this fashion, but I don't know how much time I have," Edana said. "I sent a rider to town last night with a letter for Franklyn Wells, but there's no telling how long it will take to reach him and for him to reach us."

"I hope it's a month or more."

"You do?"

"To have more time to teach you," Neal

said quickly.

"Of course." Edana placed her hand on his. "I want to thank you for standing by me. I've said it before and I'll say it again. You're the only real friend I have here."

"Does that include me?" intruded a voice from the doorway.

Edana turned. Her sister was bundled in a bulky robe and her hair was disheveled. She had obviously just woken up and not bothered to put herself together. "Go get dressed. We have company."

"Is that what you call him?" Isolda stepped to the stove and held her hand close to the coffeepot. "I'll go after I say what I came down here to say." She smiled at Neal Bonner. "Forgive my appearance. She didn't tell me we had a visitor at this ungodly hour."

"Isolda," Edana said.

"But that's always been the way with her, and Father as well." Isolda moved to the end of the table. "I've never been deemed important enough to be let in on a lot of their decisions."

"That's not true," Edana said, sitting up. "Father never did anything without consulting both of us."

"You, he consulted," Isolda said. "Me, he told me what to do based on what the two of you had decided."

"You shouldn't speak ill of the dead," Edana said angrily.

About to yawn, Isolda rolled her eyes. "Who's speaking ill? I'm saying exactly how it was. For years I put up with it. For years I was the dutiful daughter always doing as her father wanted. Well, now he's gone, and I can finally have a life of my own."

"I can't believe I'm hearing this." Edana never suspected her sister felt this way. She'd always assumed Isolda was perfectly happy in the work she did.

"You wouldn't have to hear it if you'd stopped and looked around you now and then. Father and you were too caught up in your own lives to pay any attention to me."

"I resent that."

Isolda snorted. "Resent it all you want. It's the truth. I've had it up to here" — and she touched a finger to her chin — "with ledgers and accounts. I want something new. Something different."

"What is this leading up to?" Edana wanted to know.

"Simply this," Isolda said. "I'm leaving the Diamond B. You're welcome to stay on and run it by yourself, but count me out."

Shock cleaved Edana's tongue to her mouth.

"From what I overheard, you'll have all

the help you need," Isolda went on with a smirk at Neal Bonner. "You won't really need me for anything."

"But where will you go? What will you do?"

"Whiskey Flats."

"Why on earth there? I should think New York City or Philadelphia is more to your liking."

"You'd be surprised," Isolda said. "At any rate, I'm leaving about noon and I honestly can't say when you'll see me again." She ran a hand through her hair.

"Can't we talk this out?" Edana requested. "It's all so sudden."

"Not for me."

"Father dying yesterday, and now this." Edana shook her head. "My whole world is falling apart."

"I'll only be a few hours away, and I'll come if you need me," Isolda said. "That's better than my returning to New York, isn't it?"

"I suppose," Edana said, "but I still don't like it. I was counting on you to be by my side."

"You'll be too busy with your cowboy to even notice I'm gone."

"Don't be crude," Edana said.

Isolda leaned on the table. "It's time you

grew up, sis. You're not getting any younger, and unless you want to spend the rest of your life as a spinster, you should look around and smell the roses, as they say." Turning, she moved toward the hall. "As for me, I have a whole new life and a whole new world to explore, and frankly, I can't wait." She paused in the doorway. "Don't take any of this personally. It's been building in me for a long time. I would have done this sooner or later. Later, I admit, were Father still alive. As sorry as I am that he's gone, and I truly am, I'm happy I won't have to deal with him trying to stop me."

"Oh, Isolda."

"Oh, yourself. I'm not a saint and never claimed to be. I've been a dutiful daughter. You have to grant me that much. Now that part of my life is over. I'm going out into the world my own woman." Pulling her robe tighter, Isolda departed.

"Well," Edana said.

"She speaks her mind," Neal remarked.

"She's always had an independent streak. But I didn't expect it to rear its head so soon after Father's passing." Edana bowed her head. It saddened her, her sister's decision. At the same time, she felt a certain sense of relief. It was all on her now. All on her shoulders. She could do as she pleased without any interference from anyone.

God willing, she could do her father proud by making the Diamond B one of the best ranches in the territory, or anywhere else for that matter.

"Every hand here will back you, ma'am," Neal said. "You can count on it."

"Eh?" Edana looked up. She realized she'd said that last out loud. "Will they really? They won't mind working for a woman?"

"You forget where you are," Neal said.

"I don't follow you."

Neal sat back and gestured at the window. "West of the Mississippi, menfolk hold women in high regard. For all the fancy talk those Easterners do, it's us Westerners who give women their due."

"I wish I had your confidence," Edana confessed.

"If you'd lived your whole life out here like I have, you would. Out here a man sees how hard his woman works, all the cookin' and sewin' and laundry and whatnot she does, and he sees her more as his partner than his property. It's why cowboys were the first anywhere to give women the right to vote."

Edana's interest perked. "I remember hearing about that."

"Wyoming, it was," Neal said, "ten to

fifteen years ago. Not that state where you're from, where they do a lot of talkin' about women's rights and such but never give their women the same rights the men have."

"All too true," Edana said.

"It took a bunch of ranchers and cowboys to say that their partners deserved the same as them, and now the women in Wyoming go to the polls the same as the men and can hold office if they're of a mind." Neal paused and grinned. "Or run a ranch the same as any man."

Edana was encouraged by his confidence. She'd worried that perhaps the punchers would refuse to work for her based on her gender. "Granting that all you've said is true, I have to prove worthy of their trust."

"That's where I come in."

Edana grew warm inside. He was so eager to help, so anxious to please. Her heart was stirred, and she took his hand. "I'll be forever in your debt. You don't realize how much this means to me."

"I reckon I do, ma'am. It means a lot to me, too."

They looked into each other's eyes, and for a moment Edana felt as if time were standing still. She tingled from her hand to her shoulder, and if he had leaned over to kiss her, she would have thrown herself into his arms.

Then loud pounding intruded, and the moment was gone.

"Someone is knockin' on your front door," Neal said.

"Who can it be this early?" Edana rose and hurried out and was pleased he came with her. It seemed natural having him at her side. She let him open the door.

It was Billy and Yeager, the former with his arm raised to knock again. "Neal!" he exclaimed. "We've been lookin' for you."

"You found me," Neal said. "What's so important that you have to bother Miss Jessup in her grief?"

"I'm right sorry, ma'am," Billy said to Edana. "I guess I wasn't thinkin'."

"Say why you're here," Edana said.

"Oh. Barlow just got in from the range. They found another steer like that first. It'd been shot and some of the meat taken and the rest left to rot."

"We have some of the boys ready to ride," Yeager said.

"Tell them I'll be there in a bit," Neal said. "Those as have rifles are to bring them, and grub for two days or more."

The pair jangled off.

"Must you go?" Edana said.

"Someone is goin' around killin' our

cattle. Two dead steers might not sound like much when the Diamond B has thousands of head, but it's the insult of the thing."

"No, I mean must you go *now*?" Edana said. "I have to bury my father, and I'd very much like for you to be there. Can't this wait?"

Neal looked at her. "For you, I'll stay. I'll send the others out, though, for a look-see. Maybe they can find some tracks this time." He touched his hat brim. "Ma'am," he said, and went out.

Smiling, Edana closed the door. She liked how readily he'd changed his plans at her request. It brought to mind his talk about how men and women should work as partners. She liked that a lot, too.

Neal Bonner wasn't like any man she'd ever known. She'd only been around him for a few days, yet he stirred her as no man ever had. She wasn't stupid. She recognized the signs in herself. The question now was what to do about it. A romance was the last thing she needed, on top of everything else.

Edana started down the hall, and abruptly stopped. She had a sense of being watched. Glancing at the stairs, she said, "How long have you been there?"

Isolda, still in her robe, was leaning on the

banister. "I heard the knocking, the same as you."

"What's that smirk for?"

"You, dear sister," Isolda said. "Invite me to the wedding or I'll be terribly disappointed."

"You think you know, but you don't."

"Deny it all you want," Isolda said, "but I do know one thing. We haven't been here a week and our lives have been forever changed."

25

It was well past noon when Beaumont Adams made his way to the saloon and had his first drink of the day at the bar. Half a glass, usually, was enough to jolt him out of any lingering lethargy. No sooner had he set the glass down and turned than Dyson and Stimms came hurrying up. "Trouble?"

"We've got news, boss," Stimms said.

Nodding, Dyson said, "A cowpoke from the Diamond B is in town. He told Guthrie over to the general store that Alexander Jessup has been killed."

Beaumont thought of Isolda, and how she would probably have to pack up and head back East. "Who killed him?"

"Not who. What," Dyson said. "Word is he got thrown by a horse and stomped."

Stimms nodded. "The cowpoke said he tried to ride a bronc. Why in hell would he do somethin' that stupid?"

"Beats me," Dyson said, "him bein' from

the East and all. He had as much business climbin' on a mustang as I would climbin' on a bear."

"Why would anybody climb on a bear?" Stimms asked.

"Are you two simpletons done?" Beaumont broke in. "Is that cowpoke still in town or did he leave?"

"I don't rightly know," Dyson said.

"Go find out. If he's here, ask him if he knows what the ladies will do now that their pa is gone."

"What if he won't say or doesn't know or tells us to go sit on a cactus?"

"Ask him real polite."

Dyson and Stimms looked at each other and Stimms said, "Polite? That's a new one. Do we even know how?"

"Go," Beaumont said. He didn't normally indulge in another glass so soon, but he refilled his and carried it to his reserved table. It was a shame this had to happen. He'd looked forward to getting to know Isolda Jessup a lot better.

"Damn life, anyhow," Beaumont said to the empty air, and swallowed. He couldn't complain. Things were going better than he'd anticipated. He had half a dozen businesses up and running, in addition to his three saloons. By the end of the year he'd have more. He was well on his way to becoming Whiskey Flats's one and only lord and master.

Normally that cheered him, but the thought of not seeing Isolda again depressed him so much he sat at the table drinking for over an hour. Dyson and Stimms returned to report that the cowpoke had lit out for the ranch.

Beaumont fell into a rare sulk. He told himself it shouldn't matter, that he'd only just met her and could easily forget her. He sat in on a poker game, thinking that would bring him out of himself. It didn't. The cards were in his favor and he won more hands than he lost, but he still couldn't shake his doldrums.

The clock on the wall said it was pushing six when Beaumont gathered up his winnings and strolled outside for a breath of fresh air.

A buckboard was coming down the street. Stumpy, the grizzled old hand from the Diamond B, was driving, and beside him sat a vision of loveliness in a black dress of mourning but with a parasol over her slender shoulder. Their eyes met at the same instant. She said something to Stumpy and he frowned and brought the buckboard over.

Doffing his hat, Beaumont stepped off the boardwalk. "I'll take this as an omen."

"A superstitious gambler," Isolda said, grinning. "Imagine that." She sobered and said, "My father has died."

"I've heard, and I'm sorry as can be."

"I don't need false sympathy. I do need a place to stay. This town doesn't have a hotel yet, does it?"

Beaumont shook his head. "If it's only for the night, I know some nice folks who might put you up."

"Would they put me up for a year or two?"

"You're not headin' back East?" Beaumont said in surprise.

"What gave you that idea? We have unfinished business, you and I. As a matter of fact, why don't we discuss it over supper? I'm famished, and Ma's is open. What do you say?"

Beaumont couldn't hide his delight. "First that place to stay," he said, and stepping to the front wheel, he hooked his boot on a spoke and swung up and over into the bed. He almost stepped on one of her bags but agilely jumped over it and hunkered behind the seat. "Go two blocks and turn right."

Isolda looked over her shoulder at him and smiled. "You heard the man."

Stumpy muttered and flicked the reins.

"Somethin' botherin' you, old-timer?" Beaumont asked.

"It ain't fittin', is all," Stumpy said.

"He's been grumbling since we left the ranch," Isolda said. "Apparently it's improper for a single woman to take her destiny into her own hands."

Stumpy glanced at her and shook his head. "I never said any such thing. It's just a body has to be careful who they take up with in these parts."

"He means me," Beaumont said, chuckling. "You might not have heard, but I'm an unsavory character."

"I certainly hope so," Isolda said.

"Now, see?" Stumpy said. "It's talk like that that worries me. Nothin' good will come of this, ma'am. Mark my words."

"I want to do this and I will," Isolda declared, "and no number of naysayers will persuade me otherwise." She put her hand on Stumpy's shoulder. "But I do have a request to make of you."

Stumpy stared at her hand as if it were a spider that might bite him. "Of me, Miss Jessup?"

"I want you to keep an eye on my sister for me. Whenever you come into town, look me up and let me know how things are going at the ranch."

Stumpy didn't answer right away. His jaw muscles twitching, he traveled the two blocks and swung into the turn. Finally he said, "Why me?"

"Why not?" Isolda rejoined. "I've spent more time with you than with any of the other hands. We're practically friends."

"I wouldn't go that far, ma'am," Stumpy said.

"Why wouldn't you do it? Don't you like me?"

"It's not that," Stumpy said.

Beaumont leaned forward. "How about if you do it for me? I'll pay you twenty dollars a month to be our eyes and ears out at the Diamond B. Whenever you come into town, look us up and give us the latest news."

"Twenty a month?" Stumpy blurted, and caught himself. "It doesn't sound proper, me spyin' on them."

"Who asked you to?" Beaumont said. "All you have to do is report the latest goings-on. That's not spyin'."

"Please, Stumpy," Isolda said. "I'd be ever so grateful. She is my sister, after all, and I'd like to keep up with things. Especially after what happened to our father."

Fidgeting, Stumpy said, "When you put it that way, ma'am, I reckon I can't refuse."

"Hallelujah," Beaumont said. He pointed

at a house with a yard and a picket fence, a rarity in Whiskey Flats. "Pull up there."

"Tell me about these people," Isolda said.

"Their name is Preston. A young couple, with a one-year-old girl. He's a clerk, and comes into the Three Aces now and again. Only ever has one drink, and he might play a little cards but he never lets himself lose big. I struck up his acquaintance and we're friendly enough that I'm sure they won't mind putting you up."

"I'll stay the night, but by tomorrow night I want you to find something better," Isolda said. "A place of my own. A house or an apartment. I'm not choosy so long as it's not a dump. If we had a hotel this wouldn't be an issue."

"I'll start men on building one by the end of the week," Beaumont said. He had been thinking of erecting one anyway. As the town grew, it would be a steady source of income. Hopping down, he offered his arm.

Isolda graciously took it, and lithely alighted. "You're the perfect gentleman," she teased.

"For you I am."

Beaumont ushered her to the front door, saying, "Just a suggestion, my dear, but it would please me greatly if you stayed with me."

"Why, Mr. Adams," Isolda said in mock dismay. "Think of how tongues would wag. I'd be the scandal of the territory."

"If you're seen with me often enough," Beaumont predicted, "you'll become that anyway."

"Oh, I intend to do much more than be seen with you," Isolda said. "But first we lay the ground rules."

"Mind enlightenin' me on what they are?"

Before she could answer, even before he could knock, the front door opened and Mrs. Preston stepped out holding her child. She informed them that it would be fine with her to have Isolda stay the night. She'd welcome the company of another female. But she should ask if her husband was all right with it, and he was at work.

"Tell you what, Mrs. Preston," Beaumont said. "I'll take the lady here for a meal, and by the time we get back, your husband is likely to be home. We can talk to him then, if that's acceptable?"

"We'll be looking for you," the young woman said.

"In the meantime, is it all right if we leave the lady's bags here?"

"Of course."

Isolda had Stumpy bring them to the porch. When the last had been deposited and he was climbing onto the buckboard, she plucked at his sleeve and said, "Don't forget our arrangement. You're to report on my sister's activities every time you come to town."

"I told you I would and I will," Stumpy said grumpily. Lifting the reins, he frowned down at her. "You've become awful pushy since your pa died."

"My dear sir," Isolda said sweetly, "I haven't begun to push."

"Loco female," Stumpy muttered. Calling out, "Get along there!" he rattled off, the wheels raising swirls of dust.

"Old fart," Isolda said.

Beaumont laughed and clasped her arm. "How about that meal?" Without being obvious, he studied her as they walked. He liked everything about her: the fine yet firm set of her face, the unaffected sway of her body, the superb manner in which she carried herself.

"Have a portrait made, why don't you?" Isolda said.

"You can't hardly blame me," Beaumont said. "This is all so sudden. A whirlwind has been dropped into my lap and I'm tryin' to catch up with it all."

"Catch up quick," Isolda said. "I won't have a slow-wit. We have a lot to accomplish together."

"About that," Beaumont said. "Why am I so lucky? There are millions of men in this world and out of the blue you decide on me. I'm damned if I can figure out what I did to impress you."

"Look a gift horse in the mouth, why don't you?" Isolda said with a smile. She stopped and faced him and grew solemn. "Look at me."

Puzzled, Beaumont did.

"Look me in the eye and tell me you don't want me."

Beaumont grinned and started to joke that he'd have to be crazy not to want a woman like her.

"This is serious," Isolda said. "Don't diminish it or we'll part ways here and now, forever."

Checking himself, Beaumont sobered. He looked into those lovely eyes of hers, and in some mysterious manner he couldn't fathom, it was like looking into mirror images of his own. He felt drawn into her, as if she was him and he was her. It made no sense but there it was. "I want you," he said huskily.

"And I, you. I knew you were the one the moment I first saw you. Don't ask me how. Don't ask me why. I just knew. It was as if a part of me that had been missing was in my life where it should be." Isolda swallowed. "I admit it scared me a little. I couldn't stop thinking of you, of how much I wanted you. You're the one. If you can't see that, if you don't want to be, say so now and there'll be no hard feelings."

"I just told you I want you," Beaumont said. He was having difficulty collecting his thoughts. His head was spinning, as if he'd had a bit too much to drink.

"Then we make a pact, here and now. I'm for you and you're for me. No one else. Ever. It's us against the rest of the world from here on out. Agreed?"

"Is this one of those ground rules?"

"The most important of all. What will it be? Yes or no?"

Beaumont leaned in and lightly kissed her on the lips. A mere brush of his against her, yet it sent an electric shock clear down through his body to his toes. Every sinew in his body seemed to lock up. To speak, he had to force his vocal cords to work. "The answer is yes."

Isolda was trembling. "Thank you," she said softly.

"I never heard of anything like this in all my born days," Beaumont remarked.

"People fall in love all the time."

"Is that what this is?" Beaumont said in genuine puzzlement. If so, the times he'd thought he was in love before weren't any such thing. They were insignificant in comparison.

"It's you and I until death does us part," Isolda said. "We can do it proper with a minister if you need that. I don't. I don't care if tongues wag. I don't care about anything except you, and us, and taking this town over and making it ours from top to bottom."

"You are a wonderment," Beaumont said.

"What I am is starved." Isolda took his arm and they continued along the street.

"And happier than I can ever remember being." She laughed, kissed him on the cheek, and cheerfully exclaimed, "Look out, world. Here we come."

26

Scar Wratner liked having his own saloon. He liked it a lot.

Scar had never in his life considered running a business. He didn't have a knack for sums and such. The only thing he'd ever had a knack for was pistols. Some folks would say that wasn't a knack at all, that shooting people was a sickness or a sin. He didn't see it as either.

Scar had been born in Maryland, of all places. When he wasn't quite two, his folks moved to Kansas. They'd decided to homestead and have their own farm. The only thing was, his pa was pitiful at it and his ma became sickly from all the dust and pollen. Until he was twelve, Scar spent most days tending to their milk cows and chickens and scratching at the hard earth with a plow or a hoe.

Then coyotes took an interest in their chickens, and his pa traded for an old Colt

Dragoon to do in the coyotes. It was the first revolver Scar ever set his hands on, and he took to it like a bear to honey. True, the Dragoon was a cannon, and heavy as hell. But he learned to handle it, two-handed, and the evening he shot one of the coyotes was the evening he came fully alive for the first time in his life.

Scar remembered waiting, as quiet as could be, on the roof of the coop for the coyotes to show themselves. When one skulked out of the twilight, he'd held the Dragoon as steady as he could, aimed as best he was able, and having already cocked it, squeezed the trigger. Funny thing; he hardly heard the blast, as loud as it was. He was focused on the coyote and saw, as if in slow motion, the slug core its head and blow part of its skull off.

Afterward, he stood over the dead coyote, marveling as the power the Dragoon gave him. He'd taken it to bed with him that night and slept with it under his pillow. From that day on, he was never without a revolver.

When he was thirteen he persuaded his pa to trade for a Smith & Wesson Model 1. Compared to the Dragoon, it was practically lightweight. It didn't have a trigger guard like later models, and the grips weren't that comfortable to the hand, but it was the most beautiful thing Scar had ever seen. He loved that revolver. He practiced every chance he got. To buy ammunition, he worked at neighboring farms, often until late into the night.

When Scar was sixteen, three events occurred that changed his life forever. His ma died of consumption. His pa got into an argument with a drover at the Ellsworth Saloon, where his pa went for a drink from time to time, and the drover pistol-whipped his pa into the floor. Some friends brought his pa home and then sent for the doctor.

Scar's pa, it turned out, had a cracked skull. The doc took Scar aside and said there was nothing he could do, that his pa might linger hours or days, there was no telling.

Scar sat by that bed for ten days. Ten whole days of his pa tossing and groaning and crying now and then. And finally dying.

Scar strapped on the Smith & Wesson, jammed his straw hat on his head, and rode to Ellsworth. Fortune smiled on him, in that the drover happened to be in the saloon, drinking with a couple of his pards.

Scar marched up to them and announced who he was, and that he'd come to kill the son of a bitch who had killed his pa. The drover had laughed and said he should go away and quit bothering his betters and that he was too young to act so tough.

That was the first time the killing urge came over Scar. The only way to describe it was as a great burning-hot need, like hot water being poured through him. He'd sneered at the drover and called him a yellow cur and said the drover could draw or he'd gun him where he stood.

The drover drew.

Scar shot him before he cleared leather. One of the drover's friends clawed for his hardware and Scar shot him, too.

The acrid smell of gunpowder had tingled his nose, and the gun smoke formed a small cloud.

The third man, his hands out from his sides, said he'd had no part in whatever it was that had provoked Scar and didn't want any trouble.

Scar shot him anyway.

At a nearby table, others rose and put their hands on their revolvers, but Scar whipped around and covered them, saying as how he'd put a window in the skull of the first bastard who tried anything.

That was when the marshal arrived.

Scar told the marshal that all three had gone for their guns. A few witnesses contradicted him, but since no one could deny the first two had, the marshal decided the witnesses might be mistaken. That, and the fact that the marshal knew about Scar's pa and felt sympathy for him, accounted for why Scar wasn't arrested.

Scar went back to the farm only long enough to sell it. He let it go for half of what it was worth, but that was enough to buy a new set of store-bought clothes and a new hat and boots, plus a better horse, and something he wanted even more.

He'd heard about a gun store in Dodge City, the "best gun store anywhere," and went to see for himself.

The affray in the saloon had taught him a couple of lessons. One pistol wasn't enough. He'd had five pills in the wheel and used three. If those punchers at the table had resorted to their six-guns, he'd only have been able to shoot two of the five and the rest would have finished his hash, then and there.

He also needed a better, newer model. His old one was fine for plunking targets, but it wasn't designed for an especially quick draw. He wanted a gun that fit his hand as if it were part of him.

The store was everything folks claimed. Scar walked in and thought he'd gone to heaven. Hundreds of firearms were on display, from the latest pistols to the most expensive rifles.

Scar looked at some Colts. He looked at some Remingtons. Some Merwin & Hulberts. Some Bacons. None suited him as much as the Smith & Wessons. He chose a matched pair of the newest, bought boxes of ammunition, and went out and made camp in the prairie. There, he practiced until he could draw both revolvers remarkably quick and hit what he shot at ten times out of ten.

From Dodge, Scar drifted. Because he liked to frequent saloons, and he had a temper, and because there were a lot of drunks who tested that temper, he shot four more men inside of a year. He acquired a reputation. People whispered about him behind his back.

No one called him Scar back then. He was known as Kid Wratner. That changed on a fateful night in Caldwell. He'd sat in on a card game. It was a gambler's turn to deal, and he saw the gambler deal a card from the bottom of the deck. Right away he accused the man of cheating. That was his first mistake. He should have stood and taken a few steps back and then accused him. When the gambler angrily protested he'd done no such thing, Scar made his second mistake.

He bent toward the man to accent a point by jabbing a finger at him.

The gambler exploded out of his chair, whipping a knife out of his sleeve as he rose. Not just any knife, either, but a bowie with an eight-inch blade. The gambler slashed at Scar's face and opened it like a melon.

Scar would never forget the sharp sting and awful pain and the spray of blood. He'd flung himself back and his chair had crashed to the floor. The gambler turned to flee, but Scar, heedless of his terrible wound, had risen with a pistol in each hand and put two slugs into the man before he'd taken two steps. The gambler screamed and tried to crawl and Scar walked up to him, shooting as he went, sending six more slugs into the twitching body, one after the other in a slow beat of thunder and hate.

A sawbones had done the best he could stitching Scar's wound, but it was too big to ever heal right.

At first Scar hated it. Every time he looked in a mirror he wanted to smash the mirror. Then folks took to calling him Scar instead of Kid, and they were more afraid of him than ever. He liked that. He liked that a lot.

Scar had fallen in with Grat about two years ago. Grat was from Tulsa, and had shot a couple of men down Oklahoma way.

One was the owner of a horse Grat stole, the other a townsman who refused to hand over his poke when Grat popped out of an alley late one night and demanded it. Grat was small-fry, and not all that likable. He griped about everything and wasn't much shucks with a pistol except up close.

They'd met over a card game in Longmont, Colorado. Another player had recognized Scar. Someone asked if it was true he'd bucked out over a dozen men.

Scar had said it was. Another player had asked if Scar ever had a problem with peckerwoods who figured they could acquire a reputation of their own by gunning him. Scar had answered that now and then he did.

Until that moment Grat had been silent, but then he piped up with "What you need is a pard to watch your back."

Scar had jokingly asked if Grat was volunteering, and Grat surprised him by saying he wouldn't mind partnering up if that was what Scar wanted.

Scar couldn't say what made him agree. For all he knew, Grat might want a rep of his own and put lead into his back when he least expected it. It took a couple of months for Scar to accept that Grat was in earnest, and from then on he counted on Grat to watch his back wherever they want.

Scar didn't count on Tuck for anything. Tuck didn't have a thimbleful of brains. He was slower on the draw than a snail. Left on his own, he was next to helpless. The only redeeming trait he had was that he worshipped Scar.

Ever since he was a sprout, Tuck had been fascinated by shootists. He could read, provided he went slow and mouthed the words, and his favorite reading material was those lurid dime novels about gunmen and outlaws. Never mind that they didn't contain a lick of truth. Never mind that the stories were exaggerated potboilers only simpletons would believe. Tuck *was* a simpleton, and he believed them. He could ramble by the hour about the daring exploits of Wild Bill Hickok and Black Bart and a host of shooters of every stripe. But until Tuck met Scar, he'd never come across one in real life.

Scar, to Tuck, was one of his heroes made real.

They'd met in Cheyenne. Tuck came up to Scar's table, hat in hand, and asked if Scar really was who a man at the bar claimed, "the great and wonderful Scar Wratner." Grat had snickered, but Scar gave him a look, and then asked Tuck what made him so wonderful.

"Why, you're about as famous a man-killer as there is," Tuck had gushed. "It's an honor for me to meet you."

His fawning adoration was a new experience for Scar. He hadn't known whether to laugh or rap him on the head with a pistol barrel, so he compromised and invited Tuck to sit at their table.

Grat had scowled, but even he warmed up after Tuck prattled for damn near an hour about every gunny under the sun, and then some. Scar had been amazed at how anyone so dumb could remember so much. On an impulse, when they rose to go, he asked if Tuck wanted to tag along, and you would have thought Scar had offered him his weight in gold from the way Tuck's face lit up and he babbled about how, golly, he'd do anything in the world if he could ride with them. He'd cook Scar's food and polish his boots and wash his clothes and look after his horse and whatever else Scar wanted him to do.

Scar thought for sure that after a few months the luster would wear off and Tuck would drift elsewhere, but no. If anything, Tuck became even more attached to him, especially after Scar bedded down a few sons of bitches who deserved the bedding.

Now here he was, with Grat and Tuck at his back, striding into the saloon he'd been given, as pleased as he could be. Over a week had gone by, and he'd taken to his new role with enthusiasm. So what if he had to give a percentage to Adams, and it was Deitch who handled the books and not him? The Tumbleweed was still his saloon.

On this particular night Scar was halfway to the bar when he sensed something was amiss, and he stopped. The place was too quiet. The regulars at the bar and at the tables had the subdued looks of men who were afraid trouble might break out. Scar glanced over at Deitch, who nodded toward a corner table.

A trio of newcomers were sharing a bottle between them. One look, and Scar recognized them for what they were: curly wolves on the prod. Hooking his thumbs in his gun belts, he ambled over and planted himself where he had a clear view of their hands and arms. "Howdy, gents."

They were young and had been drinking awhile, which could account for their lack of sense. The wolf in the middle tilted his head and said, "What the hell do you want, ugly?"

"I run this place," Scar informed him with undisguised pride.

319

"So?" the same one demanded.

"So I don't want you snot-nosed kids causin' trouble," Scar replied. He probably could have chosen his words more carefully, but then, he'd never given a good damn about whether he offended people.

The wolf on the left bared his teeth. "You had no call to say that. We're sittin' here mindin' our own business."

"Think of it as nippin' you in the bud," Scar said. He could be witty when he wanted to.

The third tough was as prickly as his pards. "What does that even mean, you old goat?"

Scar lost a lot of his good mood. No one had ever called him "old" before. "It means you behave or I have you tossed out on your ears."

"Why don't you try tossin' us yourself?" the first one said.

"I don't toss," Scar said. "I shoot."

"Me, too," the first one declared. "And if you're not careful, I'll put a slug into you like I did your ceilin'."

Scar looked up. Sure enough, there was a bullet hole above their table. "Son of a bitch. When did you do that?"

"About ten minutes ago when we came in. I let out a howl and shot to let everyone know they'd best step easy."

Scar felt a familiar urge come over him, that hot-water feeling he loved so much. "Any gent who will shoot another man's ceilin' doesn't deserve to go on breathin'. Go for your guns, you jackasses."

"You'd gun us over a hole?" the man on the right said.

"We should break the window while we're at it," the one on the left said.

The wolf in the middle pushed his chair back and stood. "Didn't you hear this ugly bastard? He's fixin' to try and take us."

"All three of us?" the man on the left said. He rose, too.

The third man stayed in his chair. "Hell, shoot him and let's get back to our drinkin'."

"I believe I will," the wolf in the middle said, and went for his six-shooter. So did the man on the left.

Scar had his Smith & Wessons out and cocked before either could draw. He fired both simultaneously, going for their heads.

The third man saw his friends crash down and froze. "They didn't stand a prayer!" he gulped, and thrust his arms out from his sides.

Scar trained the Smith & Wessons on him.

"Hold on!" the man cried. "I'm not goin'

to go for my gun."

"You should," Scar said, and shot him.

27

Beaumont Adams woke up but didn't open his eyes. He felt Isolda's cheek on his chest and her soft breath on his skin, and he lay savoring the miracle that had come into his life until the muffled hubbub of voices out in the street reminded him he couldn't lie there all morning.

The drawn window shade had a glow around the edges. By the clock on the dresser, it was past ten. Early, by Beaumont's standards, but he'd been in bed by eleven the night before. His usual bedtime was four a.m. or later.

Beaumont lightly placed his hand on Isolda's head and ever so gently ran his fingers over her silken hair. "You beauty, you," he whispered.

"About time you woke up," Isolda said. Raising her head, she grinned and kissed him on the chin. "I've been lying here for over an hour listening to you breathe."

"I suck in air and let it out, like everybody else," Beaumont said. Shifting, he sat up with his back to the headboard and she rose with him, her forearm on his chest, her eyes lovely pools he'd love to lose himself in.

The bedroom was nicely furnished, with feminine touches in the form of lacy curtains and a doily and a pink bedspread.

"If my father were alive, you wouldn't be breathing at all," Isolda remarked.

"Don't take this wrong," Beaumont said, "but thank God he isn't. We could never have moved in together."

"I wonder if my sister has found out yet."

Beaumont pulled her close and kissed her. "We were lucky this place was for rent."

"A whole house, all to ourselves," Isolda said dreamily. "How you found it on such short notice is beyond me."

Beaumont held his tongue. It wasn't a case of finding out the house was available so much as paying the owners a visit — with Dyson and Stimms in tow — and explaining how happy the owners would make him if they left for, say, Denver for five or six months and rented their home to him. At first the couple refused. The man couldn't possibly be away from his job for that long. Beaumont explained how much healthier they'd stay if they agreed, and the pair promptly changed their minds.

"I'll go fix breakfast and you come down in a bit," Isolda offered.

"I have a better idea," Beaumont said. "We get dressed and go down together."

He liked being in her company. In fact, he'd gotten so used to it he didn't like to be separated from her for any length of time. It was silly. He'd never felt this way about a woman. Most, he'd bedded and forgotten. Not Isolda. She'd gotten into his blood, into his very marrow, in a way he'd never have imagined a woman could.

"Why are you looking at me like that?"

Beaumont reminded himself that she didn't miss a thing. "I still can't get used to us being together."

"You disappoint me, Beau," Isolda chided. "You need to come to grips with this. We have a town to take over. I can't have you playing catch-up all the time."

"This is you we're talking about, not the damn town," Beaumont said peevishly.

Isolda smiled and touched his arm. "I wouldn't have taken you for a romantic. I forgot you're from the South."

"Southerners aren't any more romantic than Yankees."

"I beg to differ," Isolda said. "I'm a Northern girl, remember? And Northern men, by and large, are cold fish when it comes to their women. I can't recall a single instance when my father bought my mother flowers or a gift out of the fondness of his heart. He wasn't romantic whatsoever."

"You can't judge all men by your pa."

"As if I ever would. Do you rate my intelligence that low?"

"You're about the smartest female I've ever came across," Beaumont confessed. He was in awe of her ability to see to the root of a problem, and to do whatever she had to to solve it. She was also so practical she was spooky.

Isolda rose and stretched, seemingly unconscious of her nakedness. Showing no embarrassment whatsoever, she crossed to the chair she had draped her robe over and casually slipped into it. "To get back to you and me. Don't get me wrong. I like your romantic streak. Just don't let it get in the way of what we have to do."

"Why would I?" Beaumont asked.

"By confusing what we share in here with what we share out there," Isolda said, gesturing at the window. "In here it's you and me, our hearts entwined. Out there, it's you and me against the world."

"Now who is thinkin' the other one must be dumb?"

"You're anything but that, my handsome rogue," Isolda said. "The thing you lack isn't intelligence. It's your ambition that needs improving. I'm here to remedy that."

"You think that you have more ambition than I do?"

"How long have you been in Whiskey Flats but you don't control it yet?" Isolda replied. "You took a while to get started, and you've let events control you instead of controlling events. I won't. We'll seize the initiative before someone else comes along and seizes the town for themselves."

"Anyone tries and they'll regret it."

"I'm with you there, but why let it come to that? We lock Whiskey Flats down as quickly as we can."

On that note their conversation ended until they were in the kitchen and she was pouring coffee into his cup.

"The hotel is off to a good start," Isolda mentioned.

"It won't be all that long before you can have that suite you hanker after," Beaumont said, "unless you decide to stay in this house."

"A suite is more in keeping for a queen."

"Is that how you see yourself?" Beaumont said, and chuckled. "Queen Isolda does have a nice sound to it."

"Doesn't it, though?" she said, and laughed.

Half an hour later they emerged into the bright glare of the new day to find someone perched on their porch rail.

"Deitch?" Beaumont said. "What in blazes are you doin' here?"

"Waiting for you, Mr. Adams, sir." Deitch was a mousy man who wore spectacles that made his eyes seem as large as an owl's. Hopping down, he smoothed his ill-fitting suit.

"Why didn't you knock?" Beaumont asked.

Deitch averted his eyes. "I didn't want to risk disturbing you and Miss Jessup."

"That was thoughtful of you," Isolda said.

"Why are you here?" Beaumont demanded.

"It's Scar Wratner," Deitch said. "You instructed me to report to you if he did anything he shouldn't. I believe last night qualifies."

"What did he do? Shoot out the mirror or a window? Or maybe pistol-whip somebody?"

"Would that that were all," Deitch said, shaking his head. "I'm surprised you haven't heard. It's all over town."

"What is, damn it?"

"Mr. Wratner took it on himself to kill three customers."

"The hell you say."

"I saw it with my own eyes. He shot two of them so fast that if I'd blinked, I'd have missed it."

The fine morning Beaumont was having shattered by a burst of anger. He swore, then caught himself and asked, "What did they do that he shot them?"

"They swaggered in and shoved people around and pushed a couple of men at the bar to make room. Then one of them whooped and said that they were there to have a wild time, his very words, and to bring on the doves and the coffin varnish, his words again. They went over to a table and the loudmouth fired a shot into the ceiling to force the men already there to vacate their chairs."

"What was Scar doin' while this was goin' on?"

"He showed up a little later. Caught on quick that something was amiss, I must say. When I directed him to the table, he went over and talked to them. One of them mentioned he'd shot the ceiling and that's when Scar shot all three."

"Damn him, anyhow," Beaumont said. "I told him not to scare our customers off."

"Hold on," Isolda said. "How did the other people in the saloon react, Mr. Deitch, when Mr. Wratner shot them?"

"Some of them cheered and clapped. A gentleman at the bar said they had it coming. Another that they deserved it, that they shouldn't have gone around shoving and shooting."

"Then not much harm was done," Beaumont said. At least, he hoped not. When a saloon acquired a bad reputation, it was shunned.

"Do you happen to know where Mr. Wratner is right this minute?" Isolda asked.

"Probably at the boardinghouse where he and his partners took a couple of rooms. It's early yet for them to be out and about."

"Would you do me a favor?" Isolda said. "Would you go there and ask him to meet Mr. Adams and me at Ma's in half an hour? Tell him I would be ever so grateful if he isn't late, as I have a lot to accomplish today."

"You want me to wake Scar up? That could prove dangerous. He's liable to shoot me for disturbing him."

"Be discreet," Isolda advised. "Mention our names so he knows we're the ones who sent you." She smiled and said graciously, "Please. For me."

Deitch frowned and looked down at his feet and then off along the street. "For you I will, Miss Jessup."

"Thank you. Now off you go."

Beaumont watched his minion scurry away. "I hope you know what you're doin'. I'd have waited until tonight and gone over and laid down the law."

"That's exactly what I intend to do," Isolda said, "in a manner of speaking." She clasped his arm. "How about a muffin and coffee, my treat?"

Beaumont let her usher him along. He suspected she was up to something with regards to Scar, but he couldn't imagine what. She needed to be careful. Scar must be treated with care or he was liable to turn on them. Beaumont placed his free hand in his pocket, glad he had his Colts.

Deitch must have been wrong about Scar being in bed, because it wasn't ten minutes after they got to Ma's that Scar barged in with his perpetual shadows behind him. He came straight to their table. "Your errand boy told me I had to get my ass over here. I don't like bein' bossed around, gambler-man. I don't like it at all."

Isolda smiled her sweetest smile. "It wasn't Mr. Adams who sent for you, Mr. Wratner. I did. Have a seat, if you please.

We have some things to discuss."

Looking as puzzled as Beaumont felt, Scar hooked a chair with his boot, turned it around, and straddled it. "Are you talkin' for the card mechanic, lady?"

"You will address me as Miss Jessup. And yes, I am. I feel compelled to point out that Mr. Adams is far more than that, as I'm sure you realize." Isolda paused. "Now on to other matters. We've heard about the incident at the Tumbleweed last night."

"Now, look, lady —" Scar said, and caught himself. "Look, Miss Jessup. They were askin' for trouble and they got it."

"I wholeheartedly agree," Isolda said.

"You do?"

"From what we hear, you handled the situation admirably."

"I did?"

"Which is why I sent for you," Isolda said, and sat back. "We need to consolidate our power. We're going to hold an election and arrange things so Mr. Adams is Whiskey Flats's first mayor."

Now it was Beaumont who threw in "We are? Lord in heaven, but you work fast."

"We'll send out flyers in the next few days announcing that an election will be held in, say, two weeks' time," Isolda said. "You're well liked, Beau. Everyone knows you don't cheat at the table, and that you deal fairly with people. You should be a shoo-in, but we'll make sure you are by buying as many votes as we need to ensure that you're elected."

"You're awful free with my money," Beaumont said.

"Who said anything about money?" Isolda replied. "We'll quietly spread the word at each of your saloons that you're offering a free drink to anyone who votes for you. Water down your whiskey a little and it will cost you practically nothing."

Scar Wratner laughed. "Miss Jessup, I like how you think."

"Then you should like my next inspiration even more," Isolda said. "The first order of business for our new mayor will be to appoint a town marshal. For Whiskey Flats to prosper, there must be law and order. And I can't think of a better man for the job than yourself."

Scar sat back, astonishment etching his face.

Beaumont was equally dumbfounded but recovered his wits quickly. "You're forgettin' his reputation, my dear. That he just gunned down three men won't help our cause at all."

"To the contrary," Isolda said. "He took

care of some troublemakers. People will like that. The few who object won't be an issue."

"Me?" Scar said. "Tote tin?"

"Think about it, Mr. Wratner," Isolda said. "Ponder the power you'll have. You'll be able to do anything you want under the guise of the law. Anything at all, so long as you don't get carried away."

"Anything I want?" Scar said. His eyes gleamed and he broke into a slow grin.

"What do you say?"

"Lady . . . Sorry . . . Miss Jessup, you're about the craftiest female I've ever come across. If anyone had told me a year ago I'd be a marshal one day, I'd have said they were loco. But you can count me in."

"With my brains and Beau's money and your guns, we'll be unstoppable," Isolda predicted. She raised her coffee cup to them in salute. "Gentlemen, to our alliance. Very soon now, Whiskey Flats will be ours."

28

Edana Jessup threw herself into her education about ranching with a zeal that had all the hands talking. She'd told Neal Bonner she wanted to learn everything, and she wasn't kidding.

She was with him every day from sunup until long after the sun went down. They ate breakfast together, ate supper together. The only time they were apart was when Neal went to the bunkhouse to turn in.

Edana soaked up everything he had to teach her as if her life depended on it. She learned all there was to know about longhorns from birth to slaughterhouse. She saw firsthand how devoted longhorn mothers were to their calves, grinned in delight at their frisky antics, learned how when a calf was separated from its mother for whatever reason, it always returned to where it had suckled last and would stay there until its mother returned or it died of starvation.

Edana was impressed over and over by the resilience of the breed. Compared to longhorns, dairy cows were pampered dullards. The one word she would use to describe longhorns was "durable." Or, as Neal put it one day, "the toughest cattle on God's green earth."

To some people they might look ridiculous with their big ears, narrow hips, and bony flanks, to say nothing of their extraordinarily long horns. But not to her. She developed a great affection for the breed.

Edana also had Neal teach her how to rope. How to set a loop over a steer's head as neatly as you please, and how to bring one down on the fly if she had to, although she could never quite master that skill to her satisfaction.

Edana learned all there was about branding, about the irons, and how when she drew a branding iron from the fire she should smack it against her forearm to shake off the coals that sometimes stuck. She learned she must be quick at it in order not to mar the hide and to avoid unduly hurting the calf.

It wasn't enough that she immersed herself in every aspect of the cattle. She needed to acquaint herself with every particular of ranch upkeep, as well. She spent time with the cook, with the blacksmith, with the old puncher who oversaw the stable, absorbing what they knew as a sponge absorbs water.

She did it all in what she laughingly called her "man's clothes."

The second day after her father's funeral, Neal sent a cowboy into town with a list of things to buy for her.

"A dress might be fine for cookin' and sewin'," Neal had remarked, "but for workin' the range, you need duds that don't rip so easy."

The general store didn't have much of a selection. The best the puncher could find were a couple of men's work shirts that fit Edana loosely, but would do, and a pair of men's pants she took up at the hems. She also wore a narrow-brimmed hat and a brown vest and boots.

One morning not quite two weeks into her education, as she liked to think of it, Edana finished dressing and stood in front of her full-length mirror. She couldn't believe how different she was. Her face, bronzed by the sun, and her hair, which she wasn't so fussy about anymore, combined with her work clothes to lend her the look of a genuine rancher.

Edana was proud of how much she'd accomplished in so short a time. She'd been so immersed in her new role she hadn't given much thought to her sister. She did hear that Isolda had rented a house in Whiskey Flats and apparently intended to stay awhile.

One evening at supper she brought up the subject with Neal. She started by remarking, "I understand Stumpy went into town for supplies today."

Neal glanced up from the piece of beef he'd just stabbed with his fork. "That he did," he confirmed.

"Didn't he happen to hear anything new about Isolda?"

"She still stayin' at that house," Neal said, and looked away so quickly it made her suspect he was hiding something.

"What else?"

"It might upset you."

"Neal, please," Edana said. "I'm a grown woman. Treat me as such."

"Neal set down his fork and took a deep breath. "Your sister is livin' with that gambler."

"When you say living," Edana said, the implication jarring her, "do you mean as in husband and wife?"

Neal nodded. "Only they ain't married."

"My goodness," Edana said. It went against everything their parents had taught them, against everything she'd thought the two of them believed in.

"There's more," Neal said. "The town is fixin' to hold its first election, and Adams is runnin' for mayor. They say he's a shoo-in."

"And my sister will be the power behind the throne," Edana suspected. "How marvelous for her."

"Beggin' your pardon?"

"Nothing. Let's just say that when Isolda told me she wanted a new life for herself, I had no idea." Edana laughed without mirth. "Is there anything else I should know?"

"A hotel is goin' up. People are flockin' in. Oh. And there's talk that the town will have a new marshal just as soon as the new mayor is installed. You'll never guess who."

"Enlighten me."

"Scar Wratner."

Edana arched her eyebrows. "Didn't we hear he shot three men dead not that long ago?"

"Some towns like to have a man-killer wearin' the badge. They reckon there's less trouble that way. It's why Abilene hired Wild Bill Hickok, and El Paso hired Stoudenmire."

"I'm familiar with Mr. Hickok, but who is the other gentleman you mentioned?"

"Dallas Stoudenmire, ma'am. He —"

"Neal, what have I told you a hundred times about that 'ma'am' business?"

"Sorry, Edana," Neal said, abashed. "Stoudenmire is well known down to Texas. He cleaned up El Paso, and was involved in a shooting where four men were shot dead in under five seconds, or so folks say."

"How is that possible?"

"Most shootin' affrays are over right quick if the shooters know what they're doin'," Neal said. "A lot of the time, it's just a couple of drunks wavin' their six-shooters and shootin' all over the place."

"May I ask you something?"

"Anything."

"I know how fond you are of Jericho. I know you rate him as a highly competent . . . What is it? Shootist?"

"He's that and more."

"How does he stand compared to Scar Wratner? Is Jericho better? Who would prevail if they went up against each other?"

"I haven't seen Scar shoot," Neal said, "but given what folks say about him, I'd have to say it'd be a coin toss."

"They're evenly matched, in other words?"

"Sorry to say."

"Why sorry?"

"Because if there ever is trouble, and Scar is totin' a badge, it might give him an edge that would make the difference."

"I'm not sure I understand," Edana said.

"Jericho is a gun hand but he's not a bad man. If Scar comes at him in the name of the law, Jericho might hesitate and that would cost him."

"How do you think of such things?" Edama marveled. "I wouldn't have in a million years."

Neal gave her another of those smiles she liked. "I'm from Texas. We take our shootin' seriously down there."

"I still don't understand, but very well. Perhaps you should have a talk with your friend and convince him to be on his best behavior whenever he goes into Whiskey Flats."

Her suggestion seemed to surprise him. "He always is, and not just there, but everywhere."

"Still, it wouldn't hurt to have him take extra care not to be provoked into going for his gun. Ask him on my account. Tell him I put you up to it so he won't take offense."

"Jericho wouldn't anyhow," Neal said, not sounding at all pleased.

Edana assumed that was the end of it and changed their discussion to ranch business.

The next morning she was in the saddle by sunrise and heading for a new section of range to inspect the cattle. Neal was at her side, and he'd brought Jericho, Billy, and Yeager along.

Edana loved their rides, loved the spectacular mix of terrain and vegetation. Or as the cowboys liked to say, "Ride a mile and the country will change."

Ahead stretched a dry prairie dimpled with tumbleweeds. Edana couldn't get over how no two were alike. You would think all the plants would be the same, as in rows of corn, say, or a field of wheat, but each tumbleweed was different. She'd also learned that while they were picturesque at rest and even more so when they went tumbling and bouncing in the wind, she had to be careful how she handled them should the need arise. They had more thorns than a rosebush.

Past the plain rose a bevy of rock formations. The endless variety of shapes and sizes fascinated her. Here there might be an arch, there a rock shaped like a bird's beak, nearby another that resembled a mushroom.

On this particular day she experienced something else for the very first time.

Bordering the rocks was a dust plain, Neal called it. Mile after mile of flat, dusty ground. Not so much as a single plant grew. There weren't any rocks or boulders. Instead of heading straight across, Neal swung wide to skirt it. Curious, Edana asked why.

"You feel that wind?"

Edana nodded. The wind had been strong all day, so much so that she'd tightened her hat strap under her chin.

"That's why we fight shy of the plain."

"So what if the wind blows? A little dust never hurt anyone."

Behind them, Billy laughed and said, "A little, ma'am? We're talkin' dust that can blister your skin and blast your eyes."

Edana was skeptical, to say the least.

Then, when they were about halfway around, the wind intensified. Out on the plain, the dust stirred. Wisps and tendrils swirled into the air and spread to form a cloud that swiftly grew in size, the particles shimmering like so many tiny diamonds.

"Oh!" Edana exclaimed. "Isn't that pretty?"

"There's more to come," Neal said.

Other wisps rose, some thicker than before, becoming, in effect, writhing columns that curved and swayed as if they were alive. Several swiftly swelled in size until they reminded Edana of tornadoes. They rose and rose, not stopping until they were hundreds of feet high, half a dozen whirling all at once, a spectacle the likes of which she had never imagined she would behold.

"They're beautiful!"

"Not if you're caught in one," Billy said. "The dust gets into your eyes and you can't hardly see, and your horse might spook and throw you."

Neal nodded. "Don't ever get close to a dust devil."

"Is that what you call them?"

"Big or small," Neal said.

"Don't forget the invisible ones," Billy said.

Thinking he was poking fun at her, Edana shifted in her saddle. "You're joking, of course."

"I'm plumb serious, Miss Jessup," Billy assured her.

Neal nodded again. "Sometimes, not often but every now and then, the wind will be just right to raise a devil, only there's no dust to be had. Unless you hear it comin', you can be in trouble."

Edana had been aware of the keening of the wind, and of something else, a sustained sort of hiss that she realized must be the sound of the spinning dust. Suddenly it became twice as loud, and she glanced up to behold an enormous dust devil sweeping toward them.

"Ride!" Neal bawled at the others, and

bending, he smacked her bay on the rump and used his spurs on his buttermilk.

The dust devil whipped toward them faster than a horse could run, sucking more dust as it came, the middle portion bending and curling, its top lost amid the clouds.

Spiked by fear, Edana lashed her reins. The keening and the hissing grew so loud it nearly drowned out the thud of their horses' hooves. Her cheeks and neck were stung again and again, as if by scores of bees.

Edana felt a tug on the back of her vest, and looked over her shoulder. The dust devil was almost on top of them. It had to be thirty feet across and three hundred feet high. Even as she looked, part of it bulged toward her and the bay as if to envelop them in its coils. A scream rose unbidden to her lips, but she bit it off. Slapping her legs, she grabbed at the saddle horn, afraid she would be torn from her saddle.

The next moment, the keening, and the hissing, faded.

The dust devil had changed direction and was moving away, back toward its point of origin, where others twisted and contorted in incredible gyrations.

Billy let out a loud laugh.

Edana didn't share his elation. The dust devils were a reminder, as if any were needed, that the Badlands were fraught with perils. And that if she wasn't careful, she could end up like her father — in an early grave.

29

They hadn't gone a mile past the dust plain when they came on a dead steer. It lay on a ridge they were crossing.

Jericho was the first to spot it. He was listening to Neal and Edana talk about how important it was for a puncher to become familiar with every landmark and source of water on a given range when he spied the unmistakable silhouette of a steer's bulk on the crest. Spurring past them, he trotted up the slope and drew rein.

The rest were quick to join him.

Neal took one look and said, "I'll be switched."

"Why, it's the same as the other ones we found," Edana said. "Part of the haunch is missing."

"Someone carved it off, Miss Jessup," Billy said.

"And left the rest to rot," Yeager said, "same as before."

Dismounting, Jericho examined it. "Been dead less than a day," he reckoned. He pointed at a hole above an eye. "Shot through the head."

"This makes two." Neal stated the obvious.

Billy said grimly, "Someone is huntin' our cattle like they're deer or elk."

"Spread out," Neal commanded. "Search for sign."

Taking his reins in his left hand, Jericho searched on foot. He walked in a circle and discovered the tracks almost right away. "A shod horse," he reported. "It came up the other side of the ridge and left the same way."

"Then it ain't no Injun," Billy said.

"Unless it's a lone brave on a white man's horse he stole," Yeager said.

Jericho supposed that was possible but he doubted it. He suspected their quarry was a white man. Climbing onto his zebra dun, he descended the ridge to a green valley. It was like entering a whole new world. Scores of cattle were grazing. A few, the wilder longhorns, moved off at his approach, but the rest paid him no more mind than they would an antelope.

The tracks skirted the valley rather than make a beeline across it. About halfway around, the steer killer had gone off to the west.

Jericho drew rein and looked at Neal. "Do all of us go after him or only Billy and Yeager and me?" He was giving Neal a chance to keep Miss Jessup out of it.

"All of us will go," Edana said before Neal could reply. "I'm surprised you would suggest otherwise."

"There might be violence," Neal said to her.

"And you think to spare me?" Edana said. "I won't be treated like a child, Mr. Bonner. If I'm to be your boss, I'll do what any other boss would do."

"Fair enough," Neal said, "but if lead starts to fly, you're to hunt cover until it's over."

"I'm not a simpleton."

"No, you're surely not," Neal said with a smile. Sobering, he said, "Jericho, you take point."

Jericho would have done so anyway. Any trouble they ran into, he'd go up against it before they did, allowing the others to protect Miss Jessup. Tapping his spurs, he followed the tracks for more than half a mile, to an expanse of caprock that stretched into the distance.

There, the tracks vanished.

Jericho drew rein.

"Tricky varmint," Billy said when the others came up.

"Smart varmint," Yeager amended.

"He must know this country well," Neal speculated. "He always finds the rockiest ground."

"We can't keep going?" Edana asked.

"A horse doesn't leave much sign on solid rock," Neal replied.

"I don't like having our cattle killed," Edana said.

"Neither do we."

Edana frowned. "I didn't think to ask. Does something like this happen a lot?"

"Never," Neal said. "When we get back, we'll spread the word among the hands that any strangers caught on Diamond B land are to be brought to the ranch house for questionin'."

"What if those strangers refuse?"

Billy chuckled. "We'll bring 'em anyway, ma'am."

Edana had more on her mind. "Could it be someone who doesn't know any better? Who believes it's perfectly all right to kill our cows for food?"

"Even a simpleton would know better," Neal said. "No, whoever is doin' this has to know it's wrong but he does it anyhow."

"The size of the spread," Jericho mentioned, "it could go on a good long while before we catch him."

"Can't have that," Neal said.

"Then how do we stop him?" Edana wanted to know.

"We organize a huntin' party," Neal said. "Jericho there will lead it. Might as well have Billy and Yeager tag along. The next time a steer is found, we send them out and they stay on the buzzard's trail until they catch him. Or he loses them again."

"I'd like him brought back alive."

Jericho looked at her. "Do you realize what you're askin', ma'am?"

"I certainly do," Edana said. "I want to question him and find out why he's done this."

"What Jericho means," Neal said, "is that by havin' to take the varmint alive, you make it harder for them. They'll have to hold back and the steer killer won't."

"Then let me make myself clear," Edana said. "Take him alive if you can, without endangering yourselves. If that's not possible, shoot the son of a bitch." She smiled sweetly.

Jericho grinned at the startled expression on Neal. "That's the first time I've ever heard you cuss, ma'am."

"You should hear me when I stub my toe," Edana said.

Billy laughed. "Ma'am, you're a caution. You'd do to ride the river with."

"I take it that's a compliment. Thank you," Edana said.

Jericho was thinking of the steer killer. Judging by the size of the bullet holes, whoever shot them used a large-caliber rifle. Something to keep in mind when the hunt commenced in earnest.

"We might as well get back to our tour," Neal said. "We have a lot of ground to cover."

"I must say," Edana said as she raised her reins. "I never expected anything like this when my father accepted the position. The West is full of the unexpected."

"Ain't it the truth, ma'am?" Jericho said.

Neal Bonner had been wondering when Franklyn Wells would show up, and he got his answer three weeks to the day after Alexander Jessup's misguided attempt to ride the mustang.

Neal was coming out of the stable when he spotted a couple of punchers escorting a rider in, and went over. "Mr. Wells. You should have sent word. I'd've had someone meet you in town."

Franklyn Wells was weary from his long travel, and it showed. He dismounted stiffly, doffed his bowler, and mopped at his brow with a handkerchief. "I sent a letter explaining when I would arrive, but evidently you didn't receive it."

"Mail service out here is a mite spotty," Neal said.

One of the hands remarked, "We saw him crossin' our range and brought him in, like you said to do."

"We didn't know who he was," said the other cowboy.

"You did right," Neal complimented them. "Grab a bite to eat and then head out again."

The pair made for the cookhouse.

Franklyn Wells was gazing about him with an air of intent interest. "I must say, you have the ranch bustling."

"It's not my doin' so much as Miss Jessup's," Neal said. "She took over from her pa and has been handlin' things right fine."

"Yes, well." Wells unhooked his travel bag from his saddle horn. "That's what I'm here to talk about."

Neal motioned at the ranch house and they started off. "It must have come as a shock hearin' about Mr. Jessup."

"You have no idea," Wells said. "The man

353

had barely begun working for us." He shook his head. "What was Alexander thinking? He tried to ride a wild horse, I've been told."

"A mustang that had been broke," Neal clarified.

"Not broken enough, apparently," Wells said. "Why on earth did you let him do it?"

"There isn't a day my conscience doesn't prick at me," Neal confessed. "As for why, he was the big sugar." He added, in case Wells was unfamiliar with cattle lingo, "I was hired to do whatever he told me, and he hankered to ride that horse."

"His unexpected demise has thrown the consortium into disarray. They were caught completely unprepared. It never occurred to them that he might need to be replaced."

"They already have a replacement," Neal said. "Edana Jessup."

"Yes, well," Franklyn Wells said again.

Neal didn't like the sound of that.

As they climbed to the porch, the front door opened and out Edana came, smiling warmly.

Thrusting out her hand, she said, "Franklyn. It's a delight to see you again."

Wells shook with some reserve. "It's taken longer than I'd have liked to get here. The heads of the consortium didn't want me to come until they'd reached a decision about the new management. It took over a week of voting for them to come to a consensus."

"There's no need to hire someone new," Edana said. "You have me."

"Mr. Bonner is of a similar mind," Wells said, and rubbed his chin. "We need to discuss things, but first I'd like to wash up and perhaps rest a little."

"Of course. Go right ahead," Edana said. "It's only about one o'clock. Why don't you relax until supper? Say, about six we'll sit down and hash things out?"

"Hash?" Wells said, and chuckled half-heartedly. "They're turning you into a Westerner, I see, my dear."

"I've been striving my utmost to become one," Edana said. "But you'll hear all about that at supper."

Neal followed them inside and stayed in the parlor while Edana ushered Wells up to his room. He was perched on the settee, his hat in hand, when she came back down. Rising, he said, "Any hints?"

"He's holding something back," Edana said. "I suspect it will be bad news."

"You'll have your chance to make your case," Neal said. "That's what counts."

Edana placed her hand on his arm. "Thank you for your encouragement. You've stood by me through this whole ordeal. I wouldn't have been able to do it without your help."

"Shucks. I was glad to. I'd do anything you wanted of me."

"I know," Edana said, and rising onto her toes, she kissed him lightly on the mouth.

Neal thought his face had burst into flame. "What was that for?" he asked, his voice sounding ten times huskier than it usually did.

"Consider it a lady's way of expressing her gratitude," Edana said. She turned and was almost to the hallway when she stopped. Without looking back at him, she said, "No. It's time we were honest with each other. It was more than that."

"Oh?" Neal said, his tongue practically cleaving to the roof of his mouth.

"You must know how I feel," Edana said, "and if you didn't, you do now. No matter what happens with Mr. Wells, nothing will change that. It's something we should talk about . . . after." She hastened toward the kitchen.

Neal stood there a full minute, burning all over. Jamming his hat on, he walked to the front door in a daze. He could still feel her lips on his. He stepped outside, shook his head, and said to himself, "I am plumb flabbergasted."

"At what?"

Neal glanced up.

Jericho was leaning against the porch rail, his arms folded across his chest. "You look as if you just stepped on a cactus."

Going over, Neal leaned next to him. "You won't believe it."

"Try me."

Keeping his voice law in case any of the hands drifted past, Neal said, "Miss Jessup just kissed me."

"I'm shocked."

"Why did you say that as if you're not?"

Jericho responded, "You might know cattle inside out, pard, but you don't savvy women at all."

"And you do, I suppose?"

"It's been as plain as that nose on your face that you and her have been settin' the bag for weeks now."

"I've been courtin' her and didn't realize it?"

"If you didn't, you're the only one on the ranch."

Neal burned again, but this time with indignation. "That's a hell of a thing to say to me. You, of all people."

"It's the truth," Jericho said. "The other night over in the bunkhouse, Billy had everybody in stitches when he remarked that whenever you two look at each other, he expects to hear violin music."

"I will by God bean him with a brandin' iron."

"What are you so riled about? She threw her loop over you and you stepped into it."

"You, too?" Neal said.

"Deny it all you want," Jericho said. "It won't change how things are."

Wrestling with his emotions, Neal fell silent for a bit. "It came out of the blue, is all," he said quietly.

"They say the real article does that."

"Since when did you become an expert on romance?" Neal asked, grinning lopsidedly.

"I'm not. But I know you, pard. That gal is smitten. Now you have to decide what to do about it."

"Yes," Neal said, "I do."

30

Edana presented her case over supper. She became so caught up in convincing Franklyn Wells that she was qualified to run the Diamond B that she barely touched her food.

She reminded him of her long business association with her father. That everything her father knew, she knew. That everything he'd done, he did with her at his side. She pressed the point that she was as competent as any man, and more so in some respects.

Wells said that he was aware she had been her father's right hand, as it were.

He said that he knew how closely she'd worked with him, and that was why the consortium had agreed to Alexander's bringing her and her sister along.

Edana then sought to impress him with her knowledge of how the ranch was run.

For that, she gave a silent thanks to Neal, who had taught her, literally, everything he knew. She talked at length about longhorns, and the cattle trade, and the upkeep of a ranch. She threw out facts and figures that had to do with expenses and profit and every business aspect imaginable. She stressed that she knew the consortium was in the ranching business to make a profit, and she would do her utmost to see that they reaped the rewards of their investment.

Wells was pleased. He remarked it didn't surprise him that she was so well versed, given her background. Indeed that was partly why he hadn't brought someone to replace her. Or, for that matter, asked Neal Bonner to take over. He had a suspicion that Neal would say no on her account.

"Why look at all when they have me?" Edana asked bluntly. "Tell them all I've told you. Convince them I can do the job and keep me on in my father's stead. I promise I won't disappoint them."

At that point, Wells gnawed his lip and thoughtfully swirled his coffee in its cup. "I just don't know."

"What are your objections?" Edana said. She was prepared to shoot each of them down.

"That's the thing," Wells said. "If I'm honest about it, I don't really have any, other than —" He stopped.

"Other than I'm a woman?" Edana finished for him.

Wells nodded. "That's not so much my outlook as it is some of the consortium members'. They were whalers, you understand. They lived and worked in an all-male world. The idea of a woman overseeing a business venture is new to them." He paused. "To just about everybody."

Neal had been quiet a long while, but now he cleared his throat. "If you don't mind my two bits, she can do the job as good as any man ever born. Probably better than most."

"Thank you," Edana said, deeply touched.

"That may well be," Franklyn Wells said. "But it's not only me you have to convince. The consortium members must be persuaded, as well."

"Have them come here," Neal said. "Let them see for themselves."

"I'm afraid that's impractical," Wells said. "They're very busy men. They have other business ventures besides this one. And besides, it would take weeks out of their lives to make the journey and go back again."

"If the ranch is important to them, it's worth it," Neal said.

"The Diamond B is important. Never

doubt that for a moment. It's so important they hired the very best man to manage it that they could find. Alexander Jessup."

"Now they have the best in Edana."

Edana thought of the kiss she'd given him, and dipped her chin so no one could see her blush. "I thank you again, Mr. Bonner."

"I need a day or so to think," Wells said. "I'd like to look around the ranch tomorrow, perhaps have someone take me out on the range."

"I'll take you myself," Neal said.

"Once I've formulated my thoughts and made a decision, you'll be the first to know," Wells told Edana. "But, even if I decide you *are* the one for the job, I still must convince the consortium."

"Would it help if I went back with you and presented myself to them directly?" Edana proposed.

"That's difficult to say. They don't know you as well as I do. To some of them it might seem as if you're presuming too much."

"I know I can do this," Edana declared.

"I'm inclined to believe you." Wells finished his coffee in a couple of gulps. "If you don't mind, I'd like to turn in early. It's been a long day and I didn't get much sleep last night with all the bouncing around the stage did." He rose tiredly. "I will say this,

Edana. You have a lot in your favor. Were you a man, I suspect I wouldn't hesitate at all in endorsing you."

"Women are second-class, are they?"

"In my mind, no. But a lot of men think differently. They believe that a woman's place is in the home, not overseeing a business enterprise on the scale of the Diamond B."

"Ah yes. Hearth and home and kids and cooking and sewing. The woman's world," Edana said with a tinge of bitterness.

"It's just how things are."

"Maybe it's time they changed," Edana said. "In Wyoming, women even have the right to vote."

Wells grinned. "So I've heard. If the consortium were made up of cowboys, you'd be a shoo-in." He nodded at Neal and walked off. "See you both in the morning."

"Well," Edana said.

Neal refilled his cup.

"I can't tell you how it feels to have my fate in the hands of men I don't even know. My entire future rests on their decision."

"Not all of it," Neal said. "Some rests on your own."

Edana looked over. "Oh?"

"That kiss," Neal said, "and what you told me in the parlor."

"I suppose we should settle that here and now. I have enough to worry about without our relationship hanging over my head, as well." Edana took a long breath. "Where do we stand, you and I? *Is* there a you and I, or am I deluding myself?"

"Before we go on, keep somethin' in mind," Neal said. "Folks say that cowboys are a mite shy around women, and we are. Especially ladies like yourself. So if I act tongue-tied, it's only because I am."

Edana smiled. "You have no reason whatsoever to be shy around me. We've been together for weeks now and you've been perfectly fine."

"That was ranch business," Neal said. "This is personal."

"Keep your answers short, if that will help. But I need to know. What are your feelings about me?"

"I like you."

"Is that all?"

"What more do you want?"

"I want more than 'like,' " Edana said. "I want to know if you care for me as much as I care for you. Because I'll tell you right now, I feel for you as I've never felt for any man."

Neal looked away.

Edana felt a clutch of fear. Here she was,

baring her heart, and it had never occurred to her that he might not feel as deeply for her as she felt for him. "It wasn't something I planned. It just happened."

Neal didn't say anything.

"I might be making a fool of myself, but I don't care. I have to get this out while I still can. I'm not my sister. Isolda is much more frank than I am. Much more honest with herself."

Still looking out the window, Neal said, "You're as honest as the year is long."

"I like to think I am," Edana said. "And except when it comes to my feelings, that's true. A woman often hides how she feels, even from herself. I've hidden mine for a while now." She decided to let it all out, come what may. "I was attracted to you from the start. I tried telling myself it was only because you're so easy on the eyes. But it was more than that. You stirred me. You got into my heart. The first couple of weeks I put up a wall. I wouldn't let myself admit how I truly felt. But bit by bit that wall eroded away until now I'm sitting here spilling my heart to you, and I'm scared to death."

Neal turned to her. "Scared?"

"Do you realize what it takes for me to admit all this? I'm scared that I'm throwing myself at you and you won't want me. I'm scared I'm being foolish. I've never been as afraid of anything in my life as I am of what you'll say to me when I'm done baring my soul."

"That works both ways."

"How so?" Edana said.

"I'm scared, too. I'm not Beaumont Adams. I'm not a ladies' man. Words don't come easy to me. Especially when it involves women. And most especially when it involves a woman I reckon is the finest I ever came across."

"Oh." Edana wanted to say more, but it suddenly felt as if she had a lump in her throat.

"Since you're bein' so honest with me, I'll be honest with you." Neal reached across and placed his hand on hers. "I'd be honored if you'd let me court you. And after we've been at it awhile, when we both feel the time is right, I'll get down on my knee and ask you to be my wife."

"Why wait?" came out of Edana's mouth unbidden. She tried to stop herself from saying it but couldn't.

Neal blinked. "Pardon?"

Edana got the next out before she changed her mind. "How long would you court me? Three months? Six months? A year? Why wait, when we've both just admitted we care for each other? Why don't we send for a parson and get it over with? We can be man and wife by the end of the month, and run the Diamond B together."

"Ain't that kind of suddenlike?"

"Some might say so. But so what? Will the outcome be any different six months or a year from now? I'll want you as much then as I want you now."

"You don't know that."

"To the contrary. I've never been more sure of anything in my life. And if I learned anything from my father, it's that when you want something, you go after it. You don't twiddle your thumbs."

"That's for business."

"And for our personal lives, too." Edana squeezed his hand. "I fail to see the sense in my spending the next half a year alone in this big house wishing you were with me, while you're down at the bunkhouse wishing you were up here with me, too."

"But by the end of the month?"

"You'd rather not? You'd rather wait? I'll abide by whatever you want. But if I have a vote, I'd marry you tomorrow. So there."

"Lord in heaven."

"I'm sorry. Have I shocked you?"

"No," Neal said. "It's the wonder of it all.

You. Me. Together. I've dreamed of that happenin', but it doesn't seem real."

"Let's make it real. Let's send for that parson."

Pulling his hand from under hers, Neal stood and stepped to the window. "Life sure does beat all."

"What do you keeping looking at out there?" Edana asked.

"My past."

"We should be looking to the future," Edana said. "To our life as man and wife. Our pasts only count insofar as they've brought us together."

"Our pasts are part of who we are. But you're right about the rest." Abruptly turning, Neal came around the kitchen table, set his hat on it, and sank to one knee. Taking her hand in both of his, he ran a finger over her knuckles. "I can't hardly believe I'm doin' this."

Edana grappled with a sudden spike of indecision. She'd put him up to it, but now that the moment of truth had come, a small part of her balked. A tiny voice at the back of her mind warned that she was being too forward, that she was making a mistake, that she should pull her hand free and tell him she needed more time to think about it. Instead she just sat there.

"Edana Jessup," Neal said formally, "would you like to be my missus?"

Edana was trying not to be emotional, but she felt her eyes brim with tears. "Oh, Neal."

"Is that a yes or a no?"

Impulsively throwing her arms around him, Edana pressed her face to his shoulder. "Yes, yes, a thousand times, yes."

"Tarnation," Neal said, and coughed. He gently pried her off, stared longingly into her eyes, then kissed her on the mouth.

"Congratulations, you two."

Startled, Edana pulled back and rose. It bothered her that their special moment hadn't been private. "How long have you been standing there?" she demanded.

Over in the doorway, Franklyn Wells was smiling. "Quite a while. I came back for a glass of water and didn't want to intrude."

"I'd be grateful if you'd keep it to yourself for the time bein'," Neal said, standing. "I'd like to be the one the hands hear it from."

"I understand." Wells entered and went to the counter and the water pitcher. "Congratulations, my dear. A brilliant stroke, if I say so myself."

"Romantic, maybe," Edana said, "but hardly that."

"Don't you realize what you've done?"

"I've agreed to be his wife."

"Oh, much more than that." Wells took a glass from the cupboard. "You've ensured that the consortium will agree to keep you on."

Edana didn't try to conceal her confusion. "I have?"

"Don't you see? It's not just you now." Wells chuckled. "They'll be getting two for the price of one, as the saying goes. Any objection they might have had to allowing a woman to manage the ranch will fall by the wayside. It won't take much for me to convince them that the newly married Mr. and Mrs. Bonner are perfectly suitable to run the Diamond B."

"That's not why I'm doing it."

"I believe you. Permit me to be the first to congratulate the pair of you on your impending nuptials."

Neal clasped Edana's hand, looking happier than she'd ever seen him look. "Nothin' can stop us now, Mrs. Bonner."

"I sure hope not," Edana said.

31

Beaumont Adams woke at his usual time. Rolling over, he rose onto his elbow and admired the profile of the beauty sleeping next to him. He was tempted to caress her but didn't want to wake her. They'd been up until the small hours of the morning. The memory of it filled him with pleasure.

"You're staring at me again."

"I can't help it," Beaumont said. "There are days I want to pinch myself to make sure you're not a figment of my imagination."

"Not that again." Isolda cracked an eye. "I'm real and I'm yours for as long as you stay true to me."

"A match made in heaven."

"Or hell," Isolda said.

Beaumont sat up. "Is that any way to talk? Things couldn't be better. The election is comin' up. The new hotel is comin' along nicely. We're makin' more money than we know what to do with and —"

Isolda cut him off. "Oh, I know what to do with it. We use it to take over more business and start up new ones. Which reminds me. What about the feed-and-grain?"

"Jensen still refuses to sell. I've been over to talk to him twice, but he's a stubborn cuss."

"We'll go together later," Isolda said. Sliding out of bed, she stretched. She was standing in a shaft of sunlight from their bedroom window, and her lacy nightdress hid little.

"You make my mouth water," Beaumont said.

"You men. It's true what they say. You always want more."

Beaumont stood and donned his robe. He liked this part of the day. They always had a leisurely breakfast together. The rest of the time they were so busy they seldom got to relax.

"How about pancakes this morning?" Isolda asked.

"So long as we have that maple syrup I like. Which reminds me. Why don't you let me hire a cook and maybe a maid while I'm at it?"

"I've never minded cooking," Isolda said. "It's one of the few domestic duties I don't object to."

Beaumont grinned at the notion of her

being domesticated. She was about as tame as a wildcat. Only she hid her wildness from everyone save him.

They were descending the stairs when someone commenced to pound on their front door as if fit to break it down.

"Who can that be?" Isolda wondered.

Taking his derringer from his robe pocket, Beaumont went to the door and peered out. "It's your spy."

Stumpy jerked his hat off his head and showed his yellow teeth. "How do, ma'am?" he said. "And to you, too, Mr. Adams."

Isolda was frowning. "You're supposed to report to me at the Three Aces. Not here. I told you before that I don't want to chance someone from the Diamond B seeing us together."

"This is important," Stumpy said. "I reckoned you wouldn't mind just this once."

Fidgeting with excitement, he shifted his weight from his good foot to his peg leg. "Or have you already gotten an invite?"

"To what?" Isolda said.

"Why, to your sister's weddin', of course. She and Neal Bonner are gettin' hitched."

Beaumont had never seen his new love struck speechless. She looked so comical he almost laughed.

"That's right," Stumpy said, bobbing his

head. "Neal broke the news to the punchers in the cookhouse last night. You'd have thought he was walkin' on air, he was so blamed happy."

"When is the big event?" Beaumont inquired.

"The end of the month. But I figured you'd want to know right away, Miss Jessup."

Isolda had recovered her composure. "You did the right thing, Stumpy. There will be a bonus for you this week. Now hustle off before a cowboy from the ranch happens by."

"Yes, ma'am." Stumpy jammed his hat on. "Oh. One other thing. Word is, your sister and Neal expect to run the ranch as your pa was goin' to do." He smiled and clomped off.

"If I'd had a feather, I could have knocked you over," Beaumont said as he closed the door.

"My dear, wonderful Edana," Isolda said, talking to herself, not to him. "Father must be rolling over in his grave. His body is barely cold and you're taking that cowboy for better or for worse."

"You've taken me," Beaumont said.

Isolda gave a slight start. "Why, so I have. Only she's doing everything prim and proper."

Beaumont didn't know what to make of her troubled expression. "We can do it prim and proper, too."

"No. I've made my bed and I'll lie in it." Isolda laughed a short, cold laugh and made toward the kitchen as if she were mad.

"What's wrong, darlin'?" Beaumont sometimes found it hard to follow her train of thought.

Isolda didn't answer.

Taking a seat at the table, Beaumont drummed his fingers. He wasn't fond of being ignored. When she took out a pan and banged it on the stove, he decided enough was enough. "Didn't we agree there'd be no secrets between us?"

"It wasn't bad enough she was my father's favorite," Isolda said bitterly. "Things continue to break her way after he's gone."

"I thought the two of you were close."

"We got along, for his sake," Isolda said. "But we were never the best of friends." She got a bowl out. "Where our father was concerned, I was always second fiddle."

That was all Beaumont could get out of her. She clammed up. She was still in a foul mood when they left the house an hour later for the feed-and-grain. She brought her parasol along.

They stopped at the Three Aces and Beaumont was taken aback when Isolda told Dyson and Stimms that they were to tag along. They looked at him as if to ask whether they should take orders from her, and he nodded.

Ira Jensen was counting inventory in a back corner of the store when they walked in. A short, balding man, he'd opened the feed-and-grain a couple of months ago, and as the only one in town, he was doing brisk business. He heard their footsteps, turned, and scowled. "Not you again," he said to Beaumont. "I've made it as clear as I can that I have no intention of selling."

Beaumont was prepared to haggle as long as it took, but his partner had other ideas.

"You're dealing with me now, not Mr. Adams," Isolda said.

"And who are you?" Jensen asked.

"Apparently you don't keep current on local events," Isolda said. "Be that as it may, I'm tendering our final offer. Sell to us at the fair price Mr. Adams quoted, or before this day is out, you'll disappear from the face of the earth."

Beaumont glanced at her in consternation.

"What?" Jensen said.

"You heard me," Isolda said. "We're done trying to be reasonable." She gestured at Stimms, at his big Sharps. "Point that at Mr. Jensen's face."

Stimms didn't look at Beaumont for approval. He raised his rifle to his shoulder, the muzzle inches from Jensen's nose.

"Now, see here! You can't treat me like this."

"Cock it," Isolda said.

Grinning mightily, Stimms did.

Ira Jensen paled. But he wasn't a coward. "Lower that thing this instant, do you hear me? I'll report all of you to the law if you don't leave this instant."

"The nearest federal marshal is hundreds of miles away," Isolda said. "You'd never reach him. The moment we leave, I'm having someone keep an eye on you twenty-four hours of the day until you've sold to us and packed and left."

Jensen appealed to Beaumont. "Why don't you say something?"

"What the lady wants, she gets," Beaumont said, enlightening him.

"You can't force people to sell out against their will. It's not right."

"From your point of view, no," Isolda said, "but it's perfectly right for me. I won't have my will thwarted. Be at the Three Aces in

377

an hour and we'll finalize the sale. Tell no one about our visit. Should word get back to me that you couldn't keep your mouth shut, I'll have it shut permanently."

"You're despicable," Jensen declared.

"Stimms, if he insults me again, squeeze the trigger."

"Yes, ma'am. Glad to."

Jensen seemed to fold in on himself in defeat. His shoulders sagged and he lowered his arms and said in a small voice, "I'll be at the Three Aces in an hour."

"Excellent." Isolda brightened and turned. "Gentlemen," she said, and promenaded out, twirling her parasol. Once they were outside, she stopped. "Dyson, keep watch on him from across the street. If he does anything suspicious, come tell us."

"Will do, ma'am." Dyson headed across.

Isolda wasn't done. "Stimms, go to the stable. Tell the stableman that if Jensen tries to hire a horse in the next hour, he's to say he doesn't have one available and to let us know."

"On my way, ma'am," Stimms said, and left.

Looping her arm in Beaumont's, Isolda said happily, "That went well."

"You're givin' my men orders now?"

"*Our* men," Isolda said. "We might not

have done it proper, as my sister is doing, but what's mine is yours and yours is mine. Isn't that right?"

"I did say that, yes."

"Then why the hound-dog look? Things are going exactly as we want them to go."

"There are days when I'm in awe of you," Beaumont said.

"There are days when I'm in awe of myself," Isolda replied. "I'm able to be who I truly am for the first time in my life, and do you know what?"

"Tell me."

"I love it, Beau." Isolda gazed up and down Main Street. "This town is going to be ours, and no one had better try to stand in our way."

Whiskey Flats held the election on a sunny Tuesday. By Isolda's calculations, barely twenty percent of the population bothered to vote. Of that twenty, more than half were customers of Beaumont's three saloons eager to enjoy the free drink they'd been promised.

Beaumont won in a landslide. His first order of business was to pin a marshal's badge on Scar Wratner. Wratner, in turn, pinned deputy badges on Dyson, Stimms, Grat, and Tuck.

The celebration at the Three Aces continued well past midnight. Beaumont had gotten hold of some champagne, and they sat at his table drinking and making merry.

Isolda drank as if it were water. She was on her third bottle when she happened to glance over at the crowded bar and noticed a pair of cowboys at the near end. "Who are those two?" she asked, pointing.

Beaumont had his hat pushed back on his head and his chair tilted. "They're cowboys from the Diamond B."

"I know that much," Isolda said. "I don't think I was ever told their names."

"The young one is Billy and his pard is called Yeager. They've been in here plenty of times."

Isolda turned to Dyson. "Bring them over, would you? Be nice about it."

"What are you up to?" Beaumont said.

"This doesn't concern you." Isolda fluffed her hair and folded her hands in front of her. Bestowing her friendliest smile, she greeted them. "Billy! Mr. Yeager! What a delight to see you again."

The cowpokes had removed their hats. Billy shuffled his feet and said, "It's nice to see you again, too, Miss Jessup."

"Join us, why don't you?" Isolda said, motioning at empty chairs.

They were too polite to refuse. Both roosted as if they were sitting on bits of glass.

"This is some blowout you're havin', ma'am," Yeager remarked.

"Isn't it, though?" Isolda said. She slid a bottle toward them. "Have some, if you'd like."

"We're obliged," Billy said. "It's right kind of you."

"Think nothing of it," Isolda said, and then got to why she'd invited them over. "Tell me. How is my sister doing these days?"

Billy was the talkative one. He beamed and said, "Oh, she's doin' fine. Word is she's buzzin' around like a bee, gettin' ready for the weddin'. You're comin', aren't you? We heard you were invited."

"I wouldn't miss it for the world," Isolda said.

Billy drank and grinned. "Neal and her are a good pair. We'll have two big sugars instead of one."

"The hands don't mind having a woman for their boss?"

"Not at all," Billy said. "We'd do anything for her. She's the greatest gal, ever."

"You don't say."

"She'll be queen of the ranch, and that's

no lie." Billy chuckled.

"That should suit my dear sister just fine," Isolda said. "She's always seen herself as one."

"If you'd stuck around, you could have been her helper, like she was with your pa," Billy said.

Isolda resisted an urge to pick up the bottle and hit him over the head with it. "I help myself these days."

"Well, good for you, ma'am."

"Yes," Isolda said, "isn't it?" She went on. "Has she mentioned me at all to either of you?"

"We don't get to talk to her much, ma'am," Billy said.

"Not hardly ever," Yeager said. "Even when we're with her, Neal does most of the talkin'."

"What does Mr. Bonner say about me, pray tell?"

Billy shrugged. "Oh, I recollect him sayin' once that it's a shame you didn't stick around, although things sure worked out fine for Edana."

"Didn't they, though?" Isolda said.

Billy surprised her with the observation that "The important thing is that you're both happy, you and your sis. She likes what she's doin' and you must like what you're doin' or you wouldn't be doin' it."

"Why, William, you're a philosopher."

"If I am, it's news to me."

"I like what I'm doing so much I intend to do a lot more of it," Isolda informed him. "In fact, in a very short while, you shouldn't be surprised to hear that I've become a queen in my own right, as it were."

"Two queens?" Billy said, and laughed. "Ain't that somethin'?"

"As someone I'm very fond of likes to say," Isolda said, "it should prove interesting."

32

The time rushed by.

Edana had her dress made by a woman who had opened a millinery in Whiskey Flats. She would have liked to fashion the dress herself, but she had no time for sewing and stitching with all the other things she had to do.

Early on, Edana sent word to her sister, through Stumpy, that she would be grateful if Isolda would come out to the ranch and assist with the preparations. Stump returned to inform her that Isolda "respectfully declined," as Stumpy quoted Isolda, because she was too busy.

It hurt Edana's feelings. She'd always thought she could rely on Isolda. But with her typical industriousness, she barreled on. She asked the woman who ran Ma's, Mrs. Ferguson, if she would cater the wedding. Mrs. Ferguson asked how many guests Edana expected and Edana estimated over a hundred. At that, Mrs. Ferguson balked, saying she couldn't possibly provide food for so many. Neal, who was listening, mentioned that they could slaughter a few beeves for the occasion. Problem solved.

Every hand on the ranch was invited. Edana also had invitations delivered to a score of businessmen and others in town, including the new mayor and the new marshal.

"I don't know as I like the notion of Scar Wratner comin'," Neal remarked when she mentioned it.

"What harm can it do?" Edana rejoined. "He's the law now. He'll be on his best behavior. And it might result in some goodwill between him and us."

"If you say so," Neal said skeptically.

For weeks Edana hardly got any rest. There were never enough hours in the day. With only three more to go until the grand event, she sat in the kitchen sipping tea to relax, when in jangled her betrothed.

Neal kissed her on the cheek and claimed a chair. "How was your day, Mrs. Bonner?"

"Hectic," Edana said. "And you shouldn't call me that until after the wedding."

"I'm gettin' in practice," Neal teased.

"How was your day?"

"We found another steer."

Edana felt a flash of anger. "The cow killer?" That was what she'd taken to calling whoever was responsible for shooting their cattle. "How many does that make?"

"Seven that we know of," Neal answered. "There's probably more we haven't found."

"Who can be doing this?"

"I sent Jericho out. He took Billy and Yeager and they followed the tracks of a shod horse for about half a mile, then lost the trail on some shale."

"They always lose it."

"It's not their fault," Neal said. "I've said it before and I'll say it again. Whoever is shootin' our critters knows this country a heap better than we do."

"You still don't think it's an Indian?"

"It could be a warrior who stole a white man's horse," Neal said, "but my gut tells me it ain't."

"Our punchers haven't seen any strangers on our range?"

"Not a one. But if he keeps at it, sooner or later his luck will run out."

"I hope sooner. I'm starting to take this personally."

"I have from the start." Neal gave his head a slight toss. "Enough of him. How are you holdin' up? You look a little frazzled."

"I can't wait for it to be over. To be

husband and wife. To start our new life together in earnest."

"Maybe you should sleep in tomorrow. Catch up on your rest."

"I have too much to do." Edana sipped her tea and relished the minty flavor. "Mrs. Ferguson is bringing out some of the things she'll need and setting up in the kitchen. And the dressmaker is bringing my dress for a final inspection."

"Are you sorry you said you will?" Neal joked.

"Never in a million years." Setting her cup down, Edana stood and went around the table. "Push your chair back."

Puzzled, Neal did.

Edana sat in his lap and draped her arm over his broad shoulders. "This is more comfortable."

Neal coughed.

Laughing, Edana kissed his cheek and his chin. "Look at you. I hope you won't be this embarrassed on our wedding night."

"Oh, Edana," Neal said.

She rested her cheek on his shoulder and closed her eyes. "I'm so tired I could fall asleep right here."

"You've had too much to do for one person," Neal remarked. "It's a shame your sister wouldn't help."

"I'm worried about her."

Neal shifted and put his arm around her waist. "Is it that gambler she's taken up with? They say he goes around like God Almighty these days. He can shoot, too."

"The shooting's not important," Edana said. "Or even his profession. It's that she's living with him out of wedlock. Our mother raised us to be ladies, not . . ." She couldn't bring herself to finish.

"Not live below the tracks?" Neal said. "Where?"

"In some train towns they keep the saloons and such south of the tracks, so they won't disturb the good folks who live north of them."

"That's one way of putting it," Edana said. "I admit I'm disappointed. But she's a grown woman and can do as she pleases."

"Did you ask her to be your maid of honor like you were goin' to?"

"I did, and she accepted," Edana said. "She'll do that much for me, at least."

"There. You see? She does care."

"I hope so," Edana said sincerely. "I would hate for the two of us to ever be at odds."

The big day came.

The wedding was slated for one in the afternoon. That way, guests from town could leave early in the morning and be at the ranch in plenty of time. It also allowed for travel time back to town before dark.

Edana didn't sleep well the night before. She blamed it on ordinary jitters. It certainly wasn't because she was having second thoughts. She entertained no doubts whatsoever that marrying Neal was the right thing to do.

Isolda had arrived earlier that evening, with Beaumont Adams. She'd accepted Edana's offer to stay over, which pleased Edana greatly. It bothered her, though, that when they embraced in greeting, her sister was aloof, almost cold.

"It's so wonderful to see you again." Edana sought to rekindle their sisterly affection.

"I wouldn't miss your wedding for the world," Isolda said.

Edana had been somewhat relieved to hear that Marshal Wratner wasn't attending. When she asked why, Beaumont responded, "Someone has to watch over our town for us while we're gone."

Now, unable to sleep, Edana lay on her back staring at the ceiling and recalled the gambler's comment. The rumors were true. Her sister and her sister's lover saw themselves as the town's lords and masters.

Beaumont was already mayor. What next?

Did it even matter? Edana asked herself. The answer was no. She wished her sister the best in whatever she did, but it was no concern of hers. She had the ranch, and Neal, and their new life together.

Edana was so deep in thought she almost missed hearing the rooster crow. Sitting up, she shrugged into her robe and moved to the window. Stars sparkled overhead, but to the east the sky was brightening.

It wouldn't be long before others were up.

Hurrying out, Edana headed downstairs. She'd like a cup of coffee to start her day. It wouldn't take long to fix, and she could take it back to her room before anyone was about.

The parlor was dark, but the kitchen was bathed in a rosy glow. She was halfway along the hall when she smelled a familiar aroma. Someone had had the same idea and beat her to it.

Edana figured it might be Mrs. Ferguson, but she was mistaken. "You," she blurted without thinking.

Over at the cupboard, bundled in a robe of her own, Isolda was taking down a cup and saucer. "Good morning to you, too," she said.

"Sorry," Edana said. "I didn't get much sleep."

"Me, either," Isolda said.

"Anxious about the wedding?"

"Why would I be? You're the one getting married." Isolda stepped to the stove, touched the top of the coffeepot, and carried it to the counter. "I couldn't sleep because this house reminds me too much of Father. It was the last place I saw him, the last place I spoke to him."

Edana found that touching, and said so.

"There you go again. Reading more into things than there is."

"You don't miss him?" Edana said. "I do. There isn't an hour that goes by that I don't think of him."

Isolda turned and sipped her coffee. "I try not to."

Shocked at her callousness, Edana said, "You don't mean that."

"I most certainly do. If he were still alive, I'd probably still be living here, stuck doing work I didn't enjoy, and miserable as hell."

"No need to swear," Edana said.

"But I like to now and then," Isolda said. "With him gone, I can indulge my every heart's desire."

Edana regarded her with dismay. "Where did all this come from? You're not the sister

I grew up with."

"Oh, but I am," Isolda said cheerfully. "I'm more me than I've ever been and loving every minute of it." She smiled and ambled out.

Edana thought about that all morning. She tried not to. She tried to dwell on Neal and their nuptials, but her sister's statement deeply disturbed her. Isolda had gone from a bookkeeper who spent her days with her nose buried in ledgers, to . . . what exactly?

She almost came right out and asked when Isolda showed up to help her dress.

She decided not to. Today, of all days, there should be no spats between them. They would get along as sisters should.

It took an hour and a half for Edana to get ready.

The years sloughed away, their loss was put aside, and for ninety minutes the two of them were girls again, joking and laughing as they had done when they were little. They reminisced about the time Isolda got her hair caught in the fireplace grate, and the time Edana fell down the cellar stairs and fractured her leg, and the water fights they used to have in the summers when they'd take two glasses and fill a bucket and throw water at each other until they were soaked clean through.

Then came the moment when Edana stood in front of the full-length mirror while Isolda adjusted her veil.

"Thank you for your help," Edana said.

Isolda stepped back. She stared at Edana's reflection, her features hardening, and said with more than a trace of bitterness, "Look at you."

"Is something out of place?"

"You look perfect," Isolda said. Suddenly turning away, she said, "I'll see you downstairs."

"Wait," Edana said, but the door closed behind Isolda, and she was alone.

Bewildered, she tried to make sense of her sister's behavior. The only conclusion she could come to was that Isolda resented her getting married. But that was ridiculous.

The momentous event arrived, the guests assembled on the front lawn. The ceremony was to take place on the front porch where the overhang would shield the parson and the bridge and groom from the worst of the midday sun.

Edana had no aisle to walk down, and didn't want one. Without her father to give her away, what did it matter? Isolda ushered her outside, and there was Neal, dressed in a new store-bought suit. To her eyes he looked positively handsome.

Jericho was best man. He wore his usual clothes, his usual black hat. On his hip was his pearl-handled Colt.

Edana thought that was uncalled for, but she didn't make an issue of it. She stood at Neal's side, proud and straight and nearly overcome with joy, and when the time came for her "I do," she said it willingly and gladly and without reservation.

"You may kiss the bride," the parson intoned.

Neal surprised her. Where previous to this he had always been timid about showing affection, now he scooped her into his arms and planted a kiss that literally took her breath away.

Jericho distracted her by chuckling. She'd never heard him chuckle before.

Then people were whooping and clapping and some of the cowboys fired their six-shooters into the air.

Neal let out a yip of his own and scooped her into his arms. There would be no honeymoon. Not then, anyway. They'd decided to hold off until later in the year, when things slowed down.

Jericho opened the door so they could go in and she could cut the cake.

Smiling and returning the waves of the well-wishers, Edana felt her happiness suddenly shattered when she saw her sister glaring at her. Before Edana could call out and ask what the matter was, Neal whisked her indoors.

Something was wrong, terribly wrong, and for the life of her, Edana had no idea what it might be. She personally carried a piece of cake out to give Isolda and question her, and was stunned to find out that her sister and the gambler had already left for town.

Edana didn't know what to make of it. One thing she knew, though. It didn't bode well.

It didn't bode well at all.

33

Three months later

When Holland wasn't breaking broncs, he worked the range like the rest of the hands.

On a crisp autumn morning he was twenty miles from the home ranch, searching for strays in a rugged area of mostly rock and sandstone, when he heard a shot. Several bluffs caused an echo. Reining up, he cocked his head, trying to pinpoint the direction. He hoped there would be another, but there wasn't.

Gigging his horse, Holland trotted to a tract of spires and slabs. He wound through them cautiously.

Beyond stretched a flat dotted with scrub brush and mesquite. And there, out in the middle, lay a steer.

And the man who had shot it.

Holland drew rein. The shooter apparently hadn't heard him, and was intent on cutting meat from the body. Sliding his Colt from its holster, Holland cocked it. He was no gun hand. Like most cowboys, he regarded his revolver as just another tool of his trade. He'd killed a few rattlers with it and once he shot a rabbit for the supper pot, but that was all. Scarcely breathing, he moved his horse forward at a walk. He needed to be closer to be sure of not missing.

The cow killer wore a floppy hat that had seen a lot of use and, of all things, an old bear-hide coat. Hunkered down, he was slicing away with a bowie. His back was partly to Holland, and the bronc buster couldn't see the man's face.

Then the man's horse, a paint with a saddle but no bedroll or saddlebags, raised its head and pricked its ears in Holland's direction, and whinnied.

Instantly the cow killer stood and whirled. He looked to be as old as his hat and his coat, and had a mane of gray hair. Bending, he scooped a rifle off the ground, shoved the bowie into a sheath, and vaulted onto the paint with an agility that belied his years.

"Hold it right there, mister!" Holland hollered.

The cow killer did no such thing. Reining around, he flew to the north.

With a jab of his spurs, Holland gave chase. He extended his Colt but didn't shoot. He might hit the horse and he never, ever harmed a horse if he could help it.

That paint could move. Raising swirls of dust, it reached the other side of the flat and started up a rise.

Holland wasn't expecting the cow killer to turn on him, but that's exactly what the man did. Suddenly reining broadside and stopping, the man jerked his rifle to his shoulder. A Sharps, unless Holland was mistaken. No sooner had that registered than the Sharps boomed and it felt as if a sledgehammer had struck Holland in the shoulder. The impact lifted him from his saddle and sent him crashing to earth. He lost his six-shooter and his hat, and lay dazed in a welter of pain.

Shock began to set in.

Holland fought it. He was bleeding, bleeding badly, and if he passed out, he might never wake up.

Belatedly, Holland became aware of slow hoofbeats. Struggling to stay conscious, he blinked up into the glare of the sun. Without warning, it was blocked out by the cow killer and the paint.

The man pointed the Sharps. "Did you do it?"

"Do what?" Holland gasped in confusion.

"Did you kill him? Were you the one?"

"Mister," Holland got out. "I've never killed anybody in my life."

The cow killer bent down. He had gray eyes to match his gray hair, and there was a fierce glint to them. "I reckon I believe you. You get to live. Tell them others I'll find the one who did, and when I do, there'll be hell to pay." With that he straightened and reined around.

"Wait," Holland called out.

The drum of the paint's hooves faded.

With an effort, Holland rose onto his elbows. The cow killer was just going over the rise. "Hold on!" Holland tried again, but it was no use.

Gritting his teeth, Holland sat up. He saw his hat and jammed it on his head, and his Colt and jammed that in his holster. His horse had gone another dozen yards and stopped. He tried to whistle, but his mouth was too dry. Swallowing a few times, he tried again, and the roan returned, as he'd taught it. He snagged a stirrup and with considerable difficulty managed to pull himself to his feet. Leaning against the roan to keep from falling, he gripped the saddle horn with his good arm and attempted to pull himself onto his saddle. He was too weak. More from the shock than anything, he reckoned, and took deep breaths to steady himself.

Holland tried again. This time he got his leg up and over and then sat slumped in the saddle, his head pounding.

His shirt was wet with blood. He had to reach camp and get help.

The ride was a nightmare. He blacked out several times. Each time he expected to wake up on the ground, but somehow he stayed on the roan.

Holland lost all track of time. It could have been an hour, it could have been two, when he saw the wagon and the horse string and several cowboys around the fire.

He tried to call to them, but he couldn't yell loud enough to get their attention. His chest felt numb, and he was light-headed.

He blacked out again.

The next Holland knew, hands were on him, lowering him. He was aware of voices but couldn't make out what they were saying. A face floated above him, a face he should know but couldn't seem to place. As if from down a long tunnel, a voice reached him.

". . . did this to you, Holland? Who shot you?"

"The cow killer," Holland croaked. "Fetch Neal."

Blackness devoured him.

Neal Bonner was on the front porch with Edana in matching rocking chairs, enjoying the spectacle of the setting sun.

"This is one of my favorite times of the day," Edana remarked. "All the work is done and we can be together."

It was one of Neal's favorite times, too. He liked quiet moments with her, just the two of them and no one else.

Neal had never imagined married life could be so grand. They got along so well, sometimes it astounded him. He considered himself incredibly lucky to have met a gal like her. That she'd cared for him enough to marry him was a miracle.

"Who can that be in such a hurry?"

Neal looked in the direction Edana was gazing. A puncher was coming from the north, riding hell-bent, lashing his horse with his reins in a way a cowboy would only do in an emergency. "Trouble," he said, and was off the porch waiting when the puncher galloped up and came to a sliding stop.

"Neal!" the hand exclaimed. His name was Aldon. "It's the cow killer."

"He's shot another steer?"

"And Holland, too."

Edana gasped.

"Is he . . . ?" Neal said.

"He almost was," Aldon said. "He'd lost a lot of blood, but we managed to pull him through. He's weak as a kitten and can't be moved, but he'll live."

"Thank the Lord," Edana said.

Neal barked orders. He told Aldon to go to the bunkhouse and tell Jericho, Billy, and Yeager to saddle their horses and be ready to head out in half an hour. Aldon was to get a fresh horse and lead them back.

Nodding, the puncher clucked to his lathered animal.

"This is terrible, Neal," Edana said. "I should go with you."

"No." Neal turned and went up the porch steps. She caught up with him as he entered their parlor.

"I'll bring bandages. And I have some tincture in the cabinet that helps prevent infection."

"No," Neal said again. He stepped to where he had propped his Winchester a couple of days ago, picked it up, and stuck it under his arm. He turned to go, but Edana planted herself in his path.

"Why are you being so stubborn about this?"

"Do you really need to ask?"

Edana put her hands on her hips. "We run the Diamond B together. We make decisions together. We do things together."

"Not this." Neal started to go around, but she caught hold of his sleeve.

"You're being unreasonable. I want to talk this out."

"There's nothin' to talk about," Neal said. "No means no."

Edana regarded him in baffled hurt and puzzlement. "This is the first time you've ever done anything like this."

"Like what? Puttin' my foot down?"

"You're treating me as if I'm inferior somehow. As if I'm a child who must be protected from herself."

Neal was anxious to get to the stable and saddle up. Instead he grasped her hand and led her to the settee. He bid her sit and she did, but he stayed standing. "First off, when it comes to brains, I'm the one who's inferior, as you put it. You think rings around me, and I'm not ashamed to admit it." She went to respond, but he held up his hand. "I'm not done. As for you bein' a child, that's plumb ridiculous. But you are my wife, and it's a man's duty to look out for his runnin' mate."

"I don't need looking after," Edana said. "I'm perfectly capable of holding my own in a man's world."

"Us men run things? That's news to me." Neal tried to make light of her anger. "Seems to me that women do more of the bossin' than men do."

Edana wasn't amused. "Give me one good reason why you don't want me to come. And I do mean *good.*"

"Have you ever shot anybody?"

"You know I haven't."

"Could you?"

Edana hesitated.

"You see? That could get you killed."

"Nonsense."

Neal was patient with her. "Whoever this cow killer is, he has no qualms about killin' people, too. And when someone is out to shoot you, the only way to stop him is to shoot him first. Hesitate like you just did and you're dead."

"Is that your reason?"

"I care for you too much to let you be hurt, or worse," Neal said. "If that's not good enough, I'm sorry."

"I don't like being treated this way," Edana said. "I don't like it at all."

"Then stay here for my sake."

"Yours?"

"If you come with us, I'll be so worried I won't be able to do my job. We catch up to

404

that cow killer, I'll be thinkin' about you and not what needs doin', and that could get me hurt, or worse."

Edana chewed on her bottom lip, then said, "When you put it that way."

"You'll stay?"

"I will. But just so you know. The next time you want me to do something, ask. Don't order me. Don't boss me around like I'm one of the hands. I'm your wife. I deserve better. I deserve respect."

"There's no one in this whole world I respect more," Neal declared, and bending, he kissed her. "Now if you'll excuse me, Mrs. Bonner, there's a coyote who needs tendin' to."

"Give the bastard hell."

"Oh, Edana."

She laughed.

Neal grinned and was still grinning when he reached the stable. His saddle and saddle blanket were in the tack room. When he led the buttermilk out, Jericho, Billy, Yeager, and Aldon were waiting on their mounts.

Neal nodded and climbed onto the buttermilk. No one said anything as he reined to the north. Edana was on the porch, looking apprehensive. He smiled and waved. She waved, but she didn't smile.

The sun had set and twilight was falling.

The first star had appeared and it wouldn't be long before more did the same.

Jericho brought his zebra dun alongside the buttermilk. "Your missus ain't happy about you goin'?"

"You read minds now?" Neal rejoined.

"She didn't smile."

Neal sighed. "You notice everything, don't you?"

"Try to," Jericho said.

Just then Aldon brought his horse up on Neal's other side. "I almost forgot," he said. "There's more."

"I'm listenin'," Neal said.

"Holland wanted me to be sure to tell you what the cow killer said to him. He reckoned it might be important."

Neal had assumed that the killer shot Holland from a ways off. "They talked?"

"The killer did most of it. He asked Holland if he'd killed somebody. When Holland said he hadn't, the killer rode off."

Neal glanced at Jericho. "Make any sense to you?"

"Not a lick."

They settled down for a long night's ride.

Neal spent the first hour or so thinking about Edana and her sister. Edana hadn't heard from Isolda since the wedding, and she was anxious to go talk to her. He hoped she didn't do it while he was gone.

Midnight came and went. A crescent moon provided enough light to see by, and the wind, for once, was still.

Neal held to a walk in order not to tire the horses more than was necessary. It would take them until almost dawn to get there, and after a short rest, they'd head out again after the killer while his trail was still fresh.

Occasionally a coyote yipped. Once, far off, a wolf howled. Another time, a cougar screamed.

Finally they arrived. All the punchers were up and standing around looking miserable.

Neal's gut clenched when he spied a blanket draped over a body. He had no sooner drawn rein than the punchers converged.

"Holland didn't make it," one said. "We thought he was doin' all right, but he passed away in the middle of the night."

"Well, damn," Billy said.

"I liked that hombre," Yeager said.

"Grab a bite to eat," Neal directed. "We're goin' after the cow killer as soon as the sun is up, and this time we're not givin' up no matter what."

34

The spot where Holland was shot was easy enough to find. They backtracked his horse.

The dead steer lay where it had fallen, its haunch only partially cut away. Flies had swarmed to the feast and rose in a cloud when Neal climbed down.

"Doesn't stink too bad yet," Billy remarked.

"Give it a week," Yeager said.

Jericho didn't say anything.

Neal had left the rest of the hands at the camp. Why put them in danger when there wasn't any need to? was his reasoning. He walked in a circle around the steer and over to where hoofprints led to the north. They were overlaid on tracks coming *from* the north. "He went back the way he came."

"I have a feelin' about this," Billy said. "We might get lucky this time."

"Let's hope," Yeager said.

Without being asked, Jericho assumed the

lead. The tracks were plain enough that a ten-year-old could follow them, for the first mile, at least. Then, as before, the cow killer cut across rocky ground where his horse left little sign. Jericho dismounted and searched on foot. He soon found scrape marks that pointed them to the northwest.

As they resumed their hunt, Neal slid his Winchester from the saddle scabbard, jacked the lever to feed a cartridge into the chamber, and slid the rifle into the scabbard again. He liked being prepared.

Several times Jericho climbed down to examine the ground. In each instance he said, "Lost the trail." And in a minute or two he'd find it again.

Neal curbed his impatience. They mustn't slip up. They'd lost too many steers, and now one of their own.

The sun climbed and so did the temperature.

Jericho never once gave up. He stuck at it with the persistence of a coon hound on a scent.

This was the longest they'd ever been able to follow the killer's trail. Neal was encouraged, if guardedly so. They'd lost the sign too many times before to take anything for granted.

Then they came to a tableland with

patches of green. The tracks pointed up a grassy incline.

Jericho drew rein at the bottom. "I don't like it," he said, scanning the heights. "It's a good spot for an ambush."

"Oh, hell," Billy said. "The cow killer is so used to gettin' clean away, I bet you a dollar he doesn't know we're after him."

"Listen to Jericho, kid," Yeager said. "He's not wet behind the ears, like you."

"Wet, am I?" Billy retorted, and tapped his spurs to his horse. Passing them, he glanced over his shoulder. "See? You're worried over nothin'."

"Billy, wait," Neal said. He trusted Jericho's instincts.

"The last one to the top is a rotten egg," Billy said.

The boom of a heavy-caliber rifle was nearly simultaneous with part of Billy's head exploding in a shower of hair and brains. As if slammed by a battering ram, he was hurled from his saddle and crashed to earth in a heap.

"Hunt cover!" Neal bawled, hauling on his reins. He galloped toward a cluster of boulders, bent low to make less of a target.

The rifle boomed again and a horse squealed in agony.

Yeager's mount had been hit and plunged

into a roll. Yeager kicked free of the stirrups and pushed at the saddle to get clear but didn't make it. The horse came down on top of him. There was the loud crack and crunch of bones, and he cried out. The next moment both he and his mount lay still in the dust, Yeager partly under his animal, his head bent at an angle no head was ever meant to bend.

Neal reached the boulders. Galloping behind one that would shield the buttermilk, he vaulted down, shucked his Winchester, darted to a smaller boulder, and crouched.

Jericho hadn't gone for the boulders. He was racing around the incline to the north, hanging on the offside, Comanche-fashion. In less than a minute he went around a bend and was lost to view.

Taking off his hat, Neal set it at his feet, then cautiously inched his head out.

He saw no one. Nothing moved. He started to pull back and the rifle boomed. The slug struck the boulder not a hand's width from his face, sending sharp slivers into his cheek.

Up above, someone cackled.

"Did I get you, you son of a bitch?"

Neal wasn't disposed to answer until he thought of Jericho, and how it might help

411

him. "Not yet, you murderin' no-account."

"Me?" the man shouted back. "You're the ones who killed him."

"Killed who?"

"The best friend I ever had."

Neal needed to keep the man talking. Cupping his hand to his mouth, he hollered, "What are you talkin' about, mister?"

"As if you don't know."

"If I did, I wouldn't ask." When the man didn't respond, Neal yelled, "If anyone's a killer here, it's you. You've shot I don't know how many steers, and now you've killed three men, besides."

"They had it comin', them and your cows, both. I'd wipe out your whole outfit if I could. Lice meant a lot to me."

"Lice?" Neal repeated in bewilderment. "What does he have to do with this?"

"You murdered him."

Neal thought he had the man pinpointed; the shooter was behind a slab about sixty feet up. "Mister, you're loco. If not for him there wouldn't be a Diamond B."

"I know he sold his place to you. He showed me the money and invited me to go drinkin' with him."

"You and him were pards?"

"Didn't I already say that? Pay attention, you jackass."

Neal was trying to make sense of it all. "You lived with Lice?"

"God, you're dumb," the man replied. "I'm done talkin' to you."

"Who are you?" Neal tried, but the killer didn't answer. Putting his hat back on, he flattened and crawled to a different boulder. He was looking for a way to reach the top without being spotted. He crawled to another, and yet one more, and warily poked his head out.

A gully looked promising. It was deep enough to hide him. To reach it he had to snake across ten feet of open space. Girding himself, he scrambled. He made it without being shot at.

The bottom was littered with rocks. Neal crawled slowly, trying to make as little noise as possible. About halfway up, the gully took a sharp turn. He was almost to it when a gun muzzle was thrust practically in his face.

"So much as twitch and you're dead."

Neal froze. It had never occurred to him that the killer might be working his way down. His Colt was in its holster, his Winchester at his side.

The rest of the rifle appeared, a face pressed to it. The wrinkled face of a man in his sixties, or older, wearing a floppy hat and a bear-hide coat. "I've got you now, you bastard," he gloated.

The man rose onto his knees and told Neal to let go of the Winchester.

With no other choice, Neal did.

"Two fingers," the man said. "Toss the six-gun."

Again, Neal complied. He knew what a Sharps could do. That close, it would blow a hole in him the size of a melon. "Who are you?"

"What the hell do you care, you murderer?"

"You keep sayin' that," Neal said. "But as God is my witness, I'd never have done Lice any harm. I liked the old coot."

"You'd say anything to save your hide," the man said in disgust.

"I'm not that kind."

The old man chewed his lip while studying Neal intently, then gave a toss of his head. "No, you don't. You look honest enough, but looks don't always match the man."

"Mister, if it wasn't for Lice, I wouldn't have the job I do. I wouldn't be married. I wouldn't be the happiest gent alive."

"I almost believe you," the man said.

"Tell me what this is about," Neal said. "You can do that much, can't you?"

"All right. You listen, mister, and you

listen good." The man paused. "I've lived out here pretty near thirty years. I came to get away from folks. I don't like people much. Never have. And since no one else wanted to live in the Badlands, I had them all to myself until Lice came along. I struck up an acquaintance to find out why he settled so far from everywhere, and it turned out he didn't like people much, either. We became friends. I'd visit him now and again. I happened by the day after he sold his place. He couldn't stop grinnin'. He showed me his money and said as how he was goin' into town to celebrate. He invited me to go along, but I declined. I'm not much for hard liquor, and like I said, I don't like to be around a lot of people." He stopped, and scowled.

Neal glimpsed movement above and behind the old frontiersman. "Go on," he urged.

"There's not much more. Except that Lice said he'd had a brainstorm. When he got back from town, he was fixin' to move deeper into the Badlands. Maybe live near me, if I didn't mind. I said hell no, I wouldn't. He rode off and that was the last I seen of him."

"You think he was killed?"

"I know he was! He was supposed to be

back the next mornin', and when he didn't show up the whole day, I rode into town to find out why. I went to the saloon and that gambler fella told me Lice never came for that drink. I said that was peculiar, and the gambler told me it sure was. He wondered how come the fancy city feller and the cowboy who went out to see Lice had come back just a few hours ago grinnin' as if they had a big secret. He told me that he asked how the sale went, and the city feller patted his saddlebags and said they got Lice's place real cheap."

"Beaumont Adams told you that?"

"I never asked his name. But he suspicioned that they'd talked Lice into sellin', paid him the money so he'd sign his place over, then killed him and took the money back."

"And you believed him?"

"It made sense," the old man said. "So when all you cowboys came with your cows, I got back at you the only way I could think of."

"By killin' our cattle," Neal said.

"Now you know all there is," the man said, and pressed his cheek to the Sharps. "Say your prayers, mister. You're about to meet your Maker."

Not a dozen steps behind the old frontiersman, Jericho seemed to rise out of the ground. "Drop the buffalo gun, old-timer."

The old man stiffened and whipped his head around. "Son of a bitch."

"I won't say it twice," Jericho said.

The man glanced at Neal, his face twisted in fury. "Damn all you cowboys, anyhow. You kept me talkin' so he could sneak up on me, didn't you?"

"Just do as he says," Neal said.

"Like hell." The old man spun, but he wasn't halfway around before Jericho fanned his pearl-handled Colt and fired two swift shots from the hip. The old man was jolted onto his bootheels, staggered, and toppled.

Grabbing the Sharps as the man fell, Neal sprang back. He had more questions he wanted to ask, but he would never get to ask them. "Damn."

His Colt still trained on the motionless figure, Jericho came down. "I gave him his chance."

"You did."

"Who was he?"

"He never told me his handle." Neal reclaimed his Colt and his Winchester while Jericho reloaded. "Did you hear what he told me?"

"I did."

They left the old man there and walked

417

down the gully. With Jericho's help, Neal tried to roll the dead animal off Yeager, but the horse was too heavy.

"We'll take Billy's body with us but have to come back with more hands for Yeager's."

"What will you do about the other thing?" Jericho asked.

Neal had already come to a decision about that. "I'm payin' Beaumont Adams a visit."

"I reckon I'll tag along."

"Thought you might." Neal managed to smile. "I'm obliged for savin' my bacon, by the way."

"What are pards for?"

"That old man thought he was avengin' his."

"If he was right about Lice," Jericho said, "the gambler won't like you accusin' him of takin' the money."

"I suspect he won't."

"But you aim to brace him anyway?"

"I do."

"There's liable to be trouble."

"I expect so," Neal said.

"Don't forget he has the law in his pocket, and his own gunnies, besides."

"That he does."

"Then it's root hog or die?"

"It is," Neal said.

35

Neal figured his new wife would understand. He set her down in the kitchen and explained about the old man, and about Lice going missing, and what Beaumont Adams had told Lice's friend. "Tomorrow I'm goin' into town to have a talk with him," he concluded.

"I'm going with you," Edana said.

"No. You're not."

Edana sat back and folded her arms. "Not that again. I let you boss me once. I won't this time."

"Edana —" Neal began.

"Hear me out. This involves me as much as it does you."

"I must have missed that part."

"Oh, really? My sister is living with Beaumont Adams. She'll probably be at his side when you question him. I have every right to be there. I'd like to know if the man she's given her heart to is a scoundrel."

Neal would rather she didn't go. Then again, if both sisters were there, the gambler might be less likely to resort to his hardware. "I reckon you should, at that," he said reluctantly.

That evening they sat on the porch to watch the sun set. It was becoming a tradition. Neal liked how some of the clouds glowed as if they were lit from within. "Right pretty," he said.

Edana wasn't admiring the sky. She was staring absently at the porch, her forehead knit. "There's another reason I want to go with you."

"I'm all ears," Neal said.

"I haven't heard a word from Isolda since the wedding. Several times now I've had Stumpy ask her on my behalf if she'd like to come for supper some evening. She always says she's too busy."

"Doin' what?"

"From what I hear, she and Adams have bought up a lot of businesses, and what with his saloons and all, they're well on their way to becoming rich."

"Good for them," Neal said, trying to sound sincere.

"Mayor Adams is a bit heavy-handed, they say," Edana went on. "With Marshal Wratner to back him, there's nothing he can't do."

"Imagine that."

Edana raised her head. "You don't sound surprised."

"That the bad element in a town takes it over to line their own pockets?" Neal shook his head. "I'm not."

"Bad element," Edana repeated. "That's a good way to describe them. Unfortunately that element includes my sister."

Neal prudently stayed silent.

"Tell me something. You don't expect Adams to admit he killed Lice, do you?"

"Not if he has a brain, he won't."

"Then why confront him? He'll only deny it. Where does that leave you? You can't have him arrested. You don't have any proof. Just the word of a half-crazed old man who went around shooting cattle."

"Scar Wratner wouldn't arrest him, even if I had proof."

"Then I ask you again, what purpose does confronting him serve?"

"I have to do it."

"Explain it to me. I really and truly would like to understand."

Neal pondered how best to do so.

"You hardly knew Lice. You met him only that once."

"True." Neal began to slowly rock. "You're right in that I hardly knew him. But he agreed to sell largely on my say-so that it was the smart thing to do. We wouldn't be sittin' here if not for him."

"I savvy that much, as you would say."

"Franklyn Wells had already hired me to be foreman. I didn't just persuade Lice on my own account. I did it because it was part of my job."

"I get that, too." The lines in Edana's brow deepened. "So you're saying that puts some sort of obligation on you? That you're responsible, in part, for what happened to Lice?"

"Obligation is a good way to put it," Neal said.

"And you always take your obligations seriously."

"I do."

"Then I'll go along with whatever you want."

Neal felt compelled to point out, "Your sister might get mad, me accusin' her sweetheart."

"That's a polite way to describe him," Edana said. "I regard him more as an unsavory character."

"Out here we call them bad men."

"That's a little harsh, isn't it? It's not as if

he's an outlaw."

"He murdered Lice. He shot that saloon owner and those other gents. Maybe you don't see that as bein' outside the law, but I do."

"I didn't say that," Edana said defensively. "It's just that he's so personable and friendly. And he has a wonderful sense of humor."

"Maybe you should be the one livin' with him."

Edana laughed. "No, thank you. I prefer a good man like you."

"That's another thing," Neal said. "Out here, when a good man comes across a bad man doin' wrong, he does somethin' about it."

"You're worrying me."

"It has to be done."

"We should take five or six of the hands along."

"Jericho will do."

"There's safety in numbers, they say."

"And risk a full-blown battle with all those women and kids around?" Neal shook his head.

"It won't come to that, will it? Bloodshed, I mean?"

"That's up to Adams," Neal said.

■ ■ ■ ■

Beaumont had never had it so good. He had a beautiful lady for a partner, he was making money hand over fist, and he was the most powerful person in Whiskey Flats.

Beaumont had taken to being mayor like a cat taking to a bowl of milk. He ate up his newfound respect. Instead of being just another tinhorn, he was now "His Honor, the Mayor." Men doffed their hats to him. Women smiled. His world was roses, and Beaumont couldn't be more pleased. With one exception. A thorn in his side that he couldn't seem to clip.

Now, striding along Main Street with Dyson and Stimms in his wake, Beaumont struggled to control his simmering anger. He came to the marshal's office and barged in without bothering to knock. "What in hell did you think you were doin'?"

Scar Wratner sat at a desk, his boots propped up. His hat was pushed back, and he was drinking Monongahela — straight from the bottle. Tuck sat on a stool, fiddling with a shoehorn. Grat was pinning a wanted poster up over by the window.

Blinking in surprise, Scar let his boots hit the floor. "Howdy to you, too, Mayor," he said sarcastically.

Beaumont walked up to the desk. "I just heard about last night. Damn it, Wratner, you can't keep doin' things like this. It reflects badly on me. On my position as mayor."

"Why, listen to you," Scar sneered. "You sound just like a politician. Doesn't he, boys?"

"Sure does, Scar," Tuck echoed.

"I won't have it, do you hear?" Beaumont said. "Isolda and I have worked too hard to have you spoil things."

"You'd think I'd shot the parson, the way you're carryin' on. All I did was pistol-whip a drunk."

"That drunk was Guthrie, the gent who runs the general store for me. And from what I hear, you did it because you got mad when a dove paid more attention to him than to you."

"She's my dove," Scar said. "It's my saloon."

Beaumont put his hands flat on the desk. "You're only runnin' it for me. And from what I hear, lordin' it over everybody."

"Listen to the kettle callin' the pot black."

Beaumont was mad enough to shoot him. He went to slide his hands into the pockets of his frock coat.

"I wouldn't do that," Scar said, setting the bottle down. "I'm wise to your tricks, remember?"

"I won't have you underminin' me," Beaumont said. "Guthrie is the third hombre you've pistol-whipped since you pinned on that badge. Folks are talkin' behind our backs, sayin' you're unfit to be marshal and I was reckless to appoint you."

"Let them jabber," Scar said. "As if it matters."

"That jabber can get you stripped of your tin," Beaumont said. "People won't abide a rabid law dog."

"I'm foamin' at the mouth now?"

"You might as well be," Beaumont said. "Beatin' unarmed men half to death is stupid."

"I don't like bein' insulted."

"Then you should unplug those ears of yours. I can only protect you so far. Keep it up, and when a citizens' delegation shows up on my doorstep demandin' you be replaced, they'll get their wish."

"So much for backin' my play if you had to," Scar said. "Isn't that what you told me you'd do?"

"Backin' you is one thing," Beaumont said. "Ruinin' things for Isolda and me is another."

"How does the little lady feel about all this?"

"Don't bring her into it," Beaumont said.

"Might as well," Scar replied. "She's the real boss. You don't so much as belch without her say-so."

Beaumont bristled at the suggestion he was tied to Isolda's apron strings. "It's a partnership, damn you."

"Sort of like ours?" Scar said, and laughed.

"You've been warned." Wheeling, Beaumont got out of there before Wratner said something that made him even madder. He was so incensed he stormed up the street with his head down and his fists clenched.

"Boss, look out!" Dyson said.

Beaumont jerked his head up. He'd nearly collided with a mother leading two children by either hand.

"Goodness gracious!" she exclaimed. "You almost walked into us."

Beaumont bestowed his most charming smile, doffed his hat, and bowed. "My abject apologies, madam. I was entirely at fault."

The children looked at him wide-eyed, but the mother smiled and blushed. "That's all right," she said. "No harm done."

Beaumont stepped aside so they could

pass, and when they'd gone by, he replaced his hat and continued on. "That was close."

"I don't reckon I've ever seen you so mad," Dyson said.

"Me, either," Stimms said.

"There are times, gentlemen," Beaumont said, "when I regret pinnin' a star on that jackass."

"You pinned it on him," Dyson said. "You can take it away."

"There's a notion," Beaumont said. One he'd considered the last time Scar pistol-whipped someone. He'd advised Scar not to do it again, but the fool hadn't listened. Beaumont reckoned that the badge was to blame. It had gone to Scar's head. Made Scar think he could get away with just about anything.

Still fuming when he reached the hotel, Beaumont paused to admire the large sign, done in a fine cursive according to Isolda's instructions. B & I HOSTELRY. Isolda said the name had a fancy sound to it. Beaumont didn't care what they called it so long as it made her happy.

The moment he stepped foot in the lobby, the desk clerk came around to ask if he could be of any assistance. Beaumont brushed him off with a wave of his hand and went up the stairs two at a stride.

Dyson and Stimms stayed in the lobby.

The entire top floor consisted of a single suite exclusively for Beaumont and Isolda. She'd seen to the furnishings, everything from Turkish tapestries to a four-poster bed.

Beaumont had never lived in such grand style.

"Isolda?" he called out.

"Over here."

Beaumont veered to the balcony. "A little hot to be out in the sun, isn't it?" He was sweating profusely from his short walk.

Isolda was peering intently down at the far end of the street. "I happened to look out and noticed someone is paying our town a rare visit." She pointed.

Beaumont looked. "I'll be damned."

"My darling sister, her handsome husband, and their gun hand," Isolda said with disdain. "I wonder what brought her in."

"She probably came to see you," Beaumont guessed. "Should we greet them with smiles?"

"Yes, let's," Isolda said. "I can at least pretend to be the courteous hostess. Frankly I look forward to rubbing her nose in how well I'm doing."

"You're all heart, darlin'."

"Aren't I, though?" Isolda said.

They both laughed.

36

Jericho was uneasy but would never admit it to Neal. He branded it a mistake to bring Edana along. Beaumont Adams wouldn't take kindly to the accusation he'd murdered Lice.

Still, Edana was Neal's wife and Neal was his pard, so if Neal wanted to bring her, that was all there was to it.

Jericho said little on the ride into Whiskey Flats. Neither did Neal and Edana, which was unusual. Not until the spreading crop of buildings sprouted in the distance.

"We're almost there." Edana broke her long silence. "I hope my sister won't resent me for this, but I suspect I'm deluding myself."

"It has to be done," Neal said.

"You've made that plain. I'll stand by you, come what may. But I'd like to know. Do you think Mr. Adams will resort to those pistols of his?"

"He might if I came right out and accused him of killin' Lice. But I'm only goin' to tell him what the cow killer said and see how he reacts."

Edana glanced at Neal. "What was his real name again? It feels strange calling someone 'Lice.' "

"McCoy, as I recollect, was his last name," Neal replied. "Jericho, do you remember his first?"

"Isaiah," Jericho said.

"It would be horrible if Mr. Adams killed him."

"Out here," Neal said, "horrible things happen a lot."

Jericho thought of Billy and Yeager and others he had seen bucked out in gore, and said nothing. He focused on the town. People were bustling about, many on foot or horseback, some in buckboards and wagons. It was hard to believe that two years ago Whiskey Flats was a sleepy little nothing in the middle of nowhere. But then, boomtowns always sprang up quickly, whether the boom was the result of gold or silver or cattle.

Jericho placed his hand on his hip close to his Colt. They passed a butcher's and the millinery and other stores and came abreast of the marshal's office.

Grat was staring out the front window. He saw them, stiffened, and said something to someone behind him. In a few moments Tuck appeared, and then Scar Wratner. All three wore tin.

Jericho met their unfriendly stares.

Ahead reared the new hotel. At five stories high, it was the tallest building in Whiskey Flats.

"Stumpy says they have the whole top floor," Neal remarked.

Jericho drew rein and stayed in the saddle while they dismounted and tied their horses to the hitch rail. Only when Neal turned to watch the street did he climb down and do the same with his zebra dun.

"You seem a little tense," Edana said to Neal.

Neal shrugged.

Jericho went up the steps first. Striding into the lobby, he stopped.

Dyson and Stimms were over by the front desk, talking and grinning. Dyson saw Jericho and bent his head to Stimms and the pair turned, Stimms cradling his Sharps.

Dyson plastered a smile on his face and came over. "Mr. and Mrs. Bonner. Ain't this a surprise?"

"I'm here to visit my sister," Edana said.

"And I'd like a few words with your boss,"

Neal said.

Jericho noticed two other men lounging by the far wall. Both wore revolvers high on their hips. He'd never set eyes on them before, but his instincts told him they weren't there for decoration.

Dyson was saying, "I'll run upstairs and let them know you're here."

"That's not necessary," Edana said. "We'd rather just go right up."

"I'm sorry, ma'am, but I'm not supposed to let anyone on the top floor without their say-so," Dyson informed her.

"I hate to put you to any bother," Edana said.

"Go tell them we're here," Neal said.

"It won't take but a minute or two," Dyson said, and made for the stairs.

Jericho shifted so he could see Stimms and the pair by the far wall without having to turn his head.

"We're right popular," Neal said, nodding toward the lobby window.

Tuck had followed them and practically had his bulbous nose pressed to the glass.

"Scar Wratner must have sent him to keep an eye on us," Jericho figured. He was more concerned about Stimms and the pair of gun sharks.

The desk clerk was scribbling in a ledger,

oblivious of everything going on around him. Over in an easy chair, a gentleman in a suit was reading a newspaper.

Jericho noticed that Stimms had his thumb on the Sharps's hammer, ready to cock it. One of the pair by the wall had his thumb hooked in his gun belt an inch from his holster. The other shooter's arm rested on his revolver.

"I should have brought Isolda a gift of some kind," Edana said. "As a token of how much I care for her."

"The next time we come you can bring one," Neal said.

"I know. I'll invite them to the ranch. Say, for supper this weekend. Saturday, so they can stay the night if they'd like and not have to be back in town until Monday morning. Would you mind?"

"Fine by me," Neal said.

Jericho caught movement at the front window. Grat was there now, too.

"It will be wonderful to talk to Isolda again," Edana said. She sounded nervous. "I hope she's as glad to see me."

"We'll find out directly," Neal said.

Isolda was sipping a sherry cobbler on the sofa when there was a knock on the door. Beaumont was over at the bar, pouring himself a whiskey, and set the bottle and the glass down.

"I'm closer. I'll get it."

Taking another sip, Isolda leaned back. It was blistering hot outside, but here in the comfort of their suite it was warm but not unbearable.

Beaumont returned. "They're downstairs. Dyson wouldn't let them up until he'd checked with us."

"The simpleton."

"He's only doin' what we told him. Do we have him show them up or go down and meet them?"

"Make her come to me. Have him bring her up. The climb will do her good."

Beaumont grinned. "Her cowboy, too?"

"I can't say much for her taste in men, but he *is* her husband."

"Both it is." Beaumont went back into the vestibule.

Isolda debated whether to stay on the sofa or move to the plush settee with its mahogany arms. It was important she impress Edana. Show her that she could get along without her. Deciding to stay where she was, she draped an arm across the back of the sofa and adopted an air of nonchalance.

Presently Beaumont came back in and over to the side of the sofa. "You have guests, my dear," he announced with a smirk.

Edana entered, and after her, Neal Bonner.

"My dear sister and her new husband," Isolda said.

"And their gun hand, Jericho," Beaumont said. "He's out in the hall with Dyson." He didn't sound pleased.

Edana was all smiles. "Oh, Isolda. It makes me so happy to see you again. It's been much too long."

"You could have visited anytime," Isolda said.

"So could you."

Isolda reached out and took Beaumont's hand. He didn't seem pleased about that, either, and she couldn't imagine why. "We've been busy, my handsome man and I."

"So I hear," Edana said. "Your new hotel. All your other businesses. Pretty soon the entire town will be your own little fiefdom."

"Funny you should call it that," Isolda said, "when your ranch is the size of some states."

"It's not mine. I'm running it for others as you well know." Edana sat at the other end of the sofa. "But please. Let's not quibble. I want this to be a nice visit."

"Where are my manners?" Beaumont said. "Would either of you care for somethin' to drink?" He pulled his hand loose from Isolda and moved toward the bar.

"What I'd like," Neal Bonner said casually, "is to find out if it's true that you killed poor Lice McCoy."

Beaumont stopped cold.

"What's going on?" Isolda said. "What's this about a killing?"

"Ask your handsome man," Neal said.

"I don't know what in hell you're talkin' about," Beaumont retorted, facing him. "And I'd be mighty careful slingin' accusations like that."

"It's not mine," Neal said. "Someone claims Lice paid you a visit and never came back."

"That someone is a damn liar."

"He told me that when he asked you where Lice got to, you as much as claimed that Franklyn Wells and me did Lice in to get back the money Wells paid Lice for his property."

"Who is this 'he' you keep talkin' about?" Beaumont asked. He suddenly gave a start and snapped his fingers. "It's Heller, isn't it? That old loon who lives way off in the Badlands by himself."

"So you're sayin' it's not true?"

"I sure as hell am."

"We'll let the federal marshal decide, then," Neal said. "I've sent a puncher to find the nearest one and bring him back."

Isolda saw Beaumont color with fury.

"You did what?"

His tone worried her. It was the tone he used when things were about to get ugly.

"You heard me," Neal said. "He left yesterday, so don't try and send some of your gun sharks to stop him. They'd be wastin' their time."

"You shouldn't have meddled, cowboy."

"You shouldn't have killed Lice, gambler."

Isolda swore she could feel the air crackle. She needed to stop this before it went too far. Rising, she said, "I want you to leave, Mr. Bonner. You're no longer welcome."

"Isolda, no," Edana said.

"Don't you dare," Isolda snapped. "You waltzed in here with him knowing full well what he was going to do. His accusation is preposterous."

"You don't know the facts behind it."

"See?" Isolda said, her anger climbing. She pointed toward the front door. "I want you out of here, the both of you, right this instant. We won't be insulted. Will we, dear?"

Beaumont didn't respond. He was glaring

438

at Bonner.

Frowning, Edana stood. "This wasn't how I wanted our visit to go. It wasn't how I wanted it to be at all."

"Then you shouldn't have brought your husband. He has no tact." Isolda curled her mouth in a sneer. "But what else should we expect from someone who has spent his entire life nursemaiding animals as dumb as he is?"

Edana took a step and slapped her.

Isolda was so shocked she stood frozen in disbelief. "You hit me!" she exclaimed.

"To hell with this," Beaumont said, and started to slide his hands toward his coat pockets.

"Don't you . . ." Neal said.

Isolda's shock at being struck was nothing compared to the jolt of seeing Beaumont whip his hands into his coat, even as Neal Bonner grabbed for his revolver.

There was the muffled boom of one of Beaumont's pistols — still inside his pocket — and Bonner's shoulder exploded in a shower of blood.

Edana screamed.

The shot and scream were like a knife plunged into Jericho's gut. He hadn't liked waiting out in the hall, but when Beaumont Adams suggested that Dyson and he do so, Neal had agreed. He'd been leaning against the hall wall, but now he whirled toward the suite.

"No, you don't," Dyson said. He was in front of the door, his hand on his Remington.

Jericho sprang. Dyson tried to jerk his pistol, but Jericho already had his Colt out and slammed the barrel against Dyson's temple. Dyson staggered aside. In a twinkling Jericho was through the door and burst into the parlor.

Edana and Isolda were grappling by the sofa.

Neal was on his back on the floor, clutching a bleeding shoulder.

Beaumont Adams stood over him and was

pulling a pair of short-barreled pistols from his frock coat. He heard Jericho, and pivoted.

Jericho fanned two swift shots.

The slugs caught the gambler dead center and lifted him onto his bootheels. He gamely attempted to raise his pistols while stumbling back.

Jericho fanned a third shot.

Isolda Jessup screeched like a bobcat as Beaumont Adams crashed to the floor. Letting go of her sister, she ran to him.

Jericho heard someone come in behind him. Tucking at the knees, he spun just as a revolver crashed. Lead whizzed above him. He slammed two shots that impaled Dyson in the act of about to fire again and Dyson deflated like a punctured water skin.

Quickly, Jericho reloaded. He put six pills in the wheel, not the usual five. He glanced at Isolda, who had cradled the gambler's head and was weeping, and at Edana, who had rushed to Neal.

Boots pounded out on the stairs.

"Take care of my pard," Jericho said to Edana, and darted back out into the hall.

The two gun sharks from downstairs had just reached the landing. Their pistols were out, and they fired at the same instant.

Jericho fanned a shot that smashed into

the face of the foremost. The man screamed and crumpled, and his friend did the unexpected; he turned and raced back down. Jericho promptly replaced the spent cartridge. He was about to start down himself when a commotion broke out in the suite. Edana cried out as if in pain.

Jericho dashed back inside.

Edana and Isolda were grappling again. Isolda had gotten hold of one of Beaumont Adams's pocket Colts and was trying to shoot her own sister. Edana was on the bottom and had a gash on her forehead, apparently from being struck. Hissing like a sidewinder, Isolda was forcing the muzzle toward Edana's chest. A little more and she would fire.

Jericho shot her in the head.

Edana let out a wail.

Jericho ran over, grabbed Isolda by the back of her dress, and hauled her off. "Are you all right?"

Edana stared at her sibling, her mouth working but no sounds coming out.

"Neal," Jericho said. "We have to get him out of here." By now their enemies would be gathering below. Stimms and Grat and Tuck and that other gun hand and who knew how many others? And then there was deadliest of the bunch, the one real shootist, Scar Wratner.

Numbly nodding, Edana got to her knees and hooked her arm around Neal. She tried to lift him but couldn't.

Jericho helped her. They got Neal up, but Neal was weak and had to lean on Edana. "Can you two do it by yourselves? I need my hands free."

Neal, his teeth gritted, nodded. "Do what you have to, pard."

"Stay close but not right behind me." Jericho scooped up Neal's Colt and with a six-shooter in each hand led them out.

The hallway was quiet. Nor were there any sounds from below. That in itself was ominous.

Jericho paused at the landing so Edana and Neal could catch up. "Remember, not too close." He didn't want a slug to pass through him and hit them. Taking a breath, he descended. He went slowly, a step at a time. To rush would be rash and prove fatal.

No one tried to stop them at the next landing or the one after that or any of the others. He was almost to the bottom when he caught whispering from the lobby.

Stopping, Jericho looked over his shoulder.

Edana's dress was smeared scarlet with Neal's blood. Neal was pale but holding his own.

"Give me my six-gun and I'll help."

"Keep him here," Jericho said to Edana. "No matter what you hear, don't let him go out there until you hear me holler."

"What if . . ." Edana didn't finish.

"In that case it won't matter." Jericho smiled to encourage her, looked Neal in the eye, and nodded.

"Jericho . . ."

Jericho took the last steps on the fly and dived through the doorway. Somewhere the Sharps thundered and the slug thudded into the jamb. In midair Jericho banged off a shot at the partner of the man he'd shot upstairs, and the gunny grabbed for his throat. Coming down on his side, Jericho fired at Stimms, who was over by the front door. He rolled, pushed to a knee, six-guns crashing all around him. He felt pain in his left arm, but it didn't stop him from shooting Tuck, who was over by the counter. His hat was sent flying. Grat rose from behind a chair, and Jericho sent a slug into him. Guns were still going off. He launched himself at a settee. It wasn't much cover, but it was better than nothing. He emptied Neal's Colt into Stimms, shot another gun hand by a pillar. A sledgehammer seemed to slam into his back, spinning him. Grat was still on his feet. Jericho fanned a shot, hitting him smack between the eyes.

In the sudden silence, Jericho's ears rang. He slowly rose. Things were fuzzy, his vision not what it should be. Grat and Tuck and Stimms and the man by the wall and the other one were all down and none were moving. He had begun to reload when a revolver blasted, and the next he knew, he was on the floor and his right wrist hurt and his hands were empty. The fuzziness was worse.

The head and shoulders of Scar Wratner floated into view. Scar was smirking.

"Good. I get to finish you myself."

Jericho struggled to focus. The words had come as from down a long tunnel, and Scar himself was fading in and out.

"Any last words?" Scar taunted.

Abruptly Jericho's vision was crystal clear. He saw Scar's smirk, and the dark barrel of a revolver thrust near to Scar's ear. Scar went to turn, but the revolver went off and the other side of Scar's head erupted like a volcano.

Jericho felt gore splatter him and shut his eyes. When he opened them again, Neal was crouched at his side, holding the revolver.

"Grat's," Neal said, wagging it.

"I'm obliged."

"How bad?" Neal asked.

"Bad." Jericho wanted to rise but couldn't get his arms to work as they should. "Where'd your lady get to?"

"She went for the new sawbones."

"Didn't know they had one," Jericho said, and a veil of blackness fell.

The funeral was small and simple.

Edana buried her sister next to her father. When the parson finished the eulogy and moved off, the few punchers who had attended went with him. She stepped to the grave and stared down at the coffin, and a tear formed. It rolled down her cheek and off her chin. "How did it come to this?"

Neal put his left arm around her. His right was still bandaged, and he was under doctor's orders to use it as little as possible for a couple of weeks. "I never meant it to."

"I know," Edana said. "She brought it on herself, I suppose, taking up with a man like Adams."

"We dig our own graves, ma'am," Jericho said from the other side of Isolda's. He had more bandages than both of them combined.

"I reckon so," Edana said.

Neal smiled. "Listen to you. You're startin' to sound like one of us."

Edana gazed out across the ranch. Longhorns were grazing, and beyond, the buttes reared red in the afternoon sun. "I am one of you now. I'd never go back East, even if you were to ask me to."

"I wouldn't count on that happenin'," Neal said.

Breathing deep, Edana put her arm around his waist. "It gets into your blood," she said.

"What does?"

Edana motioned at the Badlands. "The West. It's more than just a place. It's a feeling that settles in your heart and becomes part of you."

"Amen to that," Neal Bonner said.

The employees of Thorndike Press hope you have enjoyed this Large Print book. All our Thorndike, Wheeler, and Kennebec Large Print titles are designed for easy reading, and all our books are made to last. Other Thorndike Press Large Print books are available at your library, through selected bookstores, or directly from us.

For information about titles, please call:
(800) 223-1244

or visit our Web site at:
http://gale.cengage.com/thorndike

To share your comments, please write:
Publisher
Thorndike Press
10 Water St., Suite 310
Waterville, ME 04901